# HEROES & VILLAINS

## DESTINY CALLS

BIRDY RIVERS

PUBLISHER'S NOTE

# HEROES & VILLAINS

## DESTINY CALLS

# CHAPTER 1

## Clara

Heroes and Villains. It's a classic story told throughout history, stories, and myths. It's supposed to be a simple black and white tale, except it's far from simple. There's a whole morally grey area that simply never gets mentioned. Nothing is truly black and white because black and white will always bleed together to create a morally grey canvas.

Oswald City is no stranger to the story of Heroes and Villains. It's deeply embedded in our history, roots, and blood. The man responsible for creating the hero and villain story in Oswald City is Wolfgang Oswald. His family built the city and like typical vain, rich assholes they named the city after themselves.

Wolfgang was wealthy and brilliant. A dangerous combination that led him to discover Aliens. The Aliens came from the planet Altron. They have more of a human appearance than one would expect. The only differences were they had pointy ears, a tail with a pointed end, their heart was on the right side, and they had all-natural white hair. Wolfgang invited a few aliens to come to Earth. Five were sent to work with Wolfgang. Their names were Crona, Cras, Salter, Tressa, and Trest.

Inevitably Wolfgang and one of the aliens, Crona, fell in love. Since the alien's anatomy is similar to a human's, Crona was able to conceive a child by Wolfgang. It was incredible the two races could make children. Everyone waited anxiously for Crona to have her baby. The child was called Thomas and he was closely studied. He appeared human, but when he hit puberty it was discovered he had superhuman abilities. He appeared completely human, but he had super abilities. Thomas has impenetrable skin and telekinesis.

The other aliens soon found human egg and sperm donors and used surrogates to further the new Bio Meta race. The original five Bio Meta's are Thomas Oswald, Janna Moore, Lois Grant, Veronica Granger, and Benji Cole. Janna had the ability to manipulate fire including creating it. Veronica could control the weather. Lois was able to communicate with animals. Benji had the deadliest superpower of them all. He could create poisonous gas that could kill any living creature.

# HEROES & VILLAINS

The goal of the Bio Meta race was to have them protect the citizens of Earth. The aliens trained the Bio Metas to use their superpowers for good. Except Benji didn't want to protect the citizens of Earth. Benji became the supervillain known as Cyanide because all heroes and villains need code names. His goal was to eliminate humans that were useless, and enslave those that were useful. It went against everything the League of Metas stood for. It was a toxic endeavor that created more chaos than anyone could have predicted. Even now, his ideas run rampant through the city. Humans are constantly targets of Bio Metas willing to carry out Cyanide's philosophies, and the League of Metas is always there to stop them.

Thomas ended up marrying Veronica, and they have a son named Collin Oswald. Lois fell in love with Harold Gavin, a human whose family works for the Oswald family. They have a daughter named Nina Gavin. Benji ended up falling in love with Janna. They never married, but they have a daughter, me, Clara Cole. I'm the daughter of a supervillain. I wish that meant something, but all it's brought me is pain and disappointment.

I haven't seen my father since my mother died when I was eleven. That was twelve years ago. Since then I've been taken in by my father's second in command, Yuri Jones. My father built himself a strong following among some of the Bio Metas. Since his disappearance, Yuri has taken over. He's responsible for almost all the crime in Oswald City. I refuse to partake in his criminal mischief because I don't believe in hurting people for fun.

After the original five were born Wolfgang got the aliens from Altron to donate sperm and eggs so that he could essentially ensure the survival of the Bio Meta race. He paid him donors and human surrogates to carry Bio Meta children. They created what is known as the Bio Meta Program. Wolfgang built Oswald Tower, which is home to the League of Metas who are superheroes trained to protect humans on Earth. Thomas is the current leader of the League of Metas. I'm sure Collin will follow in his father's footsteps and be the next honorable leader when the time comes.

I have no intentions of taking my father's place as leader of his cause. I don't care about his cause or the League's mission for world peace. Plus, I don't have a superpower, so I can't do much of anything anyway. I'm defective, but no one knows why. I'm the only Bio Meta without superpowers. In many ways, I'm grateful for being defective. I'm already a target because of who my father is. Some target me to bully me because they think I'm worthless or fear I'll turn out like my father. They call me names and taunt me trying to get me to lash out to prove

I'm a villain. Then there is the flip side of the coin that deals with my father's obsessive followers. They hunt me down to beg me to lead them or to try and fuck me. It's creepy watching them praise my dad as a way to get me to spread my legs.

My life is not glamorous. I'm an outcast who sticks to herself. I work a very basic job at a butcher shop that Yuri owns. My studio apartment is above the shop. I don't have much because there's no point in making a home here. Eventually, I plan to save enough money and have enough resources to leave Oswald City. I'll go far enough away and find a place in the middle of nowhere. I'll go off the radar. Being isolated has to be better than constantly being on edge wondering what challenge I will encounter next. I don't stray far from home. I'm usually safer if I'm in Yuri's territory. Yet, I'm not entirely sure Yuri is on my side either.

Yuri is strange. Sometimes he treats me like a daughter, and other times he keeps me on a tight leash as if he owns me or something. It creeps me out, but for the moment he's the closest thing I have to safety. It's shitty knowing I'm never truly safe. I'm paranoid with severe daddy and trust issues. I'll never feel safe until I'm out of Oswald City.

Right now, I'm trying to not focus on the three guys that have been following me since I left the store. I'm getting my time of the month soon, and I wanted to make sure I had supplies for when it came. It's midnight, no one should be out, except these assholes have been following me since I left the store. I'm two blocks away from my apartment. If I can just get there I can activate the alarm and Yuri will come with a couple of his sons to deal with these assholes.

I will my legs to move faster as my heart beats violently in my chest. It's not the first time I've been followed home, but it's usually during the day when there are more people out. It's more or less a prank to make me uncomfortable. This time it feels different. It's almost as if I can sense the malicious intent, or I'm severely paranoid, and I think I feel a panic attack threatening to overtake me. I start to run, dropping my bags. Fuck, my supplies, I'll get more later.

Terrified, I run for my life. I make the mistake of looking behind me because when I look forward again there are another four men blocking my path on the sidewalk. The street lamps cast a soft glow around the four men creating an eerie picture against the darkness of night. I do my best to halt to a quick stop, but I fail and stumble forward. I land hard on my hands and knees as I feel the concrete rip through my jeans and skin. Shit, that hurt, and certainly wasn't graceful.

Looking up, I find myself surrounded by seven men of different sizes. A few I might be able to fight off if they were by themselves, but seven men is too many. I don't stand a chance. Sinister chuckles echo in the night as they come closer.

One of them roughly grabs my hair, yanking my head back before another one kicks me in the ribs causing the air to violently leave my lungs. I feel a slap across my face followed by a punch to my left eye. I start to lose track of where they are kicking and punching as I collapse falling to the ground. I struggle to get into the fetal position, and I finally do. There is no superhero coming to save me. I'm fucked until these assholes are done doing their worst. I'm waiting for the part where they tell me I deserve this, it always comes. I try to hold on, but no one has ever beaten me for this long or badly before. The edges of my vision blur as my mind and body seek out the darkness because when there is darkness there is no more pain.

# BIRDY RIVERS

# CHAPTER 2

### Collin

The night air wraps around me as I step onto the balcony off my room. It feels good to be home. I don't care what anyone says Oswald Manor will always be my true home. It's set in the countryside near the city. It's peaceful and where I find I'm the most relaxed. Living in Oswald Tower is not relaxing. I'm always in meetings, training, doing publicity shit, or fighting crime. The only time I get to truly unwind is when I'm at the family manor.

Harold, our butler lives here full time taking care of the place. After his wife, Lois, died, he sought out solitude, so my parents offered him a job at the manor. Harold always has my room fresh and ready for when I'm here. I try to come here as often as possible, and I always ensure I come after my birthday. There's a huge party at Oswald Tower filled with eager fans. It's a total publicity thing. My birthday was yesterday. Now, I'm taking a couple of weeks at home to relax.

Looking up at the stars, I think about the home planet. We haven't had contact with them since the aliens left Earth. There are rumors that Cyanide has disappeared to the home planet, but I don't know how true that is. Still, it's strange they cut off communication. Unfortunately, my father doesn't seem too concerned with it. He's more concerned with stopping Cyanide's followers who keep causing problems.

My super hearing catches the sound of someone at the front gates. I immediately take flight, flying to the front gates. I don't know who the hell would be here at three in the morning. I'm used to staying up late because most crime happens at night. It's easier for the rats to come out in the dark and do their dirty deeds covered by the darkness of night. I doubt it's the media. I hear the intruders leave as a vehicle pulls away. As I approach the front gate I see a figure slumped against the gates.

As I get closer I realize it's a girl who appears to have been tossed over the gate. She's managed to prop herself up slightly against the gate. The light on top of the gate casts the girl in a dark light. I kneel next to her letting the gate light see her state, she's covered in bruises and cuts. Her clothes are ripped to shreds. She might as well be in her undergarments, which I can clearly see. The closer I look at the girl I realize I know her.

"Clara?" I question. I haven't seen Clara in person since we were teens at the fair. I have seen her in photos that our spies take, but other than that I don't have contact with her. My father likes to keep tabs on Clara because he is afraid she will become the next Cyanide.

"Collin?" She groans. "Is it your turn now?"

"My turn for what? What the hell happened to you?" I ask, looking over her once more to figure out if I can fly her to the Manor in my arms. I need to assess her injuries to figure out the best way to transport her.

"I don't know. Your crazy supporters attacked me. They said something about giving me as a gift for your twenty-fifth birthday so you could get answers from me." She pauses, taking a moment to catch a painful breath. "Look, I don't know what you want to know, but I assure you I don't know shit. Yuri keeps me in the dark, and I have no clue if my father is dead or alive." She explains between pained breathing. I bet she has a couple of broken ribs.

"I'm not going to hurt you, Clara. I'm going to help you." I declare as I decide to just scoop her up, bridal style.

"Always the Mighty Hero," Clara notes with a painful chuckle as I take off in the air toward the manor.

I land on the balcony that attaches to my room before heading inside. Good thing I left the damn doors open when I stepped out. I set Clara down on the couch I have in my room. Shit, she looks even worse in better lighting. I don't think there is a part of her skin that isn't covered in purple or dirt. I'm almost positive she has at least a couple of broken ribs and she will probably need some stitches. She's lucid, which is a good thing for me, but not for her. I need to get her pain medicine along with cleaning her up and addressing her injuries.

"Clara, you need to get cleaned up. You need a shower and then I need to tend to your injuries." I explain.

"You are going to have to help me, Mighty Hero. My body is screaming in pain right now. I hope you aren't bashful." She replies.

"I'm certainly not bashful, Little Villain. I'll get you pain meds to help."

I haven't called her Little Villain since the fair. It was my nickname for her. She then came up with Mighty Hero because I helped her get the food she wanted. The woman at the food stand was refusing to give Clara her food. So, I bought it for her and took it to her. She was in the parking lot crying. I don't think she liked that I saw her cry, but she was happy when I gave her the food.

Shaking the memory away, I go over to the intercom system and tell Harold what I need him to get. I'm glad we have fully stocked medical supplies at the manor. Once I give Harold my list, I go back over to Clara. I help her stand before I gently strip her of her clothes. As I strip her, I can't help but admire her.  Shit, she has a nice body. She definitely filled out her form since we were teens. I know she just had the shit beaten out of her, but it's hard to ignore her curvy hourglass figure with bigger breasts, and plump ass. Not to mention her slightly thicker thighs. Okay, I need to reign in my libido. I know it's been a while, but I'm not about to fuck a girl who clearly had the shit beaten out of her.

I help Clara to the bathroom attached to my bedroom. I settle Clara on the bench in the shower before I step out of the shower and turn the water on. Luckily, the hot water heater is top of the line and heats up within seconds. I hear Harold knocking on the door. I leave Clara before I head to answer the door. I briefly explain to Harold the situation as I take the supplies. Of course, he's not thrilled to have Cyanid's daughter here. Cyanide killed Lois and Harold hasn't let go of that. Unfortunately, I need Harold to look past it because Clara needs help.

I haven't even begun to process that this tragedy was done in my name. I know supporters of the League are getting a little extreme with their support. I never thought they would attack an innocent. I know in their eyes Clara isn't innocent. In many ways, Clara pays for her father's sins. Clara herself has never done anything wrong to be labeled a villain. Yet, she is called a villain based on who her father is. Yes, Clara is technically my enemy because she has never declared whose side she is on. However, she needs help and that's what I'm going to give her.

Harold leaves my room in an outrage, but he will get over it. I'm sure he's on his way to inform my father. I don't care, I'll deal with them both later. I take the pain meds to Clara. Clara is still sitting on the shower bench leaning against the wall as steam billows around her. I set the pain meds on the counter with the water before I pull out towels. I also pull out a washcloth. I head back to the shower with the washcloth before I strip my clothes off.

"I hope you aren't bashful, Little Villain," I say as I step in the shower.

"Like I'd let it show if I was." She counters.

"Always the smart ass," I comment as I wet the washcloth before pouring body wash on it. I hope she doesn't mind smelling like a guy, but it's what I have.

"My body feels like a crime scene," Clara comments as I gently wash her.

"Well, I hate to break it to you, but it is. I'm sorry this happened. I would never condone this." I firmly state. Tampering my anger to not scare Clara. She already thinks

I might hurt her. Being angry won't help her convince her I won't.

"Good to know. I guess that means you won't be torturing me for information." She jokes.

"No. I promise I won't hurt you unless you give me a reason to." I attempt to reassure her.

"We will see if you keep that promise, Mighty Hero."

I shake my head at her defensive comment before I focus on cleaning her up as I assess her injuries. She's mostly bruised with minor cuts. She has a few nasty looking gashes that appear to be from some type of knife. Those will definitely need stitches. Her left wrist is in bad shape. It looks as if someone stepped on it. I don't think it's broken, but it's hard to tell without an x-ray.

"They hurt you badly. Did they do anything else to you?" I inquire, wanting to know the degree these so called supporters went.

"They just beat me up. They didn't touch me sexually if that's what you're wondering."

"Good, because I'd kill them if they did." I declare possessively. I don't know why, but I've always been a little possessive of Clara. Something about our encounter when we were teens made an impression on me that I've never been able to shake. Even now, there is something about her that draws me to her.

"I guess they did technically commit a crime. Is it a crime when it's against a villain?" She bluntly questions.

"You aren't technically a villain. You're more of a villain by association, and that doesn't count in my book. However, those that did this to you, they did very much commit a crime. They better hope I don't ever find them because I won't hold back my super strength when I beat their ass."

"Justice by vengeance, how morally grey of you, Mighty Hero." Clara lightly jokes as she winces in pain as I clean a severely bruised area.

"We can debate morals later. Let's finish getting you cleaned up. You need rest so your body can begin to heal." I counter. She's a feisty one, and while I would normally love to put her feisty ass in her place, Clara needs rest. She needs to heal from these rough injuries. She's going to be here for a few weeks while she heals.

I finish cleaning Clara up. She stays quiet for the rest of the time. I can tell she is in pain and weak. Her body is craving rest. When we are done with the shower, I help dry Clara off. Once she is dried I wrap her in a towel before drying myself off. I wrap the towel around my hips before I hand Clara the pills and water.

"These are for Bio Metas." She comments, taking the pills.

"You are a Bio Meta," I reply, confused at her comment.

"I don't have a superpower. I'm defective" She firmly states.

"I don't think you are. You have the same frequency as a Bio Meta who has awakened superpowers. Still, you need these. Defective or not you still have Bio Meta genetics." I counter.

My super hearing doesn't fail me, and I know the frequency of a Bio Meta with awakened superpowers considering I spend most of my time with them. Even the young Bio Metas who don't have awakened superpowers still give off a specific frequency. I would be more worried if I didn't hear the same frequency coming off her as I do other Bio Metas.

Clara reluctantly takes the pills. I grab her some of my PJ pants and a T-shirt. I attend to her injuries the best I can before I help her dress and then help her in bed. Of course, she protests about sleeping in the bed, but she has no room to argue. Once she is settled, I dress myself before grabbing some blankets and pillows for the couch. Clara is already passed out by the time I'm ready to go to bed. I knew those pain meds would kick in quickly. They are designed that way.

I settle myself on the couch unsure of what my next moves should be. I don't know if I'm making a mistake helping her. It can't be a mistake to help her. She is a victim. Still, I don't know if I trust her just like she won't know if she can trust me. We have been taught that we were enemies and it's hard to undo that damage. Still, Clara has never posed a threat, and it's not because she believes she doesn't have superpowers. It's because she has never done anything to paint herself as the villain. It only seems to be everyone else who paints her in that light. I've never been blind to how she is viewed by others, and I've always disagreed with it.

It's never been a secret that Clara doesn't have a superpower. Some members of the League of Metas believe Clara is lying about not having superpowers. I never thought she was lying, and that was proven tonight by how she acted. She truly believes she is defective. However, I question if she does have superpowers that she simply isn't aware of. Who knows what Cyanide could have done to her? He could have found a way to suppress her superpowers. I'm not sure why he would do that to his own daughter, but Cyanide isn't known for being a man of morals.

I'm curious if Clara does have a superpower. I wonder what it is. Is it something bad and that's why

Cyanide suppressed her? Suppression is the only thing I can think of. There's no proof that it can be done, but there are theories on it. Cyanide was a dangerous genius, he might have figured out how to make one of the theories work

If Clara has superpowers then I want to help Clara discover what they are. She deserves to know what her superpowers are. I want to help her, but mostly I want to show her a world where she belongs.

One thing is clear, Clara is guarded and blunt. She's the mystery I want to unravel. I have to be careful, though. Clara is not going to come around easily. She needs guidance, but I think what she needs the most is acceptance. I can't believe she was brutally attacked. I think there was a part of her that expected me to hurt her. I don't know what those supporters were thinking. I would never condone their actions. I don't like that our supporters are taking matters into their own hands. It's dangerous. They could have killed Clara. Our supporters are committing crimes in our name. They aren't acting any better than Cyanide's followers.

Pushing the endless thoughts away, I will see what tomorrow brings. For now, I'm going to get some rest because I know Clara isn't waking up anytime soon. Those are strong pain meds that will help her rest so her body can heal. This gives me the time I need to figure shit out before my father summons me.

# BIRDY RIVERS

# CHAPTER 3

Collin

A couple of days go by before I get a concerned phone call from my father demanding I come straight to Oswald Tower. I assume Harold told him that Clara is staying here. Harold has strong feelings against Clara because he isn't over Lois's death. We still don't know why Cyanide killed her, but we know that he did because he had no problem boasting about it. It was years later when he killed Janna then he fled. No one knows where he is or if he's even alive. It would seem Clara doesn't even know where her father is. I do believe her when she says she doesn't know. It's the tone of sincerity mixed with desperation for me to believe her. I don't think she is used to people believing her.

I walk over to Clara who is currently passed out as I gave her meds not too long ago. She will be out for a bit. I've been giving her the pain meds to help her sleep so she can heal. They make her tired and knock her feisty ass out.

Shit, is she full of spirit, and blunt as fuck too. She has no problem speaking her truth. It's actually sexy the way she is bluntly honest. I admire her tough skin, but I imagine life hasn't been great for her. She's stuck between two sides who equally want her to join them. I don't think Clara wants to join either side. I get the vibe Clara wants to be left alone, but we all know that will never be an option.

"I'll be back, Little Villain," I whisper to her as I tuck a piece of her dark ash-brown hair behind her ear. Her hair is medium-length with choppy layers. Her dark blue-grey eyes compliment her hair giving her an appealing look. She looks peaceful sleeping, but the various shades of black and purple across her skin give away that she is far from peace.

I quickly get dressed to head to see my father. I tell Harold to keep an eye on Clara, which he is not pleased about. Too bad because he just had to blab to my father that Clara was here. It's not like I didn't plan on telling him, I knew there was no way I could keep it a secret for long. I wanted to be the one to tell him. I also wanted to have a few things figured out. One of which is does Clara have activated superpowers that are somehow suppressed?

Clara having superpowers changes a lot of things. For one it will make her more of a target for both sides. One side will be desperate for her to lead and the other will be desperate to stop her from leading. Cyanide is considered the original villain of Oswald City. He is the one responsible for so much violence, war, and death. The League of Metas fears Clara will be like her father and will be destructive. It's why her not having superpowers seems like a good thing. She isn't much of a threat other than sheer influence. Normally, influence can be just as dangerous, except Clara doesn't use her influence among the villains. She always sticks to her own business and doesn't interfere with the affairs of the other villains. Still, her having superpowers changes the game.

I fly to Oswald Tower. I have no intentions of staying. I need to get back to Clara. I need to figure out her agenda, and if I can trust her. I want to trust she isn't like her father or even her mother. I want to know Clara as her own person. Let's not even get into the fact that I'm attracted to her. I always have been but it was easier to admire her from afar. It's harder when she's under the same roof as me. Still, I want to help her. Maybe it is the hero in me who wants to save her because I believe she is worth saving even if no one else sees it that way. Now, I just have to convince my uptight father that Clara isn't a threat and I have the potential to connect with her. Ultimately, the goal has always been to figure out where Clara stands, and there's no better way to do that than spending time with her. Getting to know her will help us gauge whose side she's on. My argument should be solid, but my father can be stubborn. It also doesn't help that Cyanide is a sore spot for my dad.

I enter the building. As I'm on my way to my father's office I run into my best friend, Mason, whose superpower is super speed. His name while fighting crime is Bullet. Mason is tall and thin with short, yellow blond hair. Mason's girlfriend, Nina, who is also Harold's daughter, is never far from him. Nina's superpower is ice manipulation. We call her Ice Queen. The name is fitting not just because of her superpowers, but also because it fits her stone-cold personality. Nina is a certified bitch who wears the title proudly. She's also a diva. Nina has platinum blonde hair cut into a stylish bob. She has the body of a model. By all rights she's attractive, but she isn't my type. Clara is very much my type, which might become a problem.

"You just had to piss off your old man didn't you?" Mason asks as he and Nina approach me in the hall.

"I take it you two know about Clara."

"How could we not? My dad hasn't stopped fuming." Nina adds as she puts her hands on her hips while popping out her hip. Nina wears silver heels and a skin-tight silver sequin dress. Nina dresses like she is on the fucking runway. She actually has her own clothesline. I'm sure what she is wearing is something in her line. She is very influential in the fashion world.

"She was severely injured. She needed help." I defend. I'm already getting the tenth degree and I haven't even talked to my father yet.

"No, you just like fixing broken things." Mason counters.

"Clara isn't broken," I state firmly.

"Isn't she though? She doesn't have a superpower and her father is a supervillain. Her mother was a hero who chose a villain over her morals which got her killed. The girl probably has serious emotional baggage, you do not want to get involved in that." Nina adds her thoughts to the conversation as if asked for her opinion. Nina loves to give dating advice. She thinks she is some type of love expert, but I think she's full of it. Unfortunately, we are in our early and mid-twenties, and Nina still acts like she's in high school.

"Collin Wolfgang Oswald. Get your ass in my office now!" I hear my father's voice boom down the hall. I turn around and face my father. I heard him coming, he knows that. Superhearing makes it hard for people to sneak up on you.

"Someone's in trouble." Mason taunts with a laugh as Nina joins in with her own giggles. I know Mason is joking around, but I'm not in a joking mood.

Ignoring Mason and Nina, I head toward Father and follow him into his office. His office is huge with big long windows that give a spectacular view of the city. His office is modern and simple. A large cherry wood desk sits in the center with a leather office chair. To one side is a small sitting area with two leather chairs, a loveseat, and a coffee table. Not far from the sitting area is a tabletop bar cabinet complete with all kinds of liquor and even has a single serve coffee maker. The other side is nothing but shelves of books. Most of them are for aesthetic purposes, but some are important.

"You have some serious explaining to do, Collin." My father's firm voice reaches my ears. My father is tall, with short dark hair that has grey peaking through and a neatly trimmed beard.

"Be nice, Thomas." My mother warns as she enters the office through a side door that connects the main conference room. "It's nice to see you, Collin." My mother adds smiling at me.

My mom is the voice of reason for my father. She has stopped countless arguments between my dad and me. He and I tend to clash with our ideas. My poor mom is constantly playing monkey in the middle with us. Yet, somehow I don't think she minds it.

"I said I would be reasonable, not nice." My father counters before he gets a scolding look from my mom. I suppress my chuckle. My parents do know how to make me laugh. We have our issues, but we do love one another.

"It's simple, Dad. Clara was badly beaten and injured by some supporters who dropped her off at the front gates as some twisted birthday gift for me. They did it with the intention of me torturing her for information that I'm fairly certain she doesn't know. She needed help. She couldn't even walk on her own. I've never seen someone so badly beaten before. We are heroes and we help those in need." I explain.

"We have to stop these supporters from taking matters into their own hands. These extremists are getting out of hand," My mom adds. My father nods his head in agreement. I think it's time we address these extremists. They need to know we don't condone their actions. "How is Clara?" My mom questions stopping my mind from wandering. I swear she knows when I'm about to zone out on the conversation, so she asks a question to refocus me.

"In pain, and knocked out half the time because of the painkillers. She will heal with rest and time. She's not a current threat." I answer.

"She will heal and then we have to figure out what to do with her." I don't like the dark tone in my father's voice.

Cyanide broke his trust and it's caused him not to always see clearly when it comes to anything involving Cyanide, including his daughter. I think the same can be said of Harold. They are blinded by Cyanide's betrayal. My mom is more about peace, so she wants Clara to join us. My mom handled the betrayal better and is able to learn from it instead of being blinded by it.

"We train her. Show her we don't have to be the enemy because we aren't," I pause debating if I should tell my father I think Clara's superpower is suppressed. Honesty tends to work best with my father. "I think Cyanide somehow found a way to suppress Clara's superpowers or at least someone has. Clara has the same frequencies as every other Bio Meta with activated superpowers. The thing is, Clara truly believes she is defective when she isn't. She is being manipulated and lied to. No doubt Yuri has a part to play in it. Look, we have always wondered whose side she is on. To be honest, I don't think she is on anyone's side but her own. If we train and accept her then maybe we have a chance of getting her to join us. In all these years Clara has never committed a crime nor has she ever participated in Yuri's violence." My mom nods her head in agreement. I knew she wouldn't be the one I had to convince.

"She is still Cyanide's daughter." My father's voice is laced with venom. Anything involving Cyanide is a battle with my father.

"Yes, but she is also Janna's daughter. Janna might have made poor choices, but we both know she had a good heart." My mother counters defending Clara. She is eager to have Clara join us. I never understood why. I'm all for it, but her intentions are unclear. I can sense her intention is good. I simply wish I knew where she was going with her idea.

"Fine. Figure out if Clara has superpowers or not. If she does, you will bring her to Oswald Tower to train like every other Bio Meta. You will also be the one to train her. Keep a tight leash on her, Collin. We don't know what she is capable of. She might not participate in active crimes, but that doesn't mean she isn't involved in other ways. I suppose it's better to keep her close in case she turns out to be a threat." My father pauses to think for a moment. Well, at least he didn't threaten to integrate her or lock her up. Still, that doesn't mean she is free. "Clara has an influence on her father's followers and they might not take kindly to her being in our care. Yuri is someone we especially need to look out for. He might think we are holding her hostage." My father concludes.

"She is technically a hostage. She isn't free to walk away." I remind him because we all know this doesn't end with Clara walking away from us. The group of supporters did manage to be successful in one thing with their mission. Clara is our prisoner. I hope that one day she doesn't have to be because she has joined the League of Metas.

Clara isn't going to be happy about being forced to train with us, but if she doesn't my father will have no problem locking her in the secured prison in the basement of this tower. His fear that she is the next Cyanide will overtake him and even my mom won't be able to talk sense into him. I hope Clara isn't too difficult and stubborn with this. I know it's not ideal for her to be a glorified prisoner, but at least she wouldn't be locked up. Plus, I think Clara would secretly like to be included in something. She's a loner looking in on society. She is an outsider on both sides. I think Clara needs a little kindness and understanding. She needs someone to show her that she belongs somewhere. I want to do that for her because she deserves it.

"The idea is to portray that she isn't. The goal is to get her to join the League of Metas. We want her on our side. If Cyanide is alive and ever comes back, it's better if Clara is on our side. For Janna's sake, we need to try and save her daughter from Cyanide. He's taken too many lives already. I failed Janna, I don't want to fail her daughter either. You need to give Clara a reason to want to stay." My mother contributes as she finally reveals her intentions. Now it all makes sense why she is so determined to have Clara join us. She wants to save Janna's daughter.

"What do you suggest we give her as her reason to stay? It's not like we can reunite her with her parents. Janna is dead. Cyanide and her will reunite over my dead body. We could offer her a position of some sort depending on what her superpowers are, but I'm not sure that's enough. It has to be something Cyanide can't offer her as well." My father discusses. Alright, my dad is being reasonable, but he's not the one I'm currently concerned about. It's the clever smile that plays on my mother's face as she looks at me that puts me on edge. I can practically see the light bulb over her head turning on, and I'm not sure I'm going to like the idea.

"Collin, you're single. It's time you find someone to get serious with. Clara is a pretty girl. You already have a vested interest in her. Maybe you could turn that into something more." My mom casually suggests.

"Are you suggesting I make her my girlfriend?" I question dumbfounded at my mom's boldness. I know she is desperate to get Clara to join us, but I did not see her suggestion coming. I was right to be concerned.

I know I'm attracted to Clara. I want to get to know her for a reason. I've been wanting to get to know Clara since we met at the fair. I've never had an official girlfriend before. No one has ever caught my eye until Clara. I hate that I'm actually entertaining this idea but only because I think I have feelings for Clara. I don't know how I can because I barely know her. Still, I do actually like the idea of being with Clara. She does appeal to me. I wouldn't mind being the reason she stays. I can show her a place at my side.

"It wouldn't hurt to think about it as you get to know her." My mother replies like her idea isn't total madness. A madness I'm thinking of partaking in.

By the time I leave Oswald Tower my mind is swarming in different directions. Damn, my mom and her ideas. The shitty part is I know I would have come up with this on my own eventually. I've been interested in Clara for a while now. Mainly because I found her interesting as a person. There was something about her that called to me.

My mind wanders to that night. It was a few years after Cyanide killed Janna and disappeared. There was a fair that came to the outskirts of the city. We were both in our awkward teen years at the time, so when I saw her in line in front of me I wanted to find a way to talk to her. I wasn't sure how to approach her because we were supposed to be enemies. I wasn't even sure I should approach her because it was clear by how she was dressed she didn't want to be recognized. She was dressed in black skinny jeans, a black hoodie with the hood up, black canvas shoes, and she sported a black baseball cap under the hood. She never looked up until she got to the window to order.

"Can I get a funnel cake, a corndog, popcorn, cotton candy, and a lemonade?" Clara made her order.

I couldn't believe she was ordering all that food, but I also couldn't blame her for going all out at the fair since it didn't come around often. Bio Meta's do tend to have a big appetite. It was already known then that Clara didn't have a superpower. Our superpowers start showing up around eight or nine. Definitely before ten. Clara was well past the age to have superpowers. Back then I didn't have my super hearing trained enough so I couldn't hear the Bio Meta frequency.

"Sure, kid." The cashier said as she punched the order in. "That's thirty-five bucks even."

"Okay," Clara counted her money and handed it to the cashier.

"Don't I know you?" The cashier asked as she tendered the money.

"Uh, no. I just moved to Oswald City." Clara clearly lied. Her face had been plastered all over the papers just as much as I was. Everyone's a little too invested in our personal lives in my opinion. I know we are superheroes and we choose to have our identities out in the world, but that doesn't mean we don't deserve to have personal lives.

"No, I know I know you." The cashier argued as she stopped counting the change.

"Yeah, you do look familiar." A person, waiting for their order, added.

"Well, I don't know where I'd know you from since I'm new here. Uh, could I please get my change?" Clara shifted her feet. She was clearly uncomfortable.

"Wait, aren't you Cyanide's daughter?" The cashier questioned. Clara froze in her spot as I heard her suck in a breath and her heart rate picked up. She knew she had been recognized. "You are, aren't you? That's why you lied."

"Look, I just want my food. I don't want to cause any problems." Clara's voice was firm but quiet.

"We don't serve food to villains." The cashier shouted, gaining the attention of others. The cashier threw the cash in Clara's face. Clara fumbles to catch as much of the money as she can before it falls to the ground. She quickly picked up what did fall to the ground as people around whispered and pointed. No one even noticed me until I made my order. Clara ran off. I felt bad for her. I wanted to tell the cashier off, but I didn't. I simply doubled Clara's order. Of course, the cashier was sweet to me. She even gave me all the food for free and added two extra corn dogs to the order.

I listened to where Clara had run to. I found her in the parking lot slumped against a car. Her knees were against her chest and her face was buried in her knees as her arms wrapped around her legs. I could hear her sniffles as I approached her.

"Hey, Clara." I gently called.

Clara looked up, her eyes a bright blue with red rims. "What do you want?"

"I wanted to give you your food. I thought you should have it."

Clara hesitated, she was clearly unsure of my intentions. I set the food down so she knew I was genuine

he has yet to do so. I guess there are some things my father will take to his grave.

I do have my family's genetically brilliant mind. However, mine is more geared toward medicine. I helped develop several of the pills for Bio Metas including the pain meds Clara is currently taking.

Once I grab my watch, I put it on before heading to Clara's apartment. I'm hoping I don't run into Yuri. I know he will want confrontation. I also don't want to tell him Clara is with us. Yuri will surely throw a fit when he finds out Clara is being cared for by the League of Metas. I'd rather not be the one to break that news to him.

As I get closer to the Butcher Shop, I hope it's not open. Yuri has weird hours due to his many illegal operations. Plus, he doesn't have Clara to open the shop. I just don't know if he's figured out she's missing yet. Yuri and Clara don't seem overly close. Sometimes I wonder how much Clara truly trusts Yuri, but I don't think he trusts her. They don't have the father-daughter style relationship I thought they would have given the circumstances.

The butcher shop comes into my view and I listen to see if anyone is in the butcher shop. Thankfully, it's quiet. I land in the back and quickly go up the stairs to the door that leads to the apartment. I use my super strength to break the door. I don't have a choice. Yuri will know someone was here. I can't avoid that because I don't have a key.

I quickly look around the studio apartment. It's small and a little untidy. I quickly head to her closet to grab a duffle bag to fill with clothes. I look around trying to gently sort through her things for any clue. Then I spot the pill bottle sitting on the bathroom sink. I pick up the generic-looking white bottle. The label says headache pills. That's it. These clearly don't come from a doctor. I open the bottle to find basic white round pills. I dump a couple of them out. There are no words, numbers, or anything to indicate these are a legit prescription or something bought over the counter. I quickly put the pills back and close the bottle before sticking the bottle in the duffle bag. I certainly plan to ask Clara about these. I quickly grab a few more of her things that I think she might want in a tote bag before I get the hell out of her apartment. I don't want to linger and push my luck that Yuri will show up. Besides, I need to get home for Clara. She will be waking soon, and I have questions and news for her.

# HEROES & VILLAINS

## CHAPTER 4

### Clara

For the next few days, I'm in and out of it. The pain meds Collin is giving me are strong. Maybe a little too strong for my liking because right now I'm in flight mode. I need to be able to focus long enough to come up with a plan. I don't know how safe I am here. Right now, Collin is being, well, a hero. He's tending to my injuries, helping me to the bathroom, helping me eat, and taking care of me in general. It's strange having someone take care of me. I'm used to fending for myself. Although I can't lie, the help is nice because fuck me I'm in pain, which is why I don't mind taking the meds. Moving around is extremely difficult at the moment. I'm not going anywhere.

Still, I need to figure out my next move. Collin might be giving the appearance that I'm safe here, and maybe I am. The biggest problem I'm concerned about is whether Collin will let me walk away once I'm healed. If he does, I just need access to money and I can put my plan of disappearing into action. Unfortunately, I don't have as much as I would for my little disappearing act. However, what I have stashed in my apartment is enough to execute my plan. It's a little sooner than I wanted, but I know I'm no longer safe in the city. Not even with my so-called family of villains because if Yuri finds out I'm here, I'm screwed. I won't be able to get to my money.

I'm clearly not safe in Oswald City anymore. I've been jumped and attacked before, but not to this degree. I've never had broken bones, or been so badly injured that I couldn't suck up the pain and take care of myself. To be honest, I'm not sure I would be able to fend for myself with how badly I feel. I've never had stitches either. Collin ended up stitching a few of the cuts because they were a bit too deep. I think one of my attackers slashed me a few times with a butcher knife to mock the fact I work at a butcher's shop. I can't fully recall the event, and I know it's my mind's way of blocking the fear of what happened.

Thankfully, the butcher knife guy didn't go too crazy with the knife, but he did do a bit of damage. I'm sure I'll have a few scars after I heal, and luckily he didn't go near my face with the damn knife. He could have done some serious disfiguring with that knife. I hate to admit it, but Collin is saving my ass right now.

I can't get Collin off my mind, and it's not just because he holds the key to my fate because whether he wants to admit it or not, I'm his prisoner. I highly doubt I'm simply a guest here even if that's the illusion he wants me to buy. That's not the part that gets me because I've learned to anticipate all types of motivations of others over the years. What gets me is what he said about me having superpowers. I hope he's wrong. I don't want superpowers. Having superpowers blows my whole plan of fading away. Even if I tried to hide, I'd be hunted down by either the League of Metas or my father's crazy followers. I'd never be safe.

Then there is the fact that Collin is sex god hot. It's not even fair how sexy he is. His muscular build with his medium brown short hair that is floppy on the top, but neatly trimmed on the sides combined with his light facial hair, which complements his rectangular face shape. He's tall too which only adds to his slightly hulking figure. Oh, and let's not forget that the man is packing it in the downstairs region. It was hard not to notice when he was cleaning me up in the shower.

Collin entering the room breaks my thoughts. I slowly manage to painfully sit up as Collin comes striding over to the bed holding a duffle bag and tote bag.

"I see you're awake, Little Villain. How are you feeling?" He questions, setting the duffel bag and tote down at the bottom of the bed.

"Sore, like my body got hit by a bus," I reply in a snarky tone. I know he's trying to be nice, but seriously how the hell does he think I feel after being beaten within an inch of my life? I sure don't feel like a pocket full of fucking sunshine.

"I see we are feeling testy this morning." Collin mocks. "I can give you more pain meds." He suggests like he knows all the fucking answers. Actually, he probably does know more than me. Yuri truly keeps me in the dark about what goes on with my father's followers. I don't know anything about the mischief they get up to. Collin on the other hand is basically second in command of the League of Metas. He knows exactly what goes on in his city.

"No," I groan. I need to think straight. My head doesn't feel overly fuzzy at the moment due to the drugs wearing off. "If I take more, I'll end up sleeping." I use it as a lame excuse because I don't want to tell Collin I don't want it because I want to get the fuck out of here to run away. Collin might be kind but he's still a superhero, which makes him my enemy until he proves otherwise.

"You need rest, though. It will help you heal." Collin counters.

"I know. Maybe around bedtime, I'll take some more to help me sleep because I'm definitely not sleeping with the amount of pain I'm in." I do need to sleep, I just don't want to sleep all day. I need my mind to be clear some part of the day so I can figure out my next move.

"Well, at least you're trying to be reasonable. Harold is making some lunch. I also went to your apartment and grabbed you some clothes." Collin informs me. Shit, that's a problem I was hoping to avoid.

"You went to my apartment? How do you even know where I live?"

"All Bio Metas are registered. The League of Metas has a registry and knows where every Bio Meta resides, even the villains." Collin answers. That's not surprising. I surmised the League kept tabs on us. I'm sure they have spies just like the villains do.

"Did Yuri see you?" I question, secretly holding my breath.

"No, no one was around. I suspect they were looking for you."

"Well, at least I can go back home. That's if I'm even allowed to go home." I test the waters as I need to know where things are headed even if I have a gut feeling exactly where it's headed.

“You know it’s not that simple. I went to see my dad this morning. We want to help you with your superpowers. We can help you awaken your superpowers then we can help you train your superpowers.” Collin explains calmly.

“I don’t want a superpower. I don’t have one and I’m okay with that.”

“Clara, what are these?” Collin pulls out my headache pills.

“They’re for headaches. I’ve had severe headaches since I was a kid. My dad came up with a treatment for them. I need to take them at least once a week. I probably could use one now, but I can’t tell if my head is pounding due to my chronic headaches or the pain.” I answer.

“Clara there’s a very good chance these pills are suppressing your superpowers. Your headaches probably started around the time your superpowers were starting to emerge. I don’t think your dad was trying to help you when he gave you these pills.”

“Maybe he did help me because having superpowers is the last thing I want. You don’t know what superpowers would mean for me. The League of Metas would lock me up afraid that I will be like my father, and my father’s followers would force me to lead them in a cause I don’t care about. I don’t want to join either side, I just want to disappear.” I desperately try to explain out of frustration.

"We don't want to lock you up. We will train you. I will help you. Once you heal we can work on letting your superpowers emerge, which starts with tossing these damn pills. Once your superpowers emerge we can go to Oswald Tower where I will train you." Collin explains. I know his plan makes sense to him. I know that it probably seems crazy to him that I don't want superpowers. I don't care if my superpowers are being suppressed. It's the one favor my father did me before he abandoned me. I truly don't know if he's dead or alive. I know Yuri knows. I don't care if I know, it's probably better I don't know.

"I don't have a choice do I?" I question, even though I already know the answer.

"I don't think you will like the alternative option," Collin warns.

Did he really believe I would complacently agree to his plan? Well, he has another thing coming if he thinks I'm just going to accept his proposal because he's the one offering it to me. I swear the League of Metas think they are gods and we all should worship them. Then there are the assholes like my father who don't think I can handle the truth or whatever is wrong with me that he doesn't trust me with his secrets. Not that I necessarily want to know his secrets. I just want someone to be on my fucking side, but they all have their own agenda for me. What they all fail to realize is that I'm the Captain of my own damn ship.

"Are you threatening me?" I question.

Collin sighs in frustration. "No. I'm on your fucking side Clara. I'm trying to help you. You being here doesn't have to be a bad thing. All you have to do is keep an open mind." Collin tries to reason.

It's easy for him to be reasonable; he's not the prisoner. I might be a glorified prisoner, but it's very clear to me I will not be walking away freely. I don't even know if I can escape and if I do where the fuck do I go? At this rate, Yuri will find out I'm here. I won't be able to go home after this, which means no money. My worst nightmare of having superpowers is coming true unless by some grace I really am defective. Who am I kidding, I'm not that lucky.

I scoff as I wince in pain. Fuck my life right now. "Easy for you to say." I retort.

"Clara, please compromise a little. I really don't want to have to report to my dad you aren't on board with the plan."

"The plan that I had no say in. Everyone is always trying to control me and push their agenda on me. Why can't I just disappear? I'll keep suppressing my superpowers. I don't care. I just want to leave Oswald City. I'm not safe here and before you say that I am, look at my condition. I was walking home from the store with supplies that I needed when I was attacked. I wasn't doing a damn thing and I got beaten within an inch of my life. Even if I had superpowers I wouldn't have been able to fight seven men with weapons on my own. I might have done damage, but I wouldn't have walked away either. Having superpowers would make those attacks even more brutal. People would start attacking me because they think I'm dangerous. Shit, they already think I'm dangerous without superpowers. What do you think they would do out of their fear if they found out I had superpowers?" I beseech. I'm desperate for him to see my side of things.

"I can protect you. You will have the League's blessing to start training. We would make it known you were on our side. They would have no reason to attack you."

I laugh even though it's painful. "Saying I'm on your side makes me enemy number one to my father's followers. Some of them might try to abduct me and do some twisted shit to make me join the villains instead. No matter which side I pick, I lose. No one seems to realize that. Why the hell do you think I have stayed natural all these years? Why do you think I hide from everyone? I go to the store at midnight in hopes that I don't run into a soul. I don't involve myself with business on either side for a reason. Yet both sides can't accept that. I have to eventually pick a side, at least that's what you all think. Here's the thing, Mighty Hero, I don't have to pick a side because I don't want to."

"I didn't say this was easy for you. I didn't say you won the lottery with this offer. You know the League won't let you simply walk away. We also don't want to lock you up in a prison cell under Oswald Tower or send you to Nullum Island. Pick the lesser of the two evils. We are all trying to make the best of the situation. Yes, I know I have the advantage here, but I won't use it against you. Give me a chance because I'm willing to give you one. I didn't have to come up with this plan to save your ass from a prison cell. I don't have to do you favors, Little Villain. This isn't ideal for anyone involved, but I'm trying to make this less shitty for you." Collin skillfully counters.

"Fine. You win, I'll go with your stupid plan." I give in, knowing no matter what I lose. I don't know if Collin and the League of Metas are better than Yuri and my father's followers. Both sides have agendas for me, I guess I have to pick the one I can live with. Why the hell can't anyone ever leave me alone? "Oh, and those supplies I was getting were for my monthly and I'm due any day, so you might want to be prepared for that." I smugly comment knowing men hate the mention of a girl's period.

"Got it. Make me a list of what you need and I'll make sure you have it." Collin confidently replies with his own smug smile. Okay, I admit I expected him to be squeamish or something. Yuri and his sons could never stand me even mentioning my monthly. I'd have to hide my pads and tampons because they hated anything that reminded them of it. It was completely foolish. Collin on the other hand didn't even bat in eyelash.

I nod my head okay because honestly I'm done talking. I'm not going to win no matter what I do, so fuck it we will go with the dumpster fire fate has dumped on my lap. My worst fear of having superpowers is coming true because chances are Collin is right and those pills do suppress my superpowers. I'd be lying if I said the thought didn't cross my mind once or twice over the years. However, I would always shove the thoughts away. I preferred to be in ignorant bliss. The truth is overrated. Sometimes lies do more good than the truth. It's all part of the lovely morally grey area that everyone prefers to ignore. The problem is the morally grey area tends to be reality and right now my reality sucks balls.

# BIRDY RIVERS

## CHAPTER 5

### Collin

The next several days Clara fights me on just about everything. She even started refusing help to the bathroom. I think it's because she started her monthly and she wants to handle her business in private. She's vulnerable for many reasons. I'm sure she feels trapped and in a way, she is trapped. I wish this was a little different because I do want to help Clara, but I fear she is always going to think I have alternative intentions.

The problem is I might actually have alternative intentions. Damn, my mom and her suggestions. She is right, Clara will need a bigger reason to stay. She doesn't want her superpowers and the fact that she rather keep taking the pills than let her superpowers emerge speaks volumes. She is not going to join our side easily, but at least she is cooperating for the time being.

I'm nervous about bringing her to Oswald Tower. She is going to feel like an animal caught in a cage. I don't know how welcome she will be. Most of the League look at her as the enemy. It's going to take some convincing that Clara belongs with us. Everyone always remembers her as Cyanide's daughter, but they forget she is also Pyro Princess's daughter. Janna might have made poor choices in the love department. Yet I think there's more to Janna and Benji's story. Still, Janna was overall good and she had her reasons for choosing Benji.

The League needs to remember that Clara isn't either of her parents. She is her own person and I believe what she wants more than anything is to find a place she belongs. I know she claims she wants to disappear, but I don't believe she truly wants that. I understand why she doesn't want superpowers and why she may feel the need to disappear. I want to show her there is more. There is no reason Clara can't have a place in the League. It won't be an easy path as trust needs to be built, but it's doable.

My other concern is why the fuck Cyanide suppressed her superpowers in the first place. Her superpowers never fully emerged. Clara has no idea what her superpowers could be. Although, I'm not sure she would tell me if she did. Still, it makes no sense how Cyanide could have known what her superpowers were before she did. There is something I'm missing and I probably won't figure it out until Clara's superpowers emerge. Unfortunately, that won't be for several more weeks. Clara has a lot of healing to do. I'm sure the pain meds are masking her headaches. I also have no idea how long it will take for the effects of the suppressant to wear off. Clara has been taking suppression pills for close to a decade. There is no way of knowing how long it will take for it to clear her system or if there is any damage

I'm having the pills analyzed at Oswald Tower. I want to know what they are made of and if they are something any Bio Meta can take or if the pill needs to be tailored to a specific Bio Meta. I don't know how Yuri has been making these pills. We also have no way of knowing if he is using them on other people. Cyanide obviously left Yuri with instructions on how to manufacture the pills for Clara. I don't know how dangerous these pills are, but I'll find out soon enough.

Harold is still being a grumpy ass about Clara being here. He needs to get over himself. Clara didn't kill Lois, Cyanide did. I know Lois's death was incredibly hard for Harold. I also know I have no idea what it's like to be in his position. I've never fallen in love and I've never lost a wife. Still, his grief makes him a bit blind where Clara is concerned. She is innocent. Once again it's clear that Clara pays for her father's sins, and it's not fair.

I don't know how on board Mason and Nina or the rest of the League will be with this plan. Nina is a lot like her father in her views of Clara. Mason and the rest of the League could go either way. Mason will eventually catch on that I'm interested in her. Despite my mother's suggestion, I do have genuine feelings and interest in Clara. I do want to see what there is between us because there is a magnetic pull. I know she feels it too, and I'm sure it scares her. I don't know much about her dating life, but if I were to guess I would say it's similar to mine. I don't think either of us has any idea what it's like to be in a serious relationship. I've fooled around with girls and I've definitely had sex. I walked a fine line of becoming a playboy. It wasn't on purpose, I was just having fun. When I realized I was too close to being someone I didn't like, I backed off from sleeping around. Now, I only have sex a couple of times a year. I have a few go-to fuck buddies.

Unfortunately, for me, I haven't had sex in six months. I'm getting to the point where I'd call one of my fuck buddies. Except, I don't want to. I'd rather wait until Clara is ready for it, if she is ever ready for it. I want her in more ways than one. I hate that everything has to be so complicated between us. We have this barrier to cross from enemies to something else. It's going to take time because trust is built over time.

# CHAPTER 6

## Clara

It's been a few weeks since I've become a permanent guest at Oswald Manor. Almost all my injuries have healed. I can finally get around on my own. The only thing that hasn't changed is my random intense headaches. Collin seems to think the headaches are my superpower's way of trying to come through. He's probably right because he is smart when it comes to these things. Collin certainly has the brilliant Oswald mind. I don't have anything from my parents. I don't know if that's a good or a bad thing.

I can't even begin to process my dad suppressing my superpowers. I don't know why he did it. The crazy thing is I'm not sure I'm even mad about it. In many ways, he did me a favor by suppressing my superpowers. I fear what my superpowers are. What if they are similar to my father's? I don't know what I want my superpowers to be because I never bothered with it. I was content to think I didn't have superpowers. I should have known I wouldn't be able to simply disappear as I wanted.

I'm walking out of the bathroom. Thankfully, my cycle was quick and Collin wasn't freaked out that I had my monthly. Of course, I had to have it a few days after I arrived at Oswald Manor. I'm a prisoner, I'm bound to get my monthly here. At least, I was given feminine products. It could be worse. I could be locked up in a cell. I'm fairly free to roam the manor although I only recently became mobile without any help.

"You're moving around nicely." Collin comments as I walk out of the bathroom.

"I'm so glad you approve, Doctor." I retort in a smartass tone.

"You should start training before we head to Oswald Tower." Colling suggests totally skipping over my smart comment.

"We aren't going anytime soon." I counter, not in the mood to think about training. I'm still not happy that I'm stuck here. I'm pissed that I will never be able to disappear. I'm stuck as a glorified prisoner and forced to face superpowers I don't want. I'm bitter at the moment and I'm not afraid to admit it.

"Your superpowers will emerge soon enough. Your intense headaches are your superpowers trying to manifest. Without the pills suppressing you, your superpowers are going to surface sooner rather than later. I've had the pills analyzed. They require you to take them consistently to work. Your superpowers are coming and when they do we have to go to Oswald Tower. Training is going to be intense there. You are not even remotely in shape and you just healed from rough injuries. You need a head start or you won't make it through training for the League." Collin lectures me.

"Well, we all don't train to be heroes at birth." I snarkily counter.

"Take it seriously, Little Villain. You know the deal. Try not to be too difficult." Collin warns as he bridges the gap between us. Shit, it's hard to resist his charm when he's close. The hardest part about this whole fucking thing is not spreading my legs for Collin fucking Oswald, but fuck me. I can see why women swoon over him.

"I might lose the war, Mighty Hero, but that doesn't mean I won't try to win some battles along the way." There's a very tiny gap between us now. It's far too easy to fill the gap and let our bodies touch, but I won't fucking do that. "Fine, I'll start with walking." I push past Collin, not wanting to risk giving in to my desires for him.

Collin is the only guy I've been attracted to like this. I'm not a virgin. I lost my virginity when I was sixteen to some random guy at a Home Day party. He was wearing an alien mask and I was wasted. I got so drunk I barely remember having sex. Hell, I think I passed out during it or just before, but I know it happened because my thighs were blood-stained and I was sore between my legs. I felt violated after because I didn't remember it. When I was making out with the guy, I wanted to go all the way. I was tired of being a virgin and alcohol made it seem like a good idea to lose it to some random guy. It wasn't a great choice. I haven't had sex since then. One-night stands clearly weren't going to be my thing. The only guys who wanted to date me were interested in my father and fucking the all-mighty Cyanide's daughter. No one wanted to date me for me.

It's not that I haven't wanted to have sex. Fuck, I've wanted to experience sex where I remember it and enjoy it. The chance never seemed to come. Now, the chance has come and I can't take it. I can't have sex with Collin. It doesn't matter how badly I'd like to because I have a feeling the Mighty Hero knows how to pleasure a woman like a god. I need to resist. I have no clue if I can trust Collin. Plus, I still want to try to disappear. I have no idea how to disappear when I'm a prisoner and I have no money. I'm not sure there is an amount of money that would allow me to completely disappear. I want to disappear more than ever because having superpowers is a nightmare come to life.

"At least you can be reasonable, Little Villain." Collin comments.

"Only because I don't have a choice." I retort, heading straight for the couch. "Since you think I'm well enough to start exercise then I guess you should take your bed back. I can sleep on the couch or in another room." I offer.

"You still need proper rest, and I don't mind you staying in my bed. Maybe I like you in it." I stop dead in my tracks. He can't mean it in a sexual way can he? No, cool down lady parts. It doesn't matter if he does. Cold and distant is the way to go. Don't let the sexy hero break down your walls. Your walls keep you safe. I remind myself. I will not unravel. I will stand my ground.

"The bed is big enough for both of us." I taunt. Why am I taunting the Mighty Hero? I guess I like to play with fire. I am Pyro Princess's daughter after all. Maybe my superpowers have something to do with fire. Not that superpowers seem to have a rhyme or reason for what they are.

"Oh, the day I join you in my bed we won't be sleeping, Little Villain. Trust me, we will definitely not be sleeping." Collin winks at me. I have to keep my jaw from fucking dropping to the ground. Well, he's not going to make resisting his god-like charm easy. I want to hate him so badly, but he hasn't actually given me a reason to.

"Does it ever get tiring being so confident all the time?" I mock, making myself comfortable on the couch before picking up the remote to turn the TV on. At least, Collin has every streaming service and I can rent whatever I want too. It's nice having access to luxury. I definitely didn't get luxury like this living with Yuri. Perhaps I've upgraded my lifestyle by becoming a prisoner. Now that's an insane thought yet somehow it's a little true.

"No, not when it comes easy. Enjoy your last day in front of the TV. I'm going to go make sure you have everything you need. Any requests?" Collin inquires stopping in front of the TV so he's blocking my view of the menu options.

"I need to listen to music if I'm going to be forced to train. The music better be good too. I like rock and metal. Do with that as you will." I demand, looking around him to select the option I want.

"I think I can come up with something. Is that all?"

"There better be some good workout snacks and drinks. Don't give me that nasty tasting crap either. Shit better taste good or I'm not eating or drinking it." I'm not one to work out. I'm in no denial that I'm out of shape and that it's not going to suck ass getting into shape.

I'm well aware of how intense training is at Oswald Tower. They take shit seriously. Anyone training to join the League of Metas goes through intense training and tests. It's not easy to become a superhero. Most Bio Meta's get placed doing everyday type jobs. Some smart ones and other talented Bio Meta's get to work in Oswald Tower. It's not a joke there. They take being superheroes to a new level. It's like superheroes meeting celebrities. The only thing the League of Meta's is missing is starring in their own cheesy ass superhero movies or a terrible reality show about their daily life.

The League lives life in the spotlight. They are the ones the city looks up to. It's going to be intimidating as fuck going there. I'm going to be judged for everything I do and say. Half of them I'm sure will be pissed up there and try to bully me. Most of them will gossip and talk about me behind my back. I'm sure somehow I'll be made public enemy number one in the social circles there. I'm not looking forward to leaving Oswald Manor. At least here I'm tucked away from prying eyes. I only have to deal with Collin and Harold. I can handle that.

Going to Oswald Tower means dealing with a ton of other people. I'll have to meet Thomas and Veronica. I'm sure I'll meet the entire League at some point. Some of them are going to treat me like a prisoner or say that I don't deserve to be there. I'm going to be literally behind enemy lines, again. I never fully trusted Yuri. I always kept waiting for him to reveal his dark plans for me. Plans that I'm sure my father is involved with. Everyone has plans for me and no one cares about the plans that I actually want.

Technically, I'm behind enemy lines now. Somehow here it doesn't feel as intense as this is the bubble of safety. I don't know why I oddly feel safe at the manor. I don't know if it's Collin's presence or something else. All I know is that going to Oswald Tower is going to be stressful and I'm in no hurry for my superpowers to emerge. I don't care if I have to deal with mind-shattering migraines. I'd gladly suck up the torture of the headaches forever if it meant my superpowers never emerged. The day my superpowers emerge is the day that I'm truly fucked.

# BIRDY RIVERS

## CHAPTER 7

### Collin

I can't believe I'm fucking shopping for a girl. Never in my life have I gone shopping for a girl. Even when I date, the gifts I give girls aren't ones that I buy. I'm not even buying a gift for Clara, I'm buying workout gear. Clara has nothing to train in, so here I am at a sports store picking out girl shit that I know nothing about. That's why I've asked Nina here. I'm sure I'll regret it, but I need help. I've been here for over an hour trying to decide which yoga pants are the better ones. I know absolutely nothing about sports bras. Yeah, I need fucking help.

Nina arrives surprisingly quickly. She was probably nearby, shopping. Nina shops at every chance she can get. Nina stops to take a few pictures with fans while I pull my baseball cap a bit further down, trying to not be recognized. Nina loves living in the spotlight. I fucking hate it, that's why I'm trying to hide under a stupid baseball cap. It's the price to pay for being an Oswald. I do like helping people and protecting the city. I enjoy being able to use my superpowers for good. I just could do without the fame part of it.

Personally, I wish we kept our identities a secret. Wore fucking masks or something to try and hide who we are. People don't need to know who we are in real life. They only need to know our superhero names. I hate that people know that Stronghold is also Collin Oswald. My grandfather thought it was better if we were out in the open with our identities to prove we had nothing to hide. The villains had no problem putting their identities out in the open so why should the heroes hide behind masks?

Nina strides over as a few more fans snap pictures from a distance. I'm sure they will realize who I am soon enough. I take pictures and sign shit for fans. Most of our supporters are just happy to get a picture with us. Some take it to new levels with wanting to own shit that was once ours. Every year there is a huge gala fundraiser for the city's needs like education, public transportation improvement, helping the homeless, and more. Each of the League members gives something of value that we own for supporters to buy. They spend hundreds and thousands of dollars on the items. It's not just humans who participate in the auction, other Bio Metas who look up to us want a piece of us too. I really do wish we had secret identities.

"I'm all for shopping, Collin, but workout gear? I thought it was regular clothes or jewelry. Hell, I'd take lingerie over this. Seriously, I can find something sexy for your prisoner to wear." Nina suggests with a wink. I wonder if my mom had a talk with her about accepting Clara into the fold and about me potentially dating her. The last time I talked to Nina about Clara she cautioned me not to get involved with her. Now, she is suggesting I buy lingerie. I'm certainly skeptical.

"I'm sorry to disappoint you, Nina. I need training shit for Clara and I don't know what I'm buying. I didn't know there were different types of sports bras and yoga pants." I state agitated as I shift uncomfortably. The longer we are here the higher the chance we get recognized. The last thing I need is rumors getting around that I'm shopping for a mystery girl.

"Alright, grumpy pants. I'll do my best to pick some stuff out that Clara might like. I'm assuming black and dark colors are her thing?" Nina asks as if I fucking know the answer.

"Probably," I reply, hoping to move this along quickly. I can hear the whispers that aren't whispers to me. I know they know we are here and they are trying to figure out what we are doing here. Nina and I definitely don't go shopping together so this little outing is certainly gaining unwanted attention.

It takes Nina forty-five minutes to gather yoga pants, sports bras, tank tops, sneakers, and socks. By the time we check out the paparazzi have gotten wind that we are here. I quickly buy the shit and quickly leave the store while Nina stays behind to take more photos with fans. At least, she is distracting them so I can make a getaway. I dart away from the gathering crowd and when I'm safe enough away, I take off in the air with my bags.

I'm happy when I land back home. I walk into my room to find Clara resting on the couch with some action movie playing in the background. I toss the bags on the floor next to her, startling her from her trance of the TV.

"Here, Little Villain. Be ready tomorrow by seven in the morning." I command.

Clara looks at me then at the bags on the floor before rifling through the bags. "These are nice. You didn't pick them out, did you?" She taunts holding up one of the sports bras. That's when I realize the bra has lace details. Damn it, Nina. What the fuck did my mom say to Nina to change her tune? My mom is good at persuasion and it's not even her superpower.

"I had help from Nina. You'll meet Harlod's daughter soon enough." I reply casually as she continues to pull things from the bags.

"You act like I don't know who the League of Metas are. I know who Nina Gavin is, aka Ice Queen. I'm sure she will just love to be friends with the daughter of the guy who killed her mom." Clara sarcastically replies. Fuck, she makes me want to tame that attitude. Not in a way that suppresses her, but in a way that makes her mine. Shit. I didn't think it would be this hard to resist her. Our chemistry is magnetic. I know she feels it too. It's something I can't explain.

The aliens we are decedent from have destined mates on the home planet. Somehow they have the ability to sense who their soulmate is. I'm not even sure that it's a real thing and not some cute story to make people believe in love. So far, Bio Metas don't seem to share the alien ability to sense their destined mate. We are like humans taking shots in the dark hoping we hit a bullseye. However, what if we are destined mates? Is it even possible? Great, just another complex thought related to my little villain.

"I didn't say going to Oswald Tower would be easy for you. Nina will need time to come around, like Harold, but they will. You just have to prove you aren't the villain they fear you are. You're going to have to do that with a lot of people." I counter harshly.

I'm not going to sugarcoat shit for her. I don't envy what she has to face, but I'll do my best to be there for her while she does face this challenge. Her walls are so high. She is guarded because she feels the need to protect herself. She doesn't believe she is safe. How do I convince her that her enemy isn't going to harm her when she has clearly been hurt by those she calls friends? Clara is in a permanent state of paranoia that I need to snap her out of. I need to gain her trust as much as she needs to gain mine. We are trying to work past the impossible situation that we have been thrown into. I won't lie, I have the advantage. I know that. It's why I'm trying to not use the advantage I have against her, but fuck, she can make it hard sometimes with that smartass attitude.

"Even with you, Mighty Hero?" Clara challenges, raising an eyebrow.

"Yes, but I know trust is a two-way street as is respect and loyalty. I'm cocky, but I can also be down to earth too. I know I have the advantage here, but I won't use it against you. Well, that's if you don't tempt me to use it against you, Little Villain."

"Eh, what can I say? I like to live on a razor's edge." Clara says as she shrugs her shoulders before going back to sorting through the bags.

I shake my head at her. Always on the defensive as she puts on her mask that she isn't breaking on the inside. She's mastered her own masquerade. I seem to be the only one to see what she hides underneath. "Thank you for the clothes. I'm glad I don't have to work out in pajamas." She jokes as she deflects more of her hidden pain.

"We should probably get you some more clothes. I didn't grab even a portion of your clothes. I didn't have a lot of time because I didn't want to run into Yuri. When we get to Oswald Tower, I'll make sure you get a chance to go shopping for new stuff." I reply, knowing I'm not going to break down her walls right now.

"That's nice of you. I forgot Oswalds have endless money." For fucks sake she can't even take generosity. What the fuck has she endured to make her so guarded that she deflects every chance she gets? Clara has my fucking curiosity in more than one way.

"You're welcome," I say before heading to my closet to grab some workout shorts.

I need to go for a run, punch a bag, or lift some weights. I need to decompress and think. Working out is where I try to sort out my scattered thoughts concerning

Clara. Clara is increasingly becoming a complex situation. I know she is my responsibility and I don't want to fuck things up between us, but the friction between us is sure to spark a fire neither of us will be able to put out.

# CHAPTER 8

### Clara

Training with Collin isn't as horrible as I thought it would be. We work out in the gym where he blares rock and metal for us. I was surprised to find out the mighty hero and I liked the same music. I'm all the way healed now so we have moved to hand on hand combat, which Collin definitely has the advantage over me. We have only been training for a few weeks and it became clear very fast that Collin has the advantage over me in more ways than one. I'm also incredibly out of shape. I knew I was, but it's another thing having it proven.

Then there is the little fact that my headaches have completely stopped. About a week ago I woke up and they were gone. Completely gone like they were never a problem to begin with. I've told Collin they have gone, but I didn't tell him the strange things happening since they went away. The predictions of what someone will say or do. Every meal I can guess what Harold is going to make before he makes it like I've seen a glimpse of the future. It's strange and it happens every day. I don't know what it means. I'm not even sure I'm not making up the whole thing.

I haven't told Collin because I'm not sure it means anything, and I'm in no rush to have my superpower emerge. I'm sure whatever is happening is related to my superpowers, but I don't want anyone to know because that means I have to go to Oswald Tower and I'm not ready for that. I'm not ready to face everything that means. I like the bubble I'm in and I don't want it to pop.

I know my bubble will pop eventually, but I'm not going to help it pop faster. That's why every time Collin asks if anything is happening superpower-wise, I fudge the truth. I tell him there is nothing to report. I'm not going to report every little strange thing. I don't want to be analyzed like some science experiment, even if that's technically what Bio Meta's are.

It's bad enough I have to play twenty questions every day with Collin so he can figure out if my superpowers are emerging. Then I have to spend a couple of hours training and getting my ass kicked while getting it in shape. I hate to say it, but Collin was right to start me training now. I know he's going fairly easy on me to help ease me into the intense training that I will endure at

Oswald Tower. I don't know how I got stuck with him as my permanent trainer. I guess that's a good thing because I can handle Collin. I hate to admit it but I like the mighty hero even if I refuse to give in to his temptation.

Well, I say I refuse, but half the time I'm playing with fire with him. I enjoy taunting and playing hard to get with him. A little game of cat and mouse. I know I'm probably going to lose this war against my desires at some point, but I'm trying to hold out for as long as I can. Having sex with Collin is a complication I'm not ready for because with him it's not going to be a one-night stand. This isn't going to be a drunk memory that I can barely recall. This isn't going to be something I can regret.

Besides, what does having sex with Collin mean? He's a hero and I'm a villain by association. I'm the enemy and technically his prisoner. It's either train at Oswald Tower and pretend I'm there of my own free will, or actually be locked in some Bio Meta prison like a fucking animal. I'm picking the lesser of the two evils, but in doing so, I'm putting everything on the line. The worst is I'm putting my emotions and heart on the line because I don't know if Collin is interested in me and if he is, well, I don't know his intentions.

The problem with Collin is he is literally the good guy. The kind of guy you should date. He cares, is compassionate, protective, a little possessive, and considerate. He treats a woman right. Collin will fuck a woman like he owns her, but he won't control her. He respects women and treats them like an equal, but submitting to him when it comes to sex is a must. He's the ideal guy yet he's completely untouchable because we are not even in the same league. I don't deserve the hero because I'm the villain, which brings up a whole other issue.

If I'm the villain then don't I belong with the villains, not the heroes. I guess that's why I'm technically their prisoner, but it's as if they are trying to convert me or get me to join them. I'm not sure any of them would ever trust me given who my father is. To say my father has left a path of destruction that affects many is an understatement. He's killed so many people and many of them hate me for it. Harold and Nina are perfect examples and they aren't the first ones I've run into that want me to pay for the sins of my father.

I'm a villain by pure association, but most people expect me to become a true villain. My father's followers, including Yuri, expect me to become a villain, to truly live up to being the daughter of the great villain, Cyanide. I'm his daughter, therefore I must be evil too. Everyone expects me to be the villain, except fucking Collin who seems to think he can turn me into some hero.

That's the problem. Collin doesn't want a villain or even an anti-hero at his side. He wants a heroine. He wants someone that will be loved by the people, like him. He doesn't want someone like me. Whatever lust, desire, and need is between us, it can never be more than that. We can't function as a couple. I'm not the girl for him. I belong with someone like that asshole in the alien mask who took advantage of me at Yuri's Home Day party. I don't deserve to have someone treat me well. So, why don't I simply become the villain they all expect me to be?

I could. The demons deep within me would love nothing more than to become the villain I'm told I should be. I could take my father's place. Lead his followers and be a menace. If my father is alive then I could be his princess of violence. I could make him proud and be just as dark and twisted as him. I am more than capable of becoming a villain. It would be easy, like flipping a switch inside of me. A switch I've always known I've had. A switch I've ignored. Maybe I should flip it, maybe I should become the villain. I'll have my superpowers soon enough. There is no denying that something is waking up inside of me. Something radiating beneath my skin, humming in my veins, threatening to consume every fiber of my being.

"Pay attention, Little Villain." Collin criticizes me as I land hard on my back. I guess I shouldn't be so deep in thought while training. "For a minute there, you were going off instinct and doing great. Then you lost it, which is why you are on your ass."

"Yeah, I got that, thanks." I reply snarkily.

"Stay on your back, I want to see if you can counter me on the ground because despite what you might think, you might have to essentially wrestle someone on the ground. You won't always be standing." Collin directs.

I do as I am told and stay lying flat on my back. Collin gets on his belly. His ankles come under my legs, almost propping my legs up on his ankles. I'm not even sure how the fuck to counter him in this position. I guess it's good to assume I'm going to get knocked on my ass while fighting crime. If I even fight crime. I don't even fucking know why the League is even bothering training me unless they plan on me fighting with them. Perhaps it's a show or a stunt for some publicity thing. The League can sometimes get caught up in the fame of being superheroes. A problem villains don't have because we hate the spotlight. The villains that do like the spotlight, well, they are problems.

Before I even have a chance to counter Collin, he quickly flips me on my stomach. Not only does he flip himself, he's now on top of me. My back flush with his hard abs. His one arm comes around my neck as he lightly chokes me while his other hand supports him so he doesn't crush me. Fuck his super strength. While I want to be impressed, I'm distracted by the fact that he is on top of me and lightly choking me. The problem isn't that I'm afraid, I'm fucking turned on.

"Too slow, Little Villain. You need to get out of your head." Collin says lowly into my ear. His voice vibrates against my skin causing me to shiver with anticipation.

I don't know how to compete with him. The man has me outranked on so many levels. I'm in destructive mode. The villain in me wants to play and she wants to play with fire. My ass is perfectly flush with his dick right now, so I begin to move against Collin's dick. He's already semi-hard. Glad to know I'm not the only one struggling with the fucking magnetic pull between us. I rub against him some more as I feel his dick growing. Just as I start to feel smug, Collin flips me onto my back as he pins my arms to either side of my head. I swallow hard realizing I might have started a dumpster fire instead of a small trash can fire.

"We talked about this, Little Villain. Don't start games you know you can't win." Collin warns.

"What makes you think I can't win?" I challenge.

Collin puts his one knee between my legs, parting them as he slides his knee between my legs so it rests against my pussy. He rubs his knee against me causing so much friction in the right places I almost let out a fucking moan.

“I have more knowledge about sex than you do,” He rubs his knee against my pussy again and I have to fucking bite my lip from moaning. “Tell me I’m wrong, Little Villain?” Collin smugly questions.

“You’re not wrong,” I confess because shit he’s got me there.

I’ve had sex once and I barely remember it from being so drunk and the fact that I think my mind is trying to block out the fact that I was taken advantage of that night. Of course, I’d have a fucked up experience losing my virginity. I don’t have much to go on, and Collin fucking knows it. Just one more advantage he has that I don’t.

Collin brushes his lips against mine. “I’ll enjoy putting your sassy ass in line.”

“You really think you can tame me, Mighty Hero?” I challenge him because I can’t help myself. The villain in me enjoys being a temptress.

“I know exactly how to tame you, Little Villain. All I have to do is give you the one thing you want more than to disappear,” He pauses as my breath hitches in my throat as his one hand strokes my cheek. I don't even dare move my hand from the position he put it in. "I accept you for who you are, Little Villain. Every fucking damaged part." Just like that, I'm puddy in this man's hands. I know he means it too. That's what makes it strike down the walls around my heart. Fuck me, I underestimated the game I started with the mighty hero. Collin briefly brushes his lips against mine, tempting me to kiss him. Fuck, I want to, but I'm not ready to lose the game just yet. "You're not ready to submit all the way, and that is why this training session is over." Collin declares as he peels his body from mine, making me miss his touch.

Collin says nothing as he helps me up from my frozen position on the ground. I don't know how I lost control of the training session. I thought I was going to tempt him a little. I didn't think he would shatter one of my walls with his words. He only broke down one wall, though, but he is the first person to ever threaten to break them all.

We go our separate ways. I head to shower needing to gather my conflicting emotions. I hate that I'm so drawn to Collin. I hate that he knows how to break my walls down. Yet I love that he sees me. Collin actually believes in me and I don't know why I find that so terrifying. He believes I deserve to be at his side. He's not bullshitting and I don't know how to handle it. I've never been faced with someone who genuinely wanted me. I've always been wanted because of my association to my father. Collin certainly has no loyalty to my father, so he doesn't want to fuck me for that reason. I have to admit that part is refreshing and appreciated.

Fuck me, I can't fall for Collin Oswald. I don't like that Collin holds the ability to derail my plans and change my mind. I should consider him dangerous, but I don't. He's only my enemy because my father told me he was. Even as a child my father told me that the Oswald family was our enemy. What does my father fucking know? He's not even around. I hope he is dead because if he's not than that means he straight up abandoned me for his fucking mission.

My father also suppressed my superpowers. While I might have originally thanked him, I'm beginning to wonder about his intentions. I highly doubt he had my best interests at heart. I'm not even sure I want to know why he did it. All I know is that when I try to think about any memory associated with my headaches, the headache pills, or me having superpowers it's a black space as if my mind is suppressing memories to protect me. It's the same thing with that drunken night. The question becomes what was so bad my mind has to protect me?

Maybe I should keep an open mind with Collin. Maybe he can show me a life I can be happy with because he's right. All I want is to be accepted somewhere. I want a home, a family, a place where I'm safe and loved. So far, my dad or his followers haven't given me that. So what if Collin can? Is that the worst thing? What if he isn't truly my enemy? What then? Shit, I'm fucked. Yet somehow deep within my soul I know Collin and I are going to be together. How do I fucking know that? I don't know, but I know it's tied to my superpowers and it terrifies me.

# CHAPTER 9

## Collin

Fuck me, I'm getting blue balls because of my little villain. It's been a tense week of training since I almost fucked her during training. I want to fuck her so badly it's not even funny. I actually like her. I don't need to take my mom's crazy suggestion to date Clara so she will have the motivation to join the League. I truly want to date Clara because I have feelings for her. There's something between us I can't deny and I know she is struggling to not deny it herself. Clara is on a razor's edge because that's how she has had to live for most of her life. She's in survival mode and I don't know if she knows how to turn it off. Her walls are high and there are many of them. Yet I don't care. I want to know everything about her and I want to own her everything.

The problem is I can't be getting distracted right now with my desire for Clara. I'm supposed to be training her. She is not ready to go to Oswald Tower yet, and the shitty part is she might have to go soon. I know her headaches have stopped which means her superpowers might be starting to appear. If they are, she's hiding it. I know exactly why she is hiding it too and I can't blame her. For someone who wants to disappear, she is about to be cast in the spotlight. I actually hate that we have to put her in the spotlight. I don't enjoy the spotlight myself, and Clara is someone who is going to loathe it because of how private she is.

My father has an idea for a press conference where he welcomes Clara to Oswald Tower. He wants to show she is here of her own free will to the public because of Yuri's recent demands. Yuri and Cyanide's other followers are not thrilled Clara is with us. I'm not entirely sure how they figured out she was with us to begin with. The League hasn't made it known yet, but we will now because we don't have a choice. Yuri thinks we are holding Clara prisoner, and they would be somewhat right. The difference is if they know that for sure then it will spark a war. Clara knows this and if she doesn't she will when my dad essentially makes her a sacrificial lamb.

My father is planning to make a statement that he welcomes Clara with open arms to Oswald Tower to train as one of us making it appear Clara is doing all of this of her own free will, which will make her an enemy to her father's followers. It won't be easy for her to earn their trust again, if ever at all. He's doing this to cover our asses. Clara isn't going to be happy. I doubt she wants Yuri or anyone to know she is here, let alone here of her own free will. Clara knows she is technically a prisoner. Training at Oswald Tower stops her from being locked in a Bio Meta prison cell or worse taken to Nullum Island. I know why my dad wants to make it appear Clara is doing this of her own free will. It's to not give Yuri or any of Cyanide's other followers a reason to start war.

The truth is Clara does have a chance to be a part of the League. That isn't a lie. If she can prove herself, she can join. I wasn't lying when I told her I would show her a place at my side. I meant it in every way. The goal is to make Clara an ally, not an enemy. It simply won't happen overnight, but it can happen with time.

Right now, I need her superpower to emerge so we can get back to Oswald Tower. As much as I enjoy being at Oswald Manor, I need to get back to the city. I still have duties that I need to attend to. Duties I've been neglecting in favor of helping Clara heal up and prepare to go to Oswald Tower. I can't put off going back much longer. I also don't want to bring Clara to Oswald Tower until her superpowers fully emerge. That's why I'm not happy she is hiding what's going on with her. She has to be experiencing symptoms of some sort. It's fairly obvious when our superpowers are trying to emerge. It's hard to ignore and usually uncomfortable in some way, which is why I think Clara's terrible headaches were very much related to her superpowers. I think it was her superpowers trying to emerge and work past the suppression of the medicine. Now that her headaches have stopped she should be having signs of superpowers. I keep hoping I'll see a visible sign that I can point out to encourage her to tell me if there is more. Unfortunately, nothing obvious which means her superpowers might not be physical like mine.

It was fairly clear that I had super strength. I would lightly touch something and it would get crushed. I destroyed so many toys, electronics, and furniture by pure accident because I didn't know my own strength. I also had what appeared to be sensitive hearing which was really my super hearing. My superpowers are physical so the signs that they were emerging were hard to ignore. I also had extreme muscle aches and I constantly felt like my body was stretching when it wasn't. Eventually, the muscle aches and stretching feeling went away and that's when my super strength started to show.

It's like that for almost all Bio Metas. Clara should be following that pattern as well. The suppression shouldn't affect how her superpowers emerge as they had to have already emerged to suppress them to begin with. Which makes me wonder what Clara's superpowers are. She can't remember ever having superpowers, but she does remember the headaches which were the reason for her pills. I don't know what motive Cyanide had for suppressing her superpowers. I'm not even sure I want to know them because I doubt they were to protect her. Cyanide is a stressful topic for another day. He's like a guillotine that threatens us all because if he is alive and comes back who knows what that could mean? It's not something I want to deal with yet as I have to focus on Clara. She's my priority.

I have to find a way to get her to open up to me about what might be going on with her superpowers. Interrogating her is clearly not working. I don't actually mean for my questions to come off as an interrogation but Clara enjoys being stubborn. She also enjoys being a temptress and playing games she clearly is not ready for. I can't wait for her to be ready to submit to me because when she does it's going to change everything between us for the better. I know deep in my soul that Clara is meant to be mine. I think she knows that too, but she has to fight it because that's her nature. She has to fight everything because she believes everyone is against her. She's a little paranoid and rightfully so. Hopefully, with time Clara will learn she is safe with me because we aren't meant to be enemies.

# CHAPTER 10

## Clara

I'm usually glad when night comes. Sometimes I hate being awake because my thoughts never seem to stop. They bounce around everywhere trying to figure out what path I'm supposed to take, what the fuck my superpowers are, what I should do about Collin, if I'm meant to be a villain or not, and so on. It's exhausting to have them never stop. I'm also on edge constantly. That's nothing new, though. I've been on edge most of my life always guarded and ready to fight my way out of hell. Except now I'm not sure what is hell or heaven. What is my doom or my salvation?

My doom should be being behind enemy lines and going deeper into a world I don't belong in. My salvation should be with my father's followers, leading them until he returns because somehow I know that asshole is alive and on the home planet aka Altron. How do I know that? I don't fucking know, but I know it. I seem to know a lot of things these days. Something deep within my soul that tells me the absolute truth.

That soul wrenching truth deep within tells me my doom is my father and my salvation is Collin, which makes everything backward from what I've been essentially brainwashed to think. It only confuses me on what path I should take. If Collin and the League are my salvation, my safety then what the fuck does that say about my father? Shouldn't he be my safe place?

Then again, he's a true villain. He's killed hundreds if not thousands. His true agenda is terrifying. He wants to kill off the humans that he deems worthless and the ones that are worth something he wants to enslave. I have nothing against humans. Hell, Bio Metas are half human. I think there is much more to the story of why the aliens came to the human planet. They had a hidden agenda. The question then becomes were Bio Metas a part of that agenda or a happy accident? I wonder if I should share my suspicions with Collin or not. I'm not sure I can trust him. Plus, I'm not sure my theory isn't crazy. I'm not exactly sane, but my father isn't exactly known for his sanity either. My mom is questionable at best. I come from crazy genes that much is for certain.

Collin came from good genes. He seems completely sane to me. He's composed and smart. The Oswald family is known for their brilliant minds. Wolfgang, Thomas, and Collin are all known for different inventions and discoveries that have changed things for humans and Bio Metas. Collin also got the good looking genetics too. He is a true hero.

So, why the hell is he destined to be with someone like me? Destined mates are only supposed to be for those from Altron, but maybe Bio Metas have their own ways of knowing their destined mates, but we haven't figured it out yet. There is also something that no one's considered. If destined mates are a true thing then how did Crona and Wolfgang fall in love? Was Wolfgang her destined mate? I have no idea why destined mates matter but they do. It's the key to something, but I don't know what.

I need to shut my mind down. I have to get sleep because Collin kicks my ass a lot harder in training when I'm tired because I'm less focused. After today's training session got out of hand and I got my ass handed to me in more ways than one, I should probably be on my A game tomorrow. So, I curl into Collin's bed. He's still sleeping on the couch. He refuses to kick me out of his bed, and I can't decide if it irritates me or I find it sweet. Maybe both.

Somehow, I manage to fall asleep quickly, but when I am asleep I wish I hadn't fallen asleep because I find myself in one strange dream. It's like I'm viewing the world through a grainy lens like an old film. I'm outside Oswald

Tower with Collin, Thomas, and Veronica. Thomas is standing at a podium giving a speech. There are tons of cameras flashing in our faces. It's overwhelming and my heart is racing. I'm standing between Veronica and Collin. The three of us stand behind Thomas as he talks.

"I'm sorry, we had to. I'll explain later, I promise." Collin leans in as he whispers in my ear.

"I'm about to get ambushed with something I might not like, aren't I?" I hiss back at him while maintaining my fake smile. I so don't want to be here. What fucking twisted ass dream is this. Except, I don't think it's a dream.

"Keep your mask on, Little Villain. I promise we don't do this lightly." Collin replies before Thomas begins speaking.

"Thank you all for attending today. I have some exciting and positive news. Today the League of Metas accepts Clara Cole to train at Oswald Tower with the hopes that one day she will join us. Clara has come to us to train her superpowers that have freshly emerged after being suppressed by her father. We are happy to accept her and guide her on her journey." Thomas announces.

What the fuck? Thomas just made it sound like I sought the League out for help. That's not good. Well, I guess it could be good. I don't fucking know. I know why they did it. If Yuri or any of my father's followers, maybe even my father himself, finds out the League is holding my prisoner they will start a war. They will use me as a pawn to start the war against the League of Metas. A war the villains have wanted for a long time now. Both sides would use me as a pawn just in different ways. They all clearly have plans for me. Plans that I don't want to be a part of. No one cares what I want. I'm not even sure Collin cares what I want. He knew about this. He fucking knew and didn't say a damn word until a few minutes before the ambush was about to happen.

"That's a lie!" I hear Yuri scream from the crowd of people. Yuri rises up and floats closer to where we are. Yuri's superpower is to control air. His villain name is Choker because he enjoys choking the life out of people. The paparazzi camera flashes cause Yuri's bald head to glow temporarily as they snap their photos. "Clara is a prisoner. You are making her stand with you. What did you threaten her with?"

I look out in the crowd. It's easier to see now that the cameras aren't flashing in my face. Everyone is still. I know the video cameras are still rolling, but the photographers have temporarily paused.

"I don't know what you are talking about. Clara is here because she wants to be." Thomas counters.

"Oh really? Then let her speak." Yuri challenges.

Oh, fuck me. I'm not ready to pick sides. What kind of dream is this? I'm not sure it's even a dream. I want to say it's more of a nightmare, but that isn't right either. Whatever this is. I don't like it. Collin grabs my hand as we both look at one another. His eyes plead with me to do the right thing. "Stay with me, Clara." He says softly. He means his words. It's not a ploy to stop me from starting a war. He genuinely wants me to stay with him. I nod my head at him before letting go of his hand, and stepping up to stand next to Thomas.

"I'm here because I want to be." I declare.

"Don't lie, Clara. They have threatened you. They abducted you and made it seem like it was rogue supporters. They are keeping you prisoner." Yuri counters.

I never even thought about the League setting up the attack and planting me perfectly at Oswald Manor. Yet, how would Yuri know about the attack? Even I know that wouldn't be common information. No way Thomas would let it leak that I was abducted by crazy supporters of the league. So how does Yuri know? Then it hits me. Yuri has a spy somewhere within the League of Metas or close to them to know about the attack. Yuri is using me to start a war with the League. What if Yuri was really behind the attack? It's the perfect way to make me an accidental prisoner and start a war. I really am I pawn, but Yuri made me a pawn first. At least the League didn't hurt me. They could have, but they didn't. Even now they still haven't hurt me. I'm their prisoner yet they are still treating me decently.

"I'm not lying." I firmly state.

"Then they have brainwashed you." Yuri declares, gaining a boo from the crowd. I realize Yuri's sons are here. Yuri's sons aren't his biological kids. They are those who have chosen to work for him. Yuri's biological son died when he was a baby. I don't know the full details because Yuri doesn't talk about it.

"Oh come on. She has clearly stated she is here because she wants to be. You have no reason to start a war." Thomas counters.

Yuri laughs. "So you claim, but you don't get to kidnap and brainwash Cyanide's daughter without consequence."

That's when things go south real fast. Yuri and his sons attack causing a massive fight to break out. The humans gathered end up becoming collateral damage. It's a mess and it's only the beginning because this blood bath sparks the war. The war that the League has been trying to avoid. A war I'd like to avoid myself. I'm certainly not happy about being the pawn used to start the war. This is one fucking twisted dream. I keep calling it a dream, but I know it's not a dream. It's something else. It's something more.

It's the reason my superpower was suppressed in the first place.

I wake up and jolt up. I find Collin at the side of the bed. "What happened? You were shaking in your sleep."

"I think I just had a vision of the future." I state with disbelief.

"You have been having symptoms of your superpowers emerging. I knew it. Why did you keep it a secret?"

"You really need me to answer that question? How about you tell me why you are keeping your father's live press conference from me? He's planning on using me as a fucking pawn." I accuse.

"How do you know about that? I'm not hiding it from you to be spiteful. I'm trying to protect you because it involves Yuri. He knows you are here. Look, I know we are actually holding you as a prisoner. I don't like it, but I swear it doesn't have to stay that way. You know Yuri will start a war to get you back. I know you don't have a side. I know you don't care about sides, but you will have to choose."

"I know. I'm not an idiot. Don't worry, apparently, I side with the League, but that still won't stop Yuri because Yuri used me as a pawn first. I think he paid loyal supporters or loyal followers to attack me and drop me on your doorstep knowing it would force the League's hand.

He handwrapped me with a fucking bow and delivered me to the enemy all to start a war. Even when I stand with the League at the press conference, he will claim you brainwashed me. He will attack. I also hate to inform you, but  I believe Yuri has a spy amongst the League. At the press conference he gave it away that he knew information he shouldn't. The press conference can't happen, Collin. It's what will start the war the League is desperately trying to avoid." I plead with him. I need him to believe me.

"Fuck. Here my dad thought the press conference was going to stop the war. I'll have to tell him. We have to pivot and find another way to make it clear that you stand with the League and to stop the war from starting."

"You can't stop the war, but this will delay it. Don't ask me how I know, I just fucking seem to know things now." I inform him.

"Your superpowers are prophetic." Collin states.

"Yeah, I'd say so." I look away from him. I know my superpowers are super powerful. Did my father suppress my superpowers because he somehow knew what they would be? I don't know how he would know that, but there is clearly a lot I don't know. I've always been aware that I've been kept in the dark, but I never realized it went to this extent. I never realized how deep the deception went.

"I have to tell my dad. I'm sorry, Little Villain. I know what that means for you, but it's time." Collin says calmly as his hand gently strokes my cheek.

"I know. It doesn't mean I'm anymore ready to face what's to come, but I always knew the bubble had to pop." I reply, feeling defeated.

"You won't face it alone, I promise." Collin declares before he walks away to grab his cell phone.

I try to tamper the panic rising in my chest. I knew my superpowers were emerging. I knew I couldn't hold off going to Oswald Tower forever, but I'm not ready. Maybe I'll never be ready. It's too much too soon. My superpowers are more than I imagined. I'm scared of what these superpowers mean. I'm clearly not safe with the villains, but I'm not sure I'm safe with the League either. They were willing to use me as a pawn, but in their defense, they were doing it for a good reason and they wouldn't have been using me as a pawn if Yuri hadn't used me as pawn first. It's all overwhelming. It's one nasty revelation after another and on top of that my bubble has popped. My anxiety is threatening to kick into overdrive as my need to escape is increasingly becoming a need. I don't know how much longer I can hold out from fully panicking. There's no more hiding, and all I want to do is run.

# CHAPTER 11

## Collin

Clara went to bed shortly after dinner. She claimed she was tired, and I believed her. Between adjusting to getting in shape and her superpowers emerging, her body needs some extra rest. Not to mention she just got over major injuries not that long ago. She's also probably nursing her wounds from her failed attempt to play games with me.

I don't enjoy shooting her down, but until she's ready to fully submit I'm not playing games with her. Besides, there are other things going on, and I've been distracted. I still haven't figured out what Clara's superpowers might be and there are still no obvious signs. I don't know how much longer I can take before I get a little aggressive with her about it. I know she has to be having symptoms. I'm smart when it comes to medicine and biology. I even have medical knowledge on top of my scientific brain, so why the hell does she think that I haven't figured out she has to be having some signs of her superpowers emerging?

Clara isn't dumb. She has street smarts and she can put on one hell of a poker face when she wants to. She is hiding her damn superpowers or whatever hints there might be of them. I know that she knows that I know, but I haven't called her out on her bullshit yet, but I'm about to. I know she doesn't want to go to Oswald Tower. I know she doesn't want her superpowers or to train. She's trying to adjust, but my patience only goes so far. Then there is the added pressure from my dad to bring her to Oswald Tower.

My dad is insistent on this live press conference idea. He only wants Clara's superpowers to emerge so he can have this live press conference in an attempt to stop Yuri. I don't know how Yuri knows Clara is here, but he does. It raises other concerns, concerns I don't yet want to deal with because it means the possibility of a traitor. I don't fucking want to deal with that headache, and I hope it's all a fluke.

I had a meeting with my dad that ran over, so by the time I get back to the room, Clara is asleep. I don't know how to tell her about this live press conference thing. I don't want to ambush her with it, but I'm not sure how else to handle it. Telling her ahead of time will only make her more apprehensive about going to Oswald Tower. It will also give her another reason to hide her superpowers.

Clara is still sleeping in my bed. I refuse to kick her out. I know I could easily set up the couch or even one of the guest rooms, but I like her in my bed. It would be better if I could been in it with her, but I'm not pushing her. I also know I won't be able to control myself if I'm sleeping next to her. It's too much temptation and she isn't ready.

As I'm getting ready for bed, I notice Clara starts shaking in her sleep. Curious I head over to her. Sure enough her body is shaking with tremors. I don't want to wake Clara because whatever is happening is related to her superpowers. It's what I've been waiting for. Clara goes on for several minutes shaking before she suddenly stops. Seconds later, Clara shoots up from her sleep. I can hear her heart racing.

"What happened? You were shaking in your sleep." She's not going to get out of this one. I've caught her showing symptoms.

"I think I just had a vision of the future." She answers with disbelief. Well, I didn't see that coming. Nor was I expecting her to admit to her powers so quickly. I truly expected her to pretend she was fine. Whatever the vision she saw was it seems to have shaken her.

"You have been having symptoms of your superpowers emerging. I knew it. Why did you keep it a secret?" I know why, but I want her to admit it.

Clara proceeds with her smartass attitude that I desperately want to put in place. Then she proceeds to tell me about Yuri's attack. She confirms my suspicions of a traitor, which I'm not thrilled about. It's very clear Clara's superpower is prophetic and it all makes sense why her father would suppress her superpowers. Clara's ability to have visions of the future is super powerful and it could make her a weapon. I'm not sure how Cyanide would have known about her superpowers before they fully emerged. Cyanide was his own clever mind and who knows what he discovered. I don't even want to imagine what he would have needed to do in order to discover Clara's superpowers before they emerged. Cyanide is clearly full of secrets.

I feel for Clara as she knows she was used as a pawn to try and start a war between the heroes and villains. I can't imagine how horrible that makes her feel. I know we were going to use her as a pawn, but we weren't going to do it lightly. I didn't like the plan to begin with, but we had to do something to put Yuri's fire of war out. I guess it didn't matter because Yuri is dead set on starting a war no matter what we do. I don't know if Clara is able to control her visions of the future or not, but it is clear she was given this vision for a reason.

I reluctantly step away from Clara to go call my father. I just got off a conference call with him not that long ago. We have been awaiting Clara's superpowers and here they are. Who knows what else Clara can do. I know she isn't thrilled now to discover what she can do, but I hope that she gets interested. I know she fears her superpowers. I need to make her see they aren't bad. That this isn't a bad thing. However, the panicked look on her face worries me as I talk to my father about Clara's vision and her superpowers.

"Are you sure it's prophetic superpowers? Is it possible she is lying?" My father questions over the phone.

I know he is skeptical of Clara. He certainly doesn't trust her and the only reason he is willing to even let her in Oswald Tower as a trainee and not a prisoner is because of me and my mom. My mom is all about saving Janna's daughter from the same fate as her mother.

"Yes, I'm sure." I bite back annoyed at him. The man literally just lectured me about how important it is for us to figure out Clara's superpowers, and now he's going to question if I'm sure about her superpowers.

"She could be making it up. How do we know this isn't a scheme she is pulling with Yuri."

"Are you fucking kidding me right now?" I sneer, pacing toward the balcony so I can go outside because I'm not sure I want to have this conversation in front of Clara. "There is no way she knew about the live press conference. I didn't tell her because I didn't know how to tell her we were tossing her under the bus for the greater good. Plus, we both have had suspicions about a spy. Her vision confirms it. Not to mention she's literally had no contact with anyone since arriving here." I defend once I'm out on the balcony.

"I'm just trying to look at it from all angles. Her superpowers aren't something physical that can be easily proven. Look, I know your mother and you want to believe there is goodness in Clara. I want that too, but she is still Cyanide's daughter. We don't know what he has taught her. It's even possible she is brainwashed. We have to be careful." My father counters.

"She isn't brainwashed. Traumatized, yes, but not brainwashed. She's very much her own person. You are the exact reason she is terrified of going to Oswald Tower. You have all intentions of making this grand acceptance speech yet you don't actually accept her. You're being a hypocrite. You can't have it both ways. If this is going to work, if Clara is ever going to join our side then you have to stop with this bullshit. I know I don't know the full terror

Cyanide unleashed, but I do see the after effects. Part of his terror was extended to Clara. He suppressed her superpowers for a reason. Do you really think he would suppress them if he himself didn't fear she could use them against him? If he had her brainwashed he wouldn't have needed to suppress her superpowers. Look, it's going to be hard enough to get the general public to trust Clara along with the rest of the League. You being a skeptical asshole won't help. It's bad enough that Harold and Nina have sticks up their asses concerning her. You all act like she committed Cyanide's crimes for him. You're the leader so fucking be one." I attempt to reason in my frustration, running my free hand through my hair.

"You really are your mother's son." My father sighs."Fine, let's say she isn't bullshitting her superpowers. Let's say her vision is true then we have to seriously pivot in order to avoid the start of war. We also have the matter of a fucking spy working for the enemy in our ranks. That's a huge problem, Collin."

"Yeah, I know. We shouldn't do the live press conference. Do something recorded that we can broadcast. Change everything last minute so whoever the spy is doesn't get the new plan back to the enemy so they can come up with a new way to counter us." I suggest.

"That might work, but you need to get Clara on board." My dad points out as if I don't already know this.

"I can do that. You know in her vision she picked our side even after you tossed her under the bus and I let her be ambushed by it. I truly don't believe Clara supports her father's teachings. He's wronged her too. We can't wrong her as well. We need to be better. We are supposed to be the damn heroes, after all."

"I know, but it's not always black and white is it?" Dad questions.

"No, it's not, but that's still not an excuse." I counter, looking through the balcony doors at Clara who has sheer panic written all over her face.

"You need to bring Clara to Oswald Tower. We can film an announcement and release it. The sooner the better. If war is coming, like Clara claims, then we need to prepare and find out who the spy is in our ranks. We have some serious problems to figure out, Collin. No more procrastinating. It's time to come home to Oswald Tower, and you will bring Clara." My father commands.

"We'll be there tomorrow afternoon. Tell mom Clara needs to go shopping for clothes. She doesn't have anything camera ready, or really many clothes at all. Let's keep the spy in our ranks to ourselves. We don't know how high up the spy is and Mom has enough on her plate with making sure Clara fits in at Oswald Tower socially. I agreed to train her to fight. I made no agreement to make sure she is ready for the spotlight we are about to thrust her into. You know the minute we announce she is training with us the media hounds will be at our doors demanding information. We can't keep the public in the dark with everything and Clara is going to have to be an open topic for everyone's sake except for Clara's." I counter demand.

"I never said she was going to have an easy transition or that this was totally in her favor. No matter what, Clara ends up a pawn. It's better she is our pawn than theirs. I know how horrible that sounds, but we won't be cruel to Clara. She will have some freedom and eventually, she can join us, but the road to that goal isn't going to be easy. That's why you are there to help her. Whatever connection you have with her use it to benefit you both." His words have me staring at Clara who's looking at me then to the door as she chews her bottom lip. Oh shit. I don't like that look.

"Right. I'll see you tomorrow afternoon. I say we bring Clara in discreetly, allow Mom some time to get her camera ready then we film the announcement. We release it that night. We can even put a press release out saying we have big news coming. People will be on the lookout for it and as far as anyone is concerned that big news can happen any number of ways. We keep it to only those who need to know. We can't risk any more information getting to Yuri." I quickly reply, desperate to end this conversation because Clara is about to do something foolish in her panic.

"I agree. I'll see you both tomorrow." He emphasizes the word both as if I don't know my ass would be in huge trouble if I don't bring Clara tomorrow.

I don't think I've ever truly disobeyed my father in a big way. Little things, sure, but never on this scale. I know what not bringing Clara risks. It's a risk none of us can take, not even Clara who just darted for the bedroom door. Shit.

I hang up my cell before shoving it in my pocket. By the time I get into the room, Clara is out of it. I sigh. I don't know why she thinks she will get far. I can fucking fly and have super hearing so I know exactly where she is, and I know this Manor better than her. She hasn't even seen half of this place. She has no idea where she is going. She is simply acting out of pure panic. I don't even think she knows where the front door is.

I'll give it to her. She made it off the floor. I can't let her accidentally run into Harold who is still most likely in the kitchen cleaning up and prepping for tomorrow. His bedroom is off the kitchen and above the garage, so he should be contained to one area. She isn't near him now, but if she makes the right random turns she will be and that is drama no one needs. I take off and quickly see Clara in my sights. She briefly turns around to see if I'm following her. She almost trips and falls when she realizes I am. She catches her balance and attempts to propel herself fast down the hallway. At least this is good for her training.

Flying up behind her I end up pinning her to the wall with her body against the wall. Her back is against my chest as she breathes heavily. My arms rest on either side of her head. "Don't run, Clara, it's not worth it. You know there is nowhere you can hide that you will be safe from the League or Yuri. There's especially no place for you to hide if your father is truly alive." I try to reason with her.

"I know, but I had to try." She replies as her voice cracks before sobs shake her body. Shit. I turn her around and pull her into my arms. She's fracturing at the seams. I knew this would be hard for her, but I didn't think it would be like this.

"It will be okay, Little Villain. I'll be with you. I'm not going to throw you to the wolves. I promise." I attempt to calm her as I rub her back. After several minutes Clara evens out her breathing.

"When do we leave?" She asks quietly.

“Tomorrow afternoon. Come on, let's get some rest.” I reply, knowing there is no way to sugarcoat it before scooping her up in my arms bridal style.

Maybe I am the bad guy because I’m about to let my dad use Clara as a pawn. I know he is right that no matter what she is going to be used as a pawn, but she doesn’t deserve it. I know we didn’t use her as a pawn first. I wish we didn’t need to use her as a pawn at all. I hate this, but Clara does have to pick a side. She was never going to be able to be a neutral party. I hope Clara truly does join us. I want her at my side. We have a connection, something I can’t deny. Something that makes me want to protect her, make her mine, and never lose her.

# HEROES & VILLAINS

# CHAPTER 12

### Clara

Defeated is how I'd best describe how I feel at the moment. I knew I wouldn't get far with my escape, but I had to try. Maybe if I had left when he first walked out onto the balcony I would have gotten further. I might have been able to get out of the house, but beyond that Collin would have found me. He was bound to find me. He's my damn destined mate. That's something that was revealed to me that I didn't want to tell Collin yet. Being destined mates means he and I are together for better or worse. I don't know much about destined mates, but I know once you find your destined mate it's hard to leave them.

That would explain my mom and dad. My mom was a hero. She fell in love with a villain and in a way became a villain herself. I don't think my mom ever agreed with my dad's crazy plans. She knew it was wrong, as do I. So, why did she stay with him? Was it because of me? Is love really blind? Suddenly, I have all these questions that I need answers to. The past is important and I need to figure out why.

My superpowers are overwhelming me a little at the moment. I'm gaining more information than I know what to do with. It's all information I'll eventually have to share with Collin who has become a complex situation. Do I tell him we are destined mates? Would he even believe me? Fuck, this is a lot. I knew getting my superpowers would be a lot. I didn't imagine it would be on this level. My superpowers aren't done emerging either. There's more to my superpowers than visions.

I lean my head against Collin's chest as he carries me back to his room. Tomorrow is the day I've been dreading. I don't want to go to Oswald Tower, but I have to. I have to pick a side. I know I have to. I know which side I want, I just hope they truly want me too. Most importantly I hope Collin wants me. I don't know how he will be once we leave here. I want to believe he will keep his promises. I hope he doesn't throw me to the wolves. So far, he hasn't. Even though he was planning on letting me be ambushed with the League's plan, he wasn't doing it to be cruel. He didn't know how to tell me and I can understand that. I don't always know how to tell him hard things like we are destined mates.

As we enter Collin's room, I make up my mind. Tonight I give into him. Why deny him when I know he's my destined mate? I always knew I wouldn't be able to resist him forever. We only have tonight left in our bubble. Who knows what things will be like when we leave here. I might only see him for training sessions. Collin is second in command of the League, and with war coming, he's going to be busy.

Collin takes me over to his bed. He gently sets me down, but before he can pull away I wrap my arms around his neck. "What are you doing, Little Villain?" Collin questions.

"Submitting, Mighty Hero." I reply before I put my lips to his.

My lips melt against his. My hands slide down his hard chest. Collin is definitely muscular, which is his super strength showing. Collin doesn't resist. He keeps kissing me as his hands work quickly to strip me of my pajamas. I start shredding him of his clothes. We only break our kisses when we have to. When we are finally naked, Collin rearranges us on the bed so we are more comfortable. He's hovering over me as desire dances in his eyes.

"Are you sure, Little Villain? Because once you're mine there's no going back." Collin warns.

"I'm sure. Make me yours, Mighty Hero." I reply without hesitation.

Collin takes my dominant hand and places it between my legs. "Be a good girl, and touch yourself for me, Little Villain." Collin commands.

My breath hitches as I slide my fingers between my folds, finding my clit. Good thing I'm good at touching myself. I may not have much in the way of sexual experiences, but that doesn't mean I didn't learn how to pleasure myself. As I begin to rub my clit in slow circles, Collin adjusts so the tip of his hard cock, is at my entrance. He's on the big side, I won't lie, taking him is probably going to hurt because I'm tight. Yet somehow that exhilarates me. Pain and pleasure is a combination I can get behind.

Collin's lips fall on mine as I touch myself while he rubs the tip of his cock against my entrance, teasing me with what's to come. Collin's tongue slides past my lips, demanding my tongue dance with his. My free hand roams down his chest and lingers around his hips before my hand slides behind grabbing his ass in an attempt to push him in because I want to feel him inside of me. I'm getting wet at the fucking thought of him taking me like he owns me because we both know he will after this.

"Not yet, Little Villain. Don't forget who's in charge." Collin warns as he breaks our kiss. "If you can't behave with your free hand then I'll secure it for you." Collin says as pins my free arm above my head with his one hand.

I don't say a word. I simply keep touching myself, but faster because fuck that was hot. I didn't think Collin Oswald, aka Stronghold the mighty hero, could be so dominant and possessive. Collin kisses my lips briefly before kissing my jawline. He trails kisses down my neck where he nips a little, but not too harshly. He's teasing me, and I secretly love it. Collin moves his lips to my breast before he sucks one of my nipples in his mouth and swirls his tongue around. This time I don't hold back the moan. Collin takes turns sucking and licking my nipples while I rub my clit, chasing my orgasm.

"Do you want to cum for me, Little Villain?" Collin asks, moving his lips back up to my neck.

"Yes," Is all I can manage because I'm on the edge of one of the most intense orgasms I've ever had. Collin pushes the head of his cock a little more inside of me. He's no longer teasing me as he slowly enters me.

"Then be a good girl and cum for me, Little Villain." That's all it takes for me to crash over the edge as my body quakes at the intensity. It's so intense my moan gets caught in my throat.

Collin crashes his lips onto mine as he slams inside of me. My tight walls stretch all at once to accommodate him. I hiss slightly from the pain through our kiss. I don't think Collin was expecting me to be so tight because he briefly pauses allowing me to adjust. After a few seconds, the pain eases and Collin begins to move in and out of me as he furiously kisses me. I instinctively wrap my legs around his hips allowing him deeper access, and fuck he can go deep. It feels amazing. This is what I wish my first time was like, but I guess this can replace it because I barely remember my first time.

In this new position, Collin is rubbing my already sensitive clit just right. I can't help the moans that escape me. Collin breaks our kiss. "That's right, Little Villain, I'm the one giving you pleasure." Collin's husky voice reaches my ear. The man can seduce me with his words and body, it's not fair, but I'm also not complaining.

Collin picks up his speed, slamming into me harder as we both chase our release. If this is what sex is like every time with Collin then sign me up. I knew sex would be good with Collin, but I didn't think it would be out of this world. My walls clench around Collin's dick as my second orgasm sends me over the edge once more. Collin finds his release deep within me. Collin leans his forehead on mine. "You're mine now, Little Villain." Collin states possessively.

"I know, Mighty Hero." I simply reply because I am his. There's no going back, and now that I'm on cloud nine I don't want to go back. Collin rolls to the side of me before pulling me into his arms with one arm while his other arm pulls the blanket over us. I lay my head on his firm chest while his one arm wraps around me, holding me to him. I drape my one arm over his firm abs.

"What will happen tomorrow?" I ask, needing to know. If I know what's going to happen it will ease my anxiety. I guess it's a good thing I can see the future, but I don't know if I can control what I see. I suppose exploring my superpowers might be fun, maybe even interesting. I need to attempt to see the positive.

"We will go to Oswald Tower. My parents will meet us. Then my mom will sweep you off to make you ready for the camera. We are going to record the welcoming speech and broadcast it that evening. That's about as far as my dad and I got during our conversation. I'm sure we will be informed more when we get there." Collin answers honestly.

"I'm going to hate being in the spotlight." I groan.

"Want to know a secret? I actually hate it myself. I put up with it because I have to. I'll do my best to keep the media hounds away from you as much as possible. Sometimes, like tomorrow for example it's a necessary evil." Collin confesses.

"I'm sure I'll adjust. I hope everyone else adjusts as well." I comment.

"Some are going to challenge you and test you. I'm sorry you have to prove yourself to so many, but I believe in you, Little Villain."

"I'm not really a villain if I'm on the hero's side." I counter.

"No, you're more of an anti-hero because I know you will come with your own agenda, and you definitely have a problem with following the rules. You're my Little Villain. I know you have a dark side because of what you've endured over the years. Your villain only comes out to play with me, do you understand?"

"I can work with that." I agree because Collin is being reasonable.

Collin is not controlling me. He's helping me find the balance I need. A balance that will help me fit into his world. Maybe that should be a bad thing, but I don't see it that way. There's nothing wrong with Collin using his experience to guide me. I might resist it at times, but ultimately I know he's going to help me, not hinder me. I'm also not afraid to stand up if I don't agree with something.

"That's my good Little Vilain." Collin compliments before he kisses me on the head. "We should get some rest." He suggests.

I yawn, which is my agreement to sleep. I hope I don't have any more visions tonight. I do actually need some sleep. I'm sore from training because Collin decided to try a new workout that used my muscles in a different way. I also know I'm going to be sore from our intense sex. Plus, tomorrow is going to be rough. I'm going to Oswald Tower. I'm officially picking a side. On one hand I feel relief that I'm finally picking a damn side, yet I dread earning my place among the heroes. It's going to be a challenge, one that I have to be brave enough to face.

# BIRDY RIVERS

# CHAPTER 13

## Clara

The next morning, I'm sore in all the right places. I knew sex with Collin would be mind blowing. He knows what he's doing, and I'm willing to let him be my trainer in multiple ways. Unfortunately, I can't live on my own personal cloud nine for long because today is the dreaded day we go to Oswald Tower.

In some ways, I don't care that I've actually picked a side. Maybe because I know it's the right side. I'm more at peace with it. I guess seeing the future might be helpful. Still, picking a side isn't going to be easy. I'm going to be facing challenges with proving myself to the League, Collin, and everyone that I'm a hero not a villain. I might be more of an antihero. I'm never going to be loved by the public like the other League members. There will always be someone who can't look past who my father is and will hold me accountable for his sins. I'm also not joining the League purely for the greater good. I know siding with the heroes will piss Yuri and my father off. I know that asshole is alive. My father has some secret agenda for me. I just know he does. Whatever it is, he can shove it up his ass. The League might have their own plans for me as well, but I can work with their plans.

I'll do anything to toss a monkey wrench in my father's grand plan. It just so happens that my plans benefit the good side. Yuri is also someone I'd like to stick it to. He used me as a pawn. He paid a group of men to beat me within an inch of my life knowing I couldn't protect myself because my superpowers were suppressed. Yuri had the potential to be a father figure. To be a great godfather who took me under his wing. He could have had me involved in all his schemes. I would have followed because I would have belonged. It would have given me the one thing I wanted since my mom's suicide, a home.

I can't even think about my mom's suicide. That whole day was traumatic. I was eleven, and I'm the one who found her charred body. She used her superpowers to burn herself from the inside out. I was angry at her for leaving me. She was the one solid thing in my life. She was always around while my dad was off doing something for his grand plan. My mom was my rock, my safe place, and when she died all of that went with her. Now I have to question if she knew what Dad was doing to me. If she did,

did she agree with it? This whole situation raises questions, and I didn't need more questions to begin with.

I wonder if my mom would be happy that I'm joining the League. I know she was bitter toward them and that Lois betrayed her in some way. Still, she would sometimes talk fondly of her friends, especially Veronica. I guess I'll get to meet her today. She's Collin's mom, and I'm not going to lie, I'm intimidated to meet his parents. I'm nervous about everyone I'm going to meet at Oswald Tower. It's going to be like playing Russian Roulette because I'll never know what I'm going to get when I meet someone. Will they hate me because of my dad? The man has killed a lot of people and wronged many as well. Then there is the flip side that they might give me a chance. I'm sure I'll encounter everything in between as well.

We eat breakfast in Collin's room on the couch while the TV plays in the background. It's casual, which I don't mind. I'm not sure how to act after having sex with him. I don't regret it, but I also know it means there's no going back. I hope I'm ready for what it means now that we have crossed the line. It's all happening at once. Getting my superpowers, submitting to Collin, going to Oswald Tower, picking a side. It's overwhelming. I can't even begin to process one thing before I'm hit with another. My thoughts are scattered in dozens of different directions as my anxiety threatens to send me into an unnecessary panic. I tried to run last night like I actually had a chance of escaping. I hope Collin plans to keep that between us. I don't think my panicked failed escape would go over well with Thomas, Harold, or the rest of the League. I already have enough damage to undo thanks to my father. Apparently, I like to self destruct so I thought running might solve my problems.

"Does your brain ever shut off?" Collin questions as we finish our breakfast.

"No, apparently." I answer sarcastically.

"Overthinking the press conference?" Collin raises an eyebrow at me as he sets his plate on the side table next to the couch.

"Of course. I've never been on camera before. I'm probably going to make myself look like an idiot." I reply.

"You will be fine. My mom will give you plenty of pointers. It will also be short, sweet, and to the point. No one expects you to be an actress." Collin counters.

"Easy for you to say, Mighty Hero. If you mess up everyone chalks it up to a cute character flaw. If I mess up, I won't be taken seriously, and I will never live it down. You might not expect me to be the perfect performer, but everyone else will." I counter him back. He's not going to win so easily. I might have submitted to him last night, but that doesn't mean he tamed my ass overnight.

"You're siding with the League. That will carry weight. I think many will respect you openly siding with the League. It shows you have nothing to hide. I also hate to break it to you, but people will be more engrossed in the fact that you had your first TV debut than anything else. You're coming out of the shadows and that will catch people's attention in the right way. I don't think it will be as bad as you think it will be. I don't envy you being tossed into the spotlight this way, but it doesn't have to be a bad thing." Collin states as he stands up from the couch. He's probably right. I tend to build things up to be worse than they are. It's a bad habit.

"I hope you're right, Mighty Hero." I don't hide my doubt in my tone.

Collin swiftly turns around before pulling me into his arms. My chest is flush with his, and I wish we weren't wearing clothes as memories from last night flash in my mind. I can't help but rub my legs together in anticipation of what Collin might do. Collin's arms hold me securely to him. "I am right because you're going to keep your attitude in line. I know you have a dark side, Little Villain. I know you can't suppress that side all the time, so you only let it out with me in private. I can handle your dark side, Little

Villain. I know you want to sass your way through life, but that ends now. I will never put out your fire, but I will redirect it. You're my Little Villain and you will be a good girl." Collin's stern voice sends a spark of desire coursing through me. Shit, he's got me right where he wants me. What was that about him not taming my ass overnight? I might have assumed incorrectly.

"Yes, Mighty Hero." I reply submissively.

"That's my good Little Villain." Collin kisses me, and I melt into him. "Now, let's get dressed. Don't worry about what to wear or bring with you. Everything will be provided for you when we get to Oswald Tower." Collin informs me after he breaks our kiss. I would have rather kept kissing, but I can't stay on cloud nine forever.

The two of us dress casually. I'm in dark skinny jeans and a black hoodie with my canvas shoes. Collin is in jeans with a dark red v-neck t-shirt and a black leather jacket. He looks sexy. How does he look sexy in everything? It's like competing with a freaking Greek god. At least, he's mine. I don't know why Collin is my destined mate, I'm not so sure I deserve him.

"So, are we going to fly?" I question as we head to the door.

"No, that would draw far too much attention. We will drive. Plus, driving buys you more time. If I was to fly us there, we would be there in twenty minutes. Driving is more like forty or more depending on the traffic." Collin answers as we head down the hall.

We make our way to the garage where Collin selects one of the many expensive cars. The car he picks has tinted windows. I'm happy about that because then people won't see me. It's bad enough I have to be on camera today. I don't want people getting a glimpse of us together. I can only imagine what they will say if we ever go public with our relationship. I'm not sure if Collin wants people to know about us. I'm not even sure we are anything. We didn't exactly clarify our status.

On the way to the city, I'm lost in my thoughts. Collin lets me be as we listen to music. I'm not in a talking mood at the moment. My mind is running wild, my nerves are fraying at the edges because everything is about to change. My superpowers will only further emerge, I've officially sided with the League, I'll be training and living at Oswald Tower, and I'll no longer be able to hide in the shadows. Oh, and I need to tell Collin we are destined mates as if things haven't already changed between us. We are no longer enemies because now we are officially on the same side, and we've had sex. There's no going back now. This is what is meant to be.

# HEROES & VILLAINS

## CHAPTER 14

### Collin

Clara is on immediate edge as we enter the city. We still have some time to go before we get to Oswald Tower. I can't even begin to process last night and the fact that I finally fucked my little villain. It was the best sex I've ever had. I've never enjoyed myself more. Most of the time sex felt like some chore, something I'd use to take the edge off, like working out. I was never serious with anyone I fucked, until Clara. I don't want anyone else. She's it, and she's mine.

I'm glad we got our sexual tension out of the way before we came to Oswald Tower. I don't know what types of pressure we are going to face. It's better we have gotten the sex part out of the way. Now, I can focus on building a relationship with Clara without getting blue balls. I also have a lot on my plate with trying to figure out who our traitor is and what to do about them. I also need to amp up Clara's training and help her figure out more about her superpowers. They are unique and have the potential to be incredibly super powerful.

We enter a run down parking garage near Oswald Tower. I roll down the driver's window so the security guard can see me. It's actually Oliver on duty. Sometimes we have members of the League do random security around the premises. "You're here. I know what that means." He says as he leans in. I know he wants to see Clara. He's going to be curious about her. Everyone is.

Oliver and I are friendly. We aren't as close as Mason and I. Oliver is not Mason's biggest fan and vice versa. Oliver's superpower is X-ray vision. His Superhero name is X-Ray. Not overly original, but sometimes our names are that way. I can't say Stronghold is really all that much better. We don't even pick our names. Our names are picked by the current leader of the League when we become official members. Which means my dad names most of us.

"It does. We have a new trainee joining us." I reply, knowing Clara is listening like a hawk to our conversation. I'm taking her in a hidden way, which I'm sure has her suspicious. She's been bouncing her right leg up and down since we entered the city. I'm sure in her mind she's already made this out to be something bad.

"Right. Good luck." Oliver says, stepping away from my vehicle. He pushes a button at the guard stand. The wall in front of us begins to rise. It's a hidden door that blends into the parking garage walls on the first floor.

"We are going in a secret way. Only those who need to know you are here are aware that we have changed the press conference from live to recorded. It's best to avoid prying fans and the media hounds. They know something is happening today, we just didn't tell them what." I inform Clara hoping to ease her paranoia.

"Makes sense. You have no idea who the spy is, do you?" Clara pries. This is the first time she has asked me anything to do with the spy since she mentioned it last night.

"Not a damn clue," I confess. "My dad and I have been suspicious for a bit about a spy, but we weren't sure. You confirmed our suspicions."

"How did Yuri manage to get a spy close to the League?" She questions.

"I'm not sure, but he did. However, he did it was well thought out. It's certainly something we didn't see coming." I state, knowing full well it's not good that the enemy managed to successfully infiltrate our ranks.

We drive through the tunnel that leads to a hidden parking lot under Oswald Tower. We do have an intense prison under the Tower too, but that's in a different part of the vast underground level of Oswald Tower. I park the car, and we get out of. I thread Clara's fingers through mine as I lead her to the elevator. I know I'm taking her to the sixth floor. That's our media floor where we have an entire set to film interviews, announcements, and other shit. We have our own camera crew. We also have a wardrobe, makeup, and hair designated areas.

We get to the sixtieth floor, and the second the doors open my mom is there to greet us. She's in a sharp sleeveless black dress, her grey hair is pulled back in a slick bun, and she has on black pumps. "Clara, I'm so happy you are here." My mom greets with a warm smile. I knew she would be thrilled to have Clara come.

"Thank you." Clara replies awkwardly. She has no idea how to present herself. It's cute watching her take in her surroundings like she is unsure if she is going to be hauled off to a prison cell or if she is truly being welcomed.

"Don't worry about a thing. I have several outfits planned out for the announcement and for dinner tonight."

"Dinner tonight?" Clara and I both question at the same time.

"Yes, dinner tonight. It will be held at the League's private dining room. Clara needs to meet the other League members, and the best way to do that is at dinner. I would have made it a whole dinner party, but you and your father love to never give me enough time. I expect you to look nice, Collin Oswald." My mother informs us while somehow mothering me at twenty-five years old as if I don't know how to dress at different League events.

Clara suppresses a snicker next to me. "I'm going to leave you two to get ready while I go chat with Dad." I say as I let go of Clara's hand. I lean so Clara can hear me. "Behave, Little Villain." I warn before stepping back on the elevator.

As much as I don't want to leave Clara so soon after our arrival, I have to. She is in good hands with my mom. Honestly, there's not much I'd be able to help her with. Getting ready for press involved shit is my mom and Nina's territory. All I know is how I'm supposed to dress. Don't ask me to dress or give pointers to anyone else. Normally, I'd want Nina to help too, but I don't know how welcoming she is going to be. I'm not trying to intimidate Clara anymore than I know she already is.

Leaving Clara with my mom, I press the floor button that Dad's office is on. I know he's waiting for me. I might even get a lecture about being late and how I should have anticipated there would be traffic. The reality is, I took my time on purpose to give Clara as much time as possible before we came. I know how unsure she is. I might have made things more complicated for her when we had sex last night. It's not like I've exactly made it known I want to be with her. I've hinted at it, but I've never said it outright. I need to make sure I get Clara on the same page about what we are. I don't want her to think she's some fling or toy. She's more than that. Being with her makes me feel like she's the one I've been waiting for. That someone is going to be my other half. I can't even explain how I know it, but I do.

The elevator finally dings open, and I find myself heading down the hallway to my dad's office. I'm not looking forward to this particular conversation. I don't know how far up in the ranks the spy is. I don't even like thinking that it could be an actual league member, but if Cyanide taught the League anything, it's that enemies can come from anywhere even friends and supposed good guys.

I spend close to an hour with my dad, talking. Neither of us is entirely sure who it could be. We did make a list of potential traitors that we are going to try to vet. Neither of us is happy the enemy managed to sneak a spy in our ranks, and the shitty thing is we don't know how high up the fucker infiltrated our ranks. Part of me hopes Clara gets a damn vision of who the asshole is because that would make everything easier.

My dad and I head back down to the media floor. I hope Clara is holding up okay. I'm not thrilled my mom decided to do a huge dinner. I hadn't prepared for that, although, in hindsight, I should have. My mom is a social butterfly and she loves an excuse to host a party in any capacity. It's why she heads up all the charity events that the League and our family host.

Once we are on the media floor, I head to find Clara while my dad heads to make sure everything is just about ready. I think we all just want to get this press release recorded and out of the way. I'm on edge, worried that somehow our spy knows what's going on. We are trying to avoid starting a war today. I know Clara said we can't avoid it forever, but today isn't the day I want it to start.

I find Clara in a chair at one of the hair stations. Her hair is being straightened. My mom has dressed her in a dark grey quarter sleeve top with a slight v-neck, black dress slacks, and simple black flats. They kept her makeup light. She looks put together, which I know is far from how she feels. Right now, she's got her mask on and her walls up higher than I've ever seen them. Clara sits in the chair like an unwilling doll as the hairstylist continues to straighten her chocolate auburn brown hair while my mom gives her pointers.

I'm more than sure there is a script for Clara to follow to make things easier. My dad will do most of the talking and she will only have short responses. I'm glad we didn't end up ambushing her with this. I hated the damn idea of a live press conference to begin with. I need to start figuring out how to tell Clara hard things. As much as I want to protect her, I can't protect her from everything. I'll do my best to protect her from as much as I can. Plus, once she gets a hold of her superpowers and a bit further in her training she will be able to protect herself as well.

Soon Clara and my dad are set up on the two plush chairs on the stage. The stage can be arranged for different things and people. Looks like things were kept simple. The cameramen are getting the cameras set up as my parents go over things with Clara. Clara is nodding her head, trying to keep calm. I'd be over there with her, but I'd be in the way. I'll make sure I'm with her before the dinner and that she has a moment to decompress.

"What's going on?" Mason asks as he and Nina approach me off to the side.

"We heard she had arrived. At least she cleans up halfway decent. I still don't know what you see in her." Nina emphasizes with a little malice to her voice.

I'm not surprised it's gotten around the tower that Clara is here. There was no way to keep her arrival a complete secret. We just needed to keep it secret long enough to change the way we were doing the announcement from live to recorded. I'm sure Yuri and his sons are outside the building right now waiting for us to exit for the live press conference. They will be waiting for a long time for something that won't happen. I can't help the little smug smirk that forms on my face at pissing Yuri off. He causes a lot of problems for the League, almost as much as Cyanide. However, I'm not sure Yuri could outdo Cyanide. Although, Yuri tries. He got close with what he was about to with starting a war. I'm happy to have tossed a monkey wrench in his plans.

"We are doing a recorded press conference. It's better for Clara if we do." I answer Mason's question.

"We actually care about her feelings. I mean we all know she is only doing this so she doesn't get locked up in a prison cell downstairs." Nina comments.

"Yeah, how do we actually know she is on our side?" Mason questions.

"You two, like everyone else around here, need to stop looking at Clara like the enemy. She is here because she wants to be. She could have easily chosen a prison cell. Not to mention she helped us stop the start of war today with her vision that she didn't need to share with me." I inform them.

It's true, Clara didn't have to tell me her vision. She could lie about the tremors in a variety of ways. Instead, she told me. I could tell she was telling me the truth. Clara is many things, but a liar is not one of them. Clara knew what the right thing to do was. Plus, I'm not entirely sure she doesn't have her own hidden agenda behind joining the heroes. Whatever her agenda is, it's against her father, not us. I've seen the anger toward her father that she works out during our training sessions. The anger in her voice when she told me Yuri used her as a pawn to start a war. Let's not mention both her father and Yuri suppressing her superpowers and lying to her that she was fucking defective. Clara wants revenge through justice, I can work with that.

"What do you mean had a vision?" Nina asks as her forehead wrinkles in confusion.

"That's Clara's superpower, or part of it at least. She can see the future and somehow knows absolute truths. I'm sure there's more than that, but it's what we know for now. Clara is on our side. She will help us win the war that is to come. So, if I were you two, along with everyone else here, I'd get used to Clara being around. Besides, there might be some double dates in the future." I casually reply watching Clara fold her hands on her lap to stop herself from fidgeting. They are almost ready to start filming

"Double dates? Are you dating?" Nina questions in a disturbed tone totally ignoring everything else I said. Whatever kindness she was feeling when she helped me pick out workout clothes for Clara is gone. I should have known that was more or less a show for the fans snapping pictures. Nina likes drama and she knew our shopping spree would gain attention.

"We aren't official yet, but it's headed that way." I reply truthfully.

"Look at you, dating a rebel." Mason mocks. "She will never live up to your standards. This is going to end up in disaster."

"I don't have high standards, and thanks for your vote of confidence." I bite back, annoyed at Mason.

I knew I would get shit for being with Clara. I don't care. She's mine, and everyone else can fuck off. Clara is who I want because no woman has ever held me in complete captivation. Once everyone comes around and starts to realize she is truly on our side, they will be singing a different tune. I don't really care what tune they sing because it's not about them. As long as Clara and I are happy together then we will be just fine. We definitely have some obstacles to work through, but I believe we can. Some things are simply meant to be.

# CHAPTER 15

### Clara

I'm thankful when we are done filming. The entire media experience was a dreadful one. I don't know how the League deals with it. It was a controlled environment with it being recorded. I hope I don't ever have to do anything live. Unfortunately, that's the least of my problems at the moment.

After the recording, Veronica takes me back to wardrobe where she puts on a blonde wig and hands me a short red one. "Put this on. Collin tells me you need a new wardrobe. We don't have too long to go shopping, but we will get some done before I have to be back to organize for the dinner tonight," I take the wig, completely confused. "It's so we aren't easily recognized. With any luck, we won't be noticed at all. I don't like to be bothered while I'm shopping." Veronica informs me.

Veronica expertly puts her wig on, but I'm struggling because I've never worn a damn wig before. Not even for dress-up occasions. I always avoided costumes with wigs for this exact reason. Veronica ends up helping me put the wig on. Then we are heading back down to the parking garage where Oliver is still on guard duty. I didn't think the League members did basic guard duty. Maybe Oliver is in trouble or something. I clearly have a lot to learn on how things work around here. I hope someone plans on giving me a damn guide of some sort because I'm flying completely blind.

We get into a black sedan with tinted windows. Veronica gives the driver directions before he pulls out of the hidden parking garage. Veronica makes conversation with me. She's curious to know about me. I get the vibe she is happy I'm here. She and Collin might be the only ones. Thomas was all business when we were together during the announcement. I imagine the other League members might be similar to Thomas.

It doesn't take long for us to park and walk briefly to the first store. Veronica tells me there is no limit on what I can spend. I've never been clothes shopping like this before. I usually buy my shit online since I avoid the public as much as possible. The last time I went shopping in a store was with my mom, she was getting me back to school clothes. I was homeschooled for obvious reasons, but my mom tried to make the best experiences she could.

I let Veronica guide me on things I will need for League related events while I have a field day buying clothes I like. We only make it to a few stores, but I do end up with enough to get me started. Veronica even bought new training clothes for me. I have most of the basics needed for day to day stuff, a few fancy things needed for special occasions, and new shoes. I'm content with what I have even though Veronica insists we can do more shopping on another day.

When we get back to Oswald Tower, the driver takes my things to my room. A room I haven't even seen yet. I wish I was going to my room instead of this dinner. Veronica invites me to tag along with her while she gets things ready. I agree to go with her, not wanting to offend her since she has been genuinely kind to me. I want to return her efforts in building a bridge of friendship. After all, she is Collin's mom. It's probably a good idea to be on at least one of his parent's good sides.

I don't even let my mind wander to Collin or what we are. I know what we are and what we will become, it's the journey that is going to be bumpy. I haven't even told Collin about us being destined mates. I'm not sure he will even believe me because Bio Metas aren't known to have destined mates like our alien ancestors. Perhaps it's just harder for Bio Metas to sense their destined mates because we are mixed with humans. Deep down, I know Collin will accept the truth about us. It's my own insecurities eating at me.

Before I know it, it's time for the dinner with the League of Metas, the people who as of today have become my allies and not my enemies. It's still weird to have officially chosen a side. For so long I've only been on my side refusing to pick the heroes or the villains. I thought I would side with villains if I couldn't disappear because that was all I knew, all I was allowed to know. Now, Collin is in my life opening doors up that I thought I would never see open. We are destined mates, so I guess our worlds were bound to collide. The fair was just a tease of what was to come.

We are on one of the top floors. I have no idea how to find my way in the labyrinth that is Oswald Tower. The dinner is being held in a gorgeous dining room. The walls are painted maroon with hand painted golden design. The dark wood floor matches the wood of the table and chairs. The dinner chairs have maroon cushions that are extremely plush. There's a beautiful golden chandelier over the table. The table is set in fine china and glassware. I've never eaten at such a nice table before.

Dinner hasn't even started yet. Everyone has just taken their seats. I'm seated between Veronica and Collin.

I'm perfectly okay with that because I haven't fully gauged how the rest of the League members feel about me being here. Veronica clinks her class gently with a fork to gain everyone's attention. There wasn't much conversation happening anyway. I doubt there will be.

"Today is a good day. Enemies have become allies. Clara, we are so pleased you are here," Veronica beams a smile at me before addressing the rest of the table. "I know that mending whatever broken bridges there are between Clara and the League of Metas might not be easy, but I believe with the goal of looking beyond what has separated us in the past we will be just fine. Let's look forward to the bright future we can build. Now, I know it might be cheesy to some of you, but I think it will help break the ice. So, we will go around and introduce ourselves to Clara. Tell her your name, your superhero name, and what your superpowers are. I'll start. I'm Veronica Oswald. I go by Weather Witch when I'm fighting crime. My superpower is that I can manipulate the weather." Veronica directs. Damn, she has some serious charisma. The whole damn Oswald family has charisma. I also notice not one person at the table argues with Veronica. She certainly has a mother persona that makes people want to listen to her because they don't want to disappoint her.

Veronica nudges Thomas who is on her other side. Thomas awkwardly clears his throat. "I'm Thomas Oswald. I go by Impenetrable because my superpowers allow me to have impenetrable skin. I also have telekinesis." Thomas says as he puts his hand out and slowly moves his wine glass into his hand.

Next Thomas is Mason. Mason rolls his eyes. He clearly thinks this is bullshit. I agree. I know who they all are, but I appreciate Veronica trying to make me feel welcome. She's trying to break the ice, and usually, that requires something cheesy. "I'm Mason Grey. My superhero name is Bullet because I have super speed." Mason states in the most bored and unenthusiastic tone I've ever heard.

"I'm Nina Gavin. I go by Ice Queen because I can manipulate and create ice." Nina goes next.

Next to Nina is Claire. Claire smiles warmly at me. "I'm Claire Woods. I go buy Mother Nature because I can control nature and grow planets anywhere."

Oliver, Claire's twin brother is next to her. Looking at them, you'd never know they were twins. Claire has curly strawberry blonde hair to her mid back, brown eyes, and porcelain skin. She's petite. Oliver is average height, but taller than Claire. Oliver is lean, has a buzz cut, and the same brown eyes as Claire. It's probably the only thing that they have in common physically that I can see at least. They have a similar skin tone, but Claire is paler than her brother.

"I'm Oliver Woods. I go by X-Ray because I have X-Ray vision." His expression is neutral. I don't think he feels one way or another about me being here. At least he's not against it like some clearly are.

Next to Oliver is Nora. There's been rumors they are dating. Nora is pretty with dark brown hair, light olive tone skin, and honey brown eyes. "I'm Nora Jenkins. I go by Witch Doctor because I can heal others and myself." Nora says with a smile. Well, at least some of the League members seem friendly. They aren't all against me being here, but I'm sure I will still need to prove myself to them all.

"Do I seriously have to go?" Collin questions. "I think she knows who I am." Oh, I certainly know who you are, Mighty Hero, I think to myself.

"Yes, Collin. If everyone else has to do it, so do you. Including Clara." Veronica firmly replies. Shit, I didn't think I had to go. I don't have a superhero name. Only official League members have superhero names. Some of the villains do, but not many.

"Fine. I'm Collin Oswald. I go by Stronghold because I have super strength. I can also fly and have super hearing."

Then everyone looks at me. Shit. Now, I'm not a fan of this little icebreaker. "I'm Clara Cole. The only thing I know about my superpowers so far is that I have visions of the future and I seem to know truths." I say, trying to hide my nerves.

The rest of dinner is okay. Almost everyone keeps themselves in check including me. Nina and Mason do let a few snide comments out, but that's about it. Veronica and Collin are the only ones happy I'm here. Oliver, Nora, and Claire seem neutral and might be easier to get to come around to me. Thomas, though, I have no idea where he stands. He clearly is okay with me being here on some level because if he wasn't I definitely would be locked up. I understand their skepticism because I'm skeptical of them as well. Part of me is still waiting to find out this all some cruel joke, and I'm going to find myself in a prison cell.

After dinner, Collin shows me to my room. The room is huge, well huge to me as I'm used to a studio apartment above a small butcher shop. There is a round bed in the middle of the room with a dark grey comforter and matching pillows. One wall has a small entertainment center with a TV and a light grey loveseat couch. One wall has French-style doors that open to a huge walk-in closet where my clothes have been placed. I have my own full bathroom complete with a soaking tub, a shower stall, counters with a sink and mirror over it, and a toilet.

“I hope you like the room.” Collin’s voice pulls me from absorbing how nice my room is.

“It’s not a prison cell, so I’ll take it.” I joke. Collin chuckles.

“I’m a couple of doors down if you need anything. My parents are the other ones on this floor. This floor is for the Oswald family. I figured you'd feel safer on this floor than the other floor where the other League members have their rooms.”

“Thank you. I do hope you plan to give me a tour of this place. I’m fairly certain I’m going to end up lost.”

“I’ll take you on a tour tomorrow. I’ll also have a cell phone and one or two other gadgets for you. Be up and ready to go by seven AM, Little Villain. Oh, and dress casually. You are lucky and won’t have to do any training tomorrow, but we have other unpleasant things to do.” Collin informs me.

“Do I even want to know?” I question as I continue to look around my room. The windows give a nice view of Oswald City.

"It's related to your superpowers. Every Bio Meta that comes here to train, study, or work here gets a physical, blood work, and a couple of other tests that will be related to your superpowers. For example, we will do a brain scan to see if your brain shows any physical changes from your superpowers. I promise I will end the day with something fun." Collin continues ot inform me. From what I can tell he's not holding back information.

"Okay." I agree.

"That's it? Just okay? No smartass comment or arguing with me how you don't need to do the tests?" Collin questions. I giggle at him.

"Not tonight. There's always tomorrow, though." I give him a mischievous smile. "Now, can a girl get some rest?"

Collin shakes his head before coming over to me. He kisses me softly before breaking our kiss. "Goodnight, Little Villain."

"Goodnight, Mighty Hero." I reply before he leaves my room.

I don't actually want him to leave because he does make me feel safe. However, my anxiety is making me crawl out of my skin. Today has put me on edge and drained me at the same time. I need to decompress if I'm going to survive tomorrow and whatever craziness it brings. I need to get ready to face whatever backlash is going to come from siding with the heroes, and helping them stop the villains from starting war. Yuri is going to be pissed, and my father, well, he will find it unforgivable.

I might be able to see the future, but that doesn't mean I don't have uncertainties. I still have to figure out the extent of my superpowers. I know Collin will help me there. I'm sure some of the tests they will run might even help. It's probably why they run them in the first place. There is still a good amount we don't about Bio Metas. There's only a couple of generations of us and our population isn't huge.

Then there's addressing Collin and me. We might be destined mates, and Collin is clearly interested in me. However, I still don't know how far he is willing to take things with me. I'm not even sure I'm the person he wants at his side. He did promise to show me a place where I belong with him. I want to believe him, but I have some serious trust issues to work through.

There's also if and when my father decides to come back. No doubt, stopping his beloved war is going to be a problem for him. I don't know if or when he's planning to come back to Earth. I have no idea what it means if he does return. His return isn't going to be good. No one will be safe, not even me. Whatever plans he had for me, I sabotaged before he could execute them. That's not going to go over well. Daddy dearest is not going to be happy with me, and I don’t care because fuck his plans. At least the League's plans are good for me and they aren’t hiding their intentions even if some of them aren't thrilled I’m here. The sad truth is, I was always safer with my enemy than my so called allies. I’m starting to think my father never had my best interests at heart, which raises more questions. Questions I’m going to get answers to. I might have picked a side, but that doesn’t mean I won’t do things my way.

# CHAPTER 16

## Clara

The next morning I wake to a knock on my door. I spring out of bed terrified I overslept. I won't lie that round mattress bed is comfortable and the pillows are fluffy. I thought I was sleeping on a damn cloud. I scramble to the door, expecting a pissed off Collin. Instead, I find a tray of food outside my door. Whoever left it scurried away before I could make it to the door. I sigh, relieved that I didn't oversleep. I'm used to Collin waking my ass up.

I pick up the tray of food before shutting my door. I set it down on the couch by the TV. I turn the TV on and the home screen tells me the time. I have an hour before Collin shows up. I wonder if he had food brought to my door as a way of waking me up. It wouldn't surprise me. Collin somehow thinks of everything.

From the home screen on the TV, I pick one of the streaming services and pop on a show while I eat breakfast. The food isn't half bad here. I have to say

Harold is a better cook. That man might hate my guts, but he knows how to create culinary masterpieces. He could poison my ass and I'd still happily eat the food. That's how good it is.

After breakfast, I freshen up and put on black leggings, a plain midnight blue tunic top, and black combat boots. I'm not trying to stand out. I want to blend in the best I can. I'm already going to be stared at as it is. I don't need to draw any extra attention to myself. I figure the simpler the better. I'm ready just in time for there to be another knock at my door. This time when I open the door I find Collin grinning at me.

"Oh, good you can wake up on your own." Collin comments.

I roll my eyes at him. "We both know you sent food to my door to wake me up."

"Actually, that was my mom. She's in charge of that stuff. Here, take this." Collin says handing me a cell phone. "It has all the League member's numbers in it, and they have been given your number. There's also a list of the floors of the building and what's on each one. The first seventy floors are general Bio Meta territory and where most of those who work for us do their jobs. The last thirty floors are strictly for League members and those authorized to access the floors. You're training schedule and events have been added to the calendar. I've even set alarms to make sure you can move your ass in the morning since you struggle with that." Collin informs me.

"Are you ever not in superhero mode?" I joke, taking the cell phone from him. It's definitely an Oswald Tech phone which means it's top of the line.

"I don't recall being in superhero mode when I was fucking you the other night." Collin retorts. Well, damn he knows how to shut me up. "Now, come on, Little Villain, we have places to be and things to do."

Collin gives me a tour of Oswald Tower and points out the important places I need to know. Then we go to the medical floor where we spend several hours of me being poked, prodded, and scanned. Collin is clearly in his element in the labs as he talks science with the other smartypants that work for Oswald Corp. Oswald Corp is huge. They do everything from making technology advancements to medical advancements. Thomas tends to the tech stuff while Collin does the medical stuff. The two of them are prodigies of Wolfgang, who himself was brilliant.

After being examined and watching Collin show off his brain, which was sexy in ways I didn't even know were a thing, we head for a quick lunch before we head to have a meeting with Thomas. Essentially the meeting with

Thomas consists of me getting lectured for two hours about how I can't fuck this up and what is expected of me as if I didn't already know all this.

During the meeting, Thomas gives me the impression he thinks I'm lazy or not committed to this. I don't like that he is judging me before he even knows me. I should be used to people judging me. It's something I've dealt with my whole life. Everyone thinks they know me and who I am, but they don't know shit. Thomas is the first of a long list of people who I'm going to have to prove myself too while the judge and question me.

I'd like to note that I think it's complete bullshit that I have to prove myself to anyone. It wouldn't have mattered which side I chose because they both need me to prove I'm with them. I guess that's what happens when you attempt to remain a neutral party and pick your side over anyone else's. For years, I tried to make it known I didn't associate with one side over the other. I might have lived with the villains, but that wasn't by choice. As a child, I had no choice but to live with my guardian who happened to be a villain. I'm twenty-three now and I technically could have moved out, but there was no place for me to go, until now. It's why I was hell bent on disappearing. I wanted to live my life in peace, but I guess that was never a real option, only a delusion of a traumatized person running from their haunting past.

During the meeting, I realize how conceded Thomas is. Rightfully so. The man is a genius and he is responsible for creating and leading the League of Metas. Wolfgang and Crona might have accidentally created the first Bio Meta when Crona became pregnant with Thomas, but Wolfgang didn't create the League of Metas. Thomas was the one who thought it was a good idea for Bio Metas to use their superpowers to protect humans, while my father thought it was better to use their superpowers to control humans. Hence the great divide that created the first heroes and villains of Oswald City, and why it's embedded deep within its history.

I'm surprised Collin is conceded like his father. I mean he is a little arrogant, but not on the level of his father. I guess Veronica's humble genes balance Collin. I never met Wolfgang, but I've heard he was incredibly arrogant and thought he was a gift to mankind with how brilliant he was. Wolfgang did help create the surrogate program for Bio Metas so more of us could be created. He played his part in history just like Thomas and Collin.

In many ways, my father played his part in history as well. He played his part as the villain with a twisted agenda, leaving death and destruction in his path. My father killed without mercy. He destroyed and never asked questions. His agenda was the only thing that mattered. He controlled my mother and tried to control me. Benji Cole, aka Cyanide, is only out for himself and his agenda. He doesn't care who he hurts, kills, or destroys in the process, including his own family.

After being lectured by Thomas, Collin passes me off to Veronica who proceeds to show me how things run around here. She shows me how to get things I need like toiletries, getting my laundry done, if I want my room cleaned, and things like that. I'm glad Veronica is warm and sweet toward me. It makes me feel like I don't have to prove myself to everyone.

I wonder if it has something to do with my mom. From what I've been told Veronica, Lois, and my mom were best friends. The three inseparable musketeers. Clearly, some of that changed when my mom decided to leave the League to be with my dad. I still don't understand her motives for leaving the League for my dad. Is love really blind or is there something more sinister at play with their supposed twisted love story? My father is very good at twisting and morphing things to meet his needs.

To be honest, I never questioned much when it came to my parents. I simply accepted their choices and left it at that. Finding out they lied to me about my superpowers, allowing me to think I was defective, raises questions. At first, I thought they did me a favor, but now I realize how defenseless they left me. All the bullies I could have fended off. The things I could have avoided. There are pieces of the puzzle missing, and I'm not so sure I want to put the puzzle together. The truth rarely sets people free. No, the truth usually breaks us and I fear that the truth behind all my questions will only fracture me further.

Before I know it, it's dinner time. I'm okay with the day being almost over. Tomorrow I have to start training, and I'm not sure I'm ready for the intensity. I don't have a choice. The training wheels are coming off, so I better hope I know how to survive without them. I don't think Collin is going to take it as easy on me with training now that we are at Oswald Tower. I can't fuck up. I have to survive whatever intense training is thrown my way. I can't risk anyone thinking I'm slacking off.

Collin takes me off his mom's hands. I'm not sure where I expected Collin to take me for dinner, but it certainly wasn't the rooftop of Oswald Tower. There's a table set for two with string lights all around. There's a wheeling tray of covered food near the table with drinks.

"I didn't think you would like a fancy public dinner where everyone would circle us like sharks. So, I thought a private rooftop dinner would be more your ideal first date." Collin informs me.

"First date?" I question, trying to not let my jaw fully drop open at the romantic and thoughtful gesture.

Collin chuckles. "Yes, first date. We sorta skipped it and went right to the fucking. I thought we should backtrack a little and have a first date," Collin takes my hands into his as he looks deep into my soul as if he can read a secret inscription on it that only he can read. "I like you, Little Vilain. I pick you to be with and I don't care what anyone thinks. No one has captivated me the way you have."

"That's because we are destined mates, Mighty Hero. We are magnetically drawn to each other, and I wouldn't have it any other way." I confess because there is no point in hiding it from him. Especially not when he is picking me because he wants to. It's part of why I was a little hesitant to tell him  I didn't want him to be with me out of obligation. Collin just proved that isn't going to be the case.

"How do you know that? Bio Metas aren't known to have destined mates like our alien ancestors." Collin questions. I'm not even mad that he questioned it because if I were him I would too. He's also not questioning it in a bad way.

"I don't know, I just do. One of those absolute truths that I simply know to be true. It's like every fiber of my being tells me something is the absolute truth and nothing will shake it. Maybe Bio Metas do have destined mates and we haven't figured out how to tell. From what I understand Altronians just know who their destined mate is when they meet them. Maybe for us Bio Metas its clouded and harder because of our human DNA. Just another thing for us to figure out." I ponder. It's nice having someone listen to my thoughts.

"Indeed, but I'm not arguing it. I knew there was a crazy magnetic pull to you I couldn't ignore. I'm glad I didn't ignore it." Collin kisses me softly on the lips. All the man has to do is kiss me and I'm putty in his hands. "Now, should we eat?" Collin asks as he breaks our kiss. I nod my head.

We head over to the table and like a gentleman, Collin pulls out my chair for me. I take my seat and he helps me get my chair lined up better with the table so I can eat. Collin then serves us the food. It's spaghetti with meatballs and garlic bread. It smells good, and I like a simple meal. There's also wine that Collin pours. Once Collin is done serving us, he takes his seat.

I gaze out over the city, the place I've called home but it never felt like home. The sun has just set so the city is alight with its own lights that somehow are equally pretty, but to me, nothing compares to the beauty of the stars. The stars that offer answers about our alien ancestors.

"Was your first day as terrible as you thought?" Collin's question pulls me from my thoughts as I pick up my fork.

"It wasn't as bad as I chalked it up to be in my head thanks to good old anxiety. Although, your dad. Is he always so stern and serious?" I question.

Collin chuckles. "It's hard for him to turn it off. I've only ever really seen him turn it off with my mom. She has this way of getting him to put his defenses down."

"Sounds familiar." I jest and we both laugh because it's true. Collin does have a way of breaking down my walls even if I'm not sure how I feel about it.

"Maybe they are destined mates. Your parents are most likely destined mates, too." Collin comments before he takes a bite of his food.

"It's possible." I pause, wanting to shift gears. "I'm not really in the mood to talk about destined mates, and if our parents are or not."

"That's fair. So, what do you want to talk about, Little Villain." Collin prompts taking a sip of his drink.

"Do you ever find it weird that there are huge gaps of alien history missing. Almost like we don't have the full picture. I mean, why did the original aliens go back to the home planet without a word to Thomas or Crona? Isn't it strange we haven't heard anything from them in decades? They come to Earth, they live among us and learn about us, they help create Bio Metas, they even train the original five Bio Metas, and then one day they just disappear like my father."

"You are asking all the same questions me and the League have been asking for years. My dad has tried to reach out to Altron several times. They ignore us and I fear it has something to do with Cyanide's grand plan." Collin answers.

"You think the Altronians mean to hurt humans?" I question, digging into my food. It's an interesting theory and a possible one.

"I don't know. I'd like to think not, but we don't know much about them. They were here for so long. They helped create a new race. They have to have some interest in Bio Metas. After all, they donated sperm and eggs to help create more Bio Metas. The original five Altronians that came to Earth have children and grandchildren here yet they have no interest in us. It doesn't add up." Collin muses

"All good points that leave more questions than answers. Seems to be a theme." I comment.

Collin chuckles. “A serious theme that not even the brilliant Oswalds have been able to figure out” He jokes and we both laugh.

The rest of dinner is nice. We talk, joke, bullshit, and eat. Collin seems to accept that we are destined mates, which makes me happy. I still don’t fully trust him and I certainly don’t know if I’m safe here. I’m safe with Collin, but everyone else is questionable. Even sweet Veronica is questionable with her motives even though I’m sure they are genuine. I can’t help myself but fear she has a hidden agenda. She probably doesn’t, but paranoia is not an easily tamed beast.

After dinner, Collin takes me back to my room. He kisses me goodnight before I head inside my room. Once again, I hate him leaving, but I also need space to think and process. Our conversation tonight has given me some things to think about. Like I need more shit to think about. There’s also the fact that tomorrow is my official first day of training for the League. Many people train for the League here, but only a select few make the cut. There are Bio Metas that would kill for my spot, that would kill for a chance to prove they are worthy enough to be a part of the League of Metas. I’m not one who is overly thrilled about this, but it’s an opportunity that saves my ass from a worse fate. So, I'll take it even if it's not the option I originally wanted.

Plus, Collin is here, and I do want to be with him, even if I'm afraid I'm not worthy of him. I'm damaged, fractured, and I don't know if I'll ever be a full blown hero. An anti-hero, sure, but doesn't Collin deserve someone who can be the whole package? There's also the possibility this is my own insecurities eating at me. I've never had anyone believe in me or accept me for who I am, so for Collin to do it so willingly throws me off kilter.

I shower and then get ready for bed before curling into my bed. I need rest. If anything Collin has drilled it into my head that I need rest, hydration, and carbs for all the training I'm about to do. Not to mention trying to figure out the extent of my superpowers. I know there's more them and everyone else seems to know that as well. It takes time for us to fully gauge our the extent of our superpowers. Since mine were suppressed for so long, I don't know how long it will take for us to figure out the full extent of them. Just another thing to figure out.

# HEROES & VILLAINS

## CHAPTER 17

**Clara**

It's been a couple of weeks since I came to Oswald Tower. I've managed to get into a routine with training, testing my superpowers, figuring out what exactly is between Collin and me, and trying to make friends. The last two have proven to be a bit harder. While Collin is aware we are destined mates and seems to accept that, I only see him for training and meals. That's it. I know he's busy being a superhero, and I know Yuri has been causing even more problems than usual for the League.

Still, I wish Collin would spend a little more time with me. If we are going to make something like a relationship work we need to see each other more than just training and meals. Our first date was so romantic and great. It was literally the stuff out of a book or movie. That was it though. I mean that can be the only romantic thing her does, can it? I'm certainly no relationship expert, but shouldn't there be more?

When Collin and I are training or working on figuring out my superpowers, he's all business. Then when we are done, he goes off to do his superhero thing and I'm left on my own. We haven't had much in the way of conversation either. I'm starting to fear maybe Collin is second guessing his feelings for me. It could be that he truly is just busy, but my anxiety says it's not.

Besides my love life, I'm trying to make friends or at least be friendly to the League members. Of course, Nina accused me of being a suck up. She's certainly not my biggest fan. Mason is no better. Thomas is still clearly waiting to see if I fuck up. As for Nora, Oliver, and Claire, they are fairly neutral still. Claire is the friendliest of the so-called neutral bunch. Veronica has totally taken me under her wing like some mother goose. I don't mind it. It's actually nice having a mother figure, but I do wonder why she is so intent on helping me settle and feel welcomed. Although, I do know Veronica is known for being kind and keeping the peace, so it's more to do with personality than some ulterior motive.

I just finished a training session with Collin who left before I could even ask if I'd see him for dinner. I usually go shower after I'm done training because I always feel so sticky from sweat after. Fucking Collin knows how to push a gal to her limits and he does every fucking training session. He wasn't lying when he said training for the League would be intense. Once we know more about superpowers, Collin will incorporate that into our training. We still haven't figured out much about my superpowers other than what we already knew. Collin said my brain functions are off the charts. Then he proceeded to speak in medical and science terms which is where he lost me.

As I'm stepping off the elevator onto the floor my room is on, something quickly swooshes past me from one of the hallways that branches off to the other rooms on this floor. What the hell? I ignore it as I head down the hall but as I do something speeds behind me, picking me up, and moving too fast. One second I'm in the hallway, the next I'm in my room being pinned to the door by Mason, aka Bullet. Well, super speed makes one's stomach queasy. I feel like I just got the worst motion sickness of my life. Mason cages me in with his body while his hands rest beside my shoulders.

"What do you want Mason?" I question. Seriously what the fuck?

"For you to stop helping the fucking enemy, Clara. You are supposed to be your father's daughter, not the League's pet project."

I suck in a breath at his words as relaxation crashes over me in waves making me a little bit more nauseous than I already was. "You're the spy? How? You're a League member." The words rapidly flow from my mouth.

An evil grin spreads across Mason's face. "At least you're quick. Maybe you can keep up after all. Your father asked my father to put me in the Bio Meta program, so he did. They both paid my mom handsomely to let them visit so they could eventually tell me my purpose. My mom claimed she was raped by a Bio Meta and was pregnant, so she qualified for the Bio Meta program that would guarantee me a place to work my way into the League. She claimed she wanted to keep me, but needed the program's help to raise me. Thomas agreed, taking pity on her since she was supposedly raped. It all worked out according to Cyanide's plan until you fucking had to use your superpowers for the League. Now they know for sure there is spy in the ranks."

"Who is your father?" I don't know why, but I feel this is important, and I know I won't like the answer one damn bit.

"Grey is just a fake last name. Jones is my real last name."

"You're Yuri's supposed dead son?" Yeah, I don't like the answer.

"Look at you putting all the pieces together. You weren't supposed to have your superpowers yet.

Unfortunately, Yuri's plan to use you to start a war backfired. Without your suppression pills, your superpowers emerged, and they came faster than we thought. You weren't supposed to have your superpowers until after we fucking attacked. Somehow, you got them sooner. Now, I have to leave sooner rather than later, and the war is delayed. You are not on your father's good side, young lady." Mason scolds. So that confirms my dad is alive.

"What makes you think I won't march right to Thomas's office and tell him about this?" I question because Mason is a little too confident that I won't turn him.

Mason gives me another evil smirk before he pulls out his cell phone and begins to search for something. "Because I'll tell Collin you and I are secret lovers then I'll show him this as proof." Mason smugly states as he turns his phone so I can see it before pressing play.

I almost vomit right then and there. It's a video of him fucking me the night of the Home Day party. The alien mask is pulled up on his head so his face is showing while he fucks me. I'm clearly drunk and maybe drugged because I only appear half conscious. "It was you. You were the guy in the alien mask? Why?" My voice is quiet and a little breathless at the terrible retaliation of what happened that night. I preferred it when the guy was anonymous.

“You are mine, Clara. For my loyalty to Cyanide, I have been promised the ultimate prize. You. Collin can have his fun with you for now, but at the end of the day, you belong to me. When I leave here, you will come with me.” Mason demands.

“I’m not going anywhere with you! What about Nina? Why date her?”

“Nina is a lesbian and doesn't know how to come out of the closet, so she asked me to be her fake boyfriend. She will have no choice but to come out when it’s known that I’m a villain and not a hero. In a way, I’m doing her a favor. Oh, and you will come with me. I own your pretty ass.” Mason firmly states as his hands firmly come around my neck. This isn’t a sexy choke, not that I’d want him to choke me in a sexy way. I don’t want his hands on me period. This choke is threatening. “You will do what I say. You will not say a fucking word to Collin or Thomas about me, and when I say so, you will leave with me. You belong with me, Clara. You’re the daughter of a villain. You belong with a villain, not a superhero. I staked my claim on you years ago, and you are promised to me. Now, be a good bitch and suck my dick.”

Mason uses his super speed to push me to the ground while his other hand undoes his pants before I come face to face with his raging hard dick that's pierced. He has a Jacob's Ladder. Mason roughly shoves his dick in my mouth. Mason roughly fucks my mouth while I gag on him. I can't even breathe. His fingers painfully dig into my scalp as he harshly grips my hair in his hands.

I don't know how long this goes on as my mind chooses to not keep track. It's like that night all over again, except this time I'm painfully sober. I can't even begin to wrap my mind around the violation of that night let alone what is happening now.

Once Mason cums in my mouth, I quickly swallow as choke on the sweet air I now have with his dick removed. "Don't forget who you belong to. You will always be controlled, Clara. Your father will hand me your chains soon enough, and I will make sure you use your superpowers for the correct side. Don't think you won't be punished for your betrayal before you are put in chains." Mason threatens before he bolts out of my room.

The second he is gone, I run to the bathroom where I proceed to vomit until there's nothing coming out but my stomach bile. I end up leaning against the cool porcelain of the toilet after I flush it. Fuck. My father is the toxic gift that keeps on giving. I don't even know where to begin to process the mind fuck Mason just dropped on my lap.

I peel my body from the toilet and decide to take a hot bath in the soaking tub. I put in some soaking salts that will help with soreness and help me relax because I need to relax. What I really want is to get wasted and pretend that nothing has happened. Wait, isn't drinking part of what got me in this situation? Hell, that video was horrifying. I didn't know it was recorded. I was clearly taken advantage of. My mind was blocking that night to protect me from the harsh truth. I never consented to having sex.

It all comes flooding back to me. Mason tore down a protective wall my mind placed around the memories when he showed me the video. It's not just that night of the Home Day party, which I scarcely remember. I remember when he took me to the bedroom that I told him I wasn't sure I wanted to have sex. He called me a tease because we had been making out and touching each other all night long. He shoved something in my mouth, a pill I think. He used his super speed to shove the pill down my throat so I had no time to react.

The pill is what really made me feel funny like I had no control over my body. I don't think I was as drunk as I initially remember. It was the pill that incapacitated me. One minute I was dressed the next I wasn't. Then he shoved me onto the bed. I couldn't move. I felt paralyzed Too bad he didn't use his super speed to fuck me. That's when he took his time. I don't remember him setting up a camera. He must have had it all set up in the room when he took me there. The whole night was set up so he could take advantage of me. The worst part is this was at Yuri's home, which means Yuri most likely knew what Mason was up to proving I'm nothing but an object to the villainous men that surround me.

Mason wasn't Bullet the superhero then. Mason didn't join the League until a few years later, but he was training at Oswald Tower. He was friends with Collin at that point. Shit, Collin. I can't imagine him seeing that video. Mason's words play in my mind that Collin can play with me for now like I'm so toy to be shared. I know Collin has no idea what Mason is up to. I doubt he or Thomas thinks the spy is an actual League member. I have to tell them, but I risk losing Collin. Mason will show him that video and tell lies. Mason could even spin it that I too have been playing them the entire time. Mason will do anything to make Collin toss me aside.

I don't even want to imagine what punishment would await me if I went with Mason. If I tell Collin and he believes Mason's lies then I will either end up locked up or worse with Mason when he goes back to the villains. My future was looking decent when I woke up today and now it looks grim. I can see the future, how did I not see this coming? I don't know if I can pick what I see or if it's random. I don't know much about my superpowers yet and I might now get a chance to.

Mason also blew the lid on all the childhood memories I had suppressed of my father controlling me. He somehow knew about my superpower. He suppressed my superpowers to control me. He force fed me the suppression pills. Even then I must have known it wasn't right, but I guess over time my mind blocked the bad out and created the illusion that I took the pills for my headaches. Of course, my father would want me with some psycho asshole like him. How did my mom willingly choose my dad? Either they were destined mates or my mom was insane herself.

This is so fucked up. I don't know what my move should be. I certainly don't want to go with Mason. I want to tell Collin everything, but I fear he's going to believe Mason's lies. Oh, there's also Thomas who will certainly believe Mason's lies. Thomas doesn't trust me. He already assumes I'm a villain and questions my loyalty to the League. I know there is a part of Thomas that doesn't believe I've truly picked the hero's side. It won't take much to convince him I'm still the enemy when I'm not.

My anxiety is spiraling out of control threatening to develop into a full-blown panic attack. Shit! This isn't good. I need to keep Collin at arm's length until I figure out what my next moves should be. I also need to avoid Mason and Thomas. I'm not safe, and I was foolish to think I might be.

# BIRDY RIVERS

# CHAPTER 18

## Collin

The last few weeks have been insane. Yuri got pissed that we deterred his plan, so he's been living up to his name, Choker. He's been going around killing innocent people, destroying businesses, and creating more crime than he ever has. His sons, those that follow him, are also making mayhem in their wake. It's been a nightmare, but it's nothing compared to what is to come because all of this is building toward war.

Dad and I have been trying our best to prepare for war even though we don't know exactly what type of war we are planning for. Between war planning, fighting the increase of crime, and training Clara I've been spread out leaving me no real time for Clara who for the last week has been acting strange.

The first week Clara was here, she was on edge as she was trying to adjust to her new routine. Then she seemed to relax for a couple of weeks. I knew she wasn't fully comfortable or feeling totally welcoming as I know some of the League members have been less than friendly. I haven't even had a chance to talk to Mason and Nina and tell them to back off. They really need to change their attitude, but no one needs to more than my father who is waiting for Clara to fuck up. He still doesn't believe she is serious about her training or if she is really on our side.

About two weeks ago, Clara suddenly started acting distant and on edge like she was waiting for something terrible to happen. I know I haven't been around much on a personal level for her, and I fear she's starting to think I'm having second thoughts about us. I can't blame her. We had sex then a romantic dinner where she tells me we are destined mates then I essentially ghost her on a personal level. I've only spent time with her for training, figuring out her superpowers, or eating quick meals that are usually with other people. It's not on purpose, but I'm not sure she knows that.

That's why I asked for tonight off from fighting crime. My dad wasn't overly thrilled, but my mom was on my side. Of course, my mom is on my side. I did tell her about Clara and I being destined mates. I'm not so sure she believed me, but then again she did admit that there isn't much known about destined mates for Bio Metas. She also said she felt a magnetic pull to my dad, and so she understood what I was talking about when I described it. Either way, my mom is all for Clara and I being together, so she basically scolded my father for not giving me a break so I could take care of things in my personal life.

I know it's after dinner and Clara is in her room, which is where I'm headed. Clara is a creature of habit and doesn't seem to drift too far from her routine. I'm sure she has reasons and I'm sure they are good ones. Clara doesn't seem to do anything without reason. I get to Clara's door and knock. It takes several minutes before she opens the door, but she doesn't open it all the way. She cracks the door and has her whole body behind it to protect herself minus her head.

"Mighty Hero, how can I help you?" She questions clearly skeptical of my visit.

"Can I come in?"

She looks around the hallway to see if anyone is around. Strange. "Sure." She says opening the door when she is satisfied no one is around. I walk into her room as she shuts the door. "To what do I owe this visit, Mighty Hero?"

"I wanted to see you. I've missed you." I reply standing close to her, but I'm not sure I should touch her.

She has her arms crossed against her chest. "Is everything okay? You seem edgy."

"I'm fine. It's just my paranoia." She bites back.

"You still don't feel safe here do you?" Clara shakes her head no. "What can I do to make you feel safe, Little Villain?" I ask, my tone soft as I step closer to her, bridging the gap between us.

Clara is quiet for a few moments before she speaks, letting her arms fall from her chest. "I don't know. No one has ever asked me that question before."

"Then we can figure it out together." I reply, cupping her cheek. Clara leans into my hand.

"You being here helps." She confesses quietly.

I pull her into my arms and she lets me. Clara puts her head on my chest and I hold her close to me, wrapping my arms around her. "I'm sorry I've been so busy. Being a superhero and a leader can be time consuming when things are going haywire. I'm also not used to being in a relationship with someone. I need to learn to make time for you too because you are just as important as my duties. I don't want you to think I've changed my mind about us." I say as I stroke her back.

Clara lifts her head so she can look at me. "I know you have responsibilities. I just don't know where I exactly fit into your life. I didn't have much of a life before you, but you had a whole successful life before me. We don't come from the same world, Mighty Hero. Besides, you might change your mind after I tell you something. I need you to believe me, Collin." Her eyes plead with me to believe her. Did she have another vision? As far as I know, she hasn't had any major ones since we came to headquarters. I know she's had minor ones, but that's it.

"I'll believe you, I promise." I reply keeping my tone soft as to not spook her because I can sense she isn't sure she tell me anything.

"I know who the spy is. It's Mason Grey or you should really call him Mason Jones. He's Yuri's biological son. My father asked Yuri to use Mason to infiltrate the League. They took advantage of the Bio Meta program and had Mason's mom claim she was raped when she wasn't. They paid her to let Yuri see him, so they could brainwash him into being the perfect spy. It gets worse because my father promised me to Mason as some sort of reward for being his spy. Mason confronted me almost two weeks ago and told me everything. He is angry that I helped the League. I wasn't supposed to have my superpowers yet. Mason informed me that my father gave me the suppression pills to control my superpower so that eventually he could use it to further his cause. When they set the attack up and dumped me on your door, they didn't think my superpowers would emerge as fast as they did, so Yuri's plan backfired. I would have told you sooner, but Mason has something on me." Clara pauses and swallows hard. "He has a video of him and I having sex, except I don't remember giving him my consent. He drugged me and I didn't even know it was him because he wore a mask for the Home Day party Yuri was throwing. He also used the dimly lit room to his advantage. I did willingly make out with him, but when he took me to the room, I told him no. I was sixteen and I thought I wanted to have sex, but something felt wrong. That's when he used his super speed to shove a pill in my mouth. It made me woozy and it made it hard to move. I didn't even remember much from that night because my mind was blocking it, but when he showed me the recorded video of him…" Her voice breaks as she pauses. She can't bring herself to say the word rape. "It brought it all back like a flood of memories that I had been suppressing. He told me that if I told you or your dad he would show you that video and tell everyone he and I were secret lovers. He will convince everyone I'm the villain they think I am. Please, Collin, you have to believe me. I know he's your best friend, but he's not who anyone thinks he is." Clara pleads.

I take a deep breath because that's a lot to unpack on many levels from the betrayal of my best friend to finding out my destined mate was raped and threatened by said best friend. “I believe you, Clara. It’s a lot to digest, but I believe you.” I hold her closer to me as anger spreads through me at Mason’s betrayal. Somehow, it all clicks into place as my mind pieces together that Mason is indeed the spy.

“He’s going to go back to the villains soon. He didn’t say when, but when he does he’s taking me with him. I don’t want to go with him, I told him no, but he obviously doesn’t care what I want. I want to stay with you.”

“I won’t let him take you. Despite what he might think, you are mine and I will protect you. I’m sorry for what he did to you that night, you didn’t deserve that.” I hold her a little closer, hating that she had to have such a traumatic thing happen to her. I’ve never been in denial that Clara is traumatized, I just never realized the extent of it.

“I wish that was the only time he touched me. He forced me to suck his dick when he confronted me and after promised me I would be punished for my betrayal.” Clara informs me, which sends a new wave of anger surging through me. I’m going to kill him. I should have been here to stop him. I need to control my anger because I don’t want to scare Clara.

"I'm sorry, Little Villain. I should have been here. He won't touch you again, and if he tries, so help me I will fucking rip him apart."

"Be with me tonight and help me forget what he did. I want to feel your hands on my skin, not the memories of his."

"I will erase his touch so you only remember mine. Don't ever believe Mason's lies. You are mine and only mine, Little Villain." I reply before I let my lips land on her soft ones.

I will think about and deal with Mason later. Right now, I want to be with Clara. She needs me and I want her to feel loved right now because she needs it. She needs to feel safe, accepted, and loved by her destined mate. That is exactly what I'm going to do. Tonight is about her and her needs. I hate what Mason did to her, and he will pay for it, I'll make sure he does.

Our hands make quick work stripping us both of our clothes in between our passionate kisses. There is something intoxicating about being skin to skin with Clara. Everything draws me to her, from her scent, looks, personality, body, and the way her body perfectly molds to mine like two puzzle pieces coming together. She's the vision of my dream girl that I never even knew I wanted.

I slide my hands to her cute ass, grabbing it to lift her up as her arms instinctively snake around my neck. I carry her to the bed then lay us down on the bed with Clara under me. My arms go to either side of her head while her arms remain loosely wrapped around my neck. I kiss her softly before kissing my way slowly down her body making sure to spend extra time on her sensitive areas like her neck and nipples before I land at my destination.

Lowering my head between Clara's legs, I let my tongue slide between her folds finding her clit. My tongue swirls around her clit causing Clara to let out a sensual moan of pleasure. I let my tongue work her clit while I insert two of my fingers inside of her. I begin to pump fingers in and out of her while my tongue licks her clit giving me a taste at how sweet my little villain tastes. Clare begins to buck her hips slowly to the rhythm of my tongue and fingers as her moans of pleasure fill my ears. I continue pleasuring her, allowing her to feel worshiped. Clara's walls clench around my fingers, but I don't stop. I keep licking her and pumping my fingers out of her until a second orgasm shakes her body. I remove my finger and reposition myself so I'm back on top of her with my dick hard and ready at her entrance.

Clara nudges her pussy entrance against my tip, begging me to slam into her so I do. Fuck, she feels good.

I've fucked my share fair of women, but not one of them felt like this because there weren't my destined mate. There is something super powerful in the connection that links us in unexplainable ways.

I drape Clara's legs over my shoulders allowing me much deeper access to her. I slow my pace not wanting to go as rough when I'm this deep because I want to enjoy how good this feels. I move slowly letting us both revel in the feeling of being intertwined this way, allowing the bond to grow stronger as our feelings for one another develop into something neither of us can fathom.

After several moments, I need more, I need to consume her. I drop her legs, pick up the pace, and let lips crash to hers allowing my tongue to demand entrance in her mouth. Clara place her hands on my chest before expanding them out to my shoulders. She moves her hands up behind my neck before tangling her fingers in my hair. I pump into her at a rapid rate chasing my release while reveling in the feel of Clara wrapped around my dick. My mouth catches Clara's sweet moans while our tongues dance with one another. My release surges out of me causing me to have one hell of an orgasm.

Clara and I take a moment to catch our breaths before I roll to her side, laying on my back. "Thank you for believing me." Clara says as she curls up in my arms, laying her head on my chest.

"I'll always believe you, never doubt that." I reply, holding her close.

"You believe me, but will your dad or the rest of the League? Mason has weaved his way into their lives and gained their trust. They might not want to believe he's a traitor."

"Don't worry about my dad or the rest of the League. I will handle them. I promise I will protect and keep you safe, Clara."

"I know you will. I need to train a little harder. I don't want Mason to ever get the upper hand on me again. The next time he tries to make me do anything, I want to fight because I might just have to fight for my life. Mason isn't going to let me go and neither is my dad."

"He's alive, isn't he?" I ask even though I've suspected he wasn't dead for a while now.

"I believe he is. One of those things I just know. I don't know where he is, though. I have a feeling he's on Altron, which begs to question Altron's motives."

"I know. This war might be bigger than we want it to be. We can up your training. I have some self-defense moves I can teach that are particularly for fending off a predator like Mason. I know he has super speed, but I do know his weaknesses. Mason lets his guard down when he thinks he's won. He's cocky, and it's cost him many duals with me. The key is to never let your guard down even when you are winning. Somehow, I don't think you will have a problem with that."

Clara giggles. "My guard is only ever down when I'm with you." She playfully pokes my chest. "Are you going to leave to tell your dad?"

"I'll tell him tomorrow. I always met with him, and we need to keep things exactly the same. If I go to him now, Mason might get suspicious. He might be out fighting tonight, but that doesn't mean he won't hear about me going to my dad in the middle of the night. It's best to keep everything the way it normally is as to not raise suspicions. Besides, I want to be with you tonight." I answer.

"Do you think Mason will be suspicious if you spend the night in my room?"

"Maybe, but that's easier to get around. We are dating and I can tell him we fell asleep after sex. Trust me, I can play it off in a way that he will understand as a man. Now, get some rest, Little Villain." I reply, kissing the top of her head.

Clara doesn't say another word she just curls more into me, settling herself. I manage to grab the edge of the blanket and pull it over us. It doesn't take Clara long to fall asleep. Unfortunately mind is wide awake ready to go over details.

All this time Mason has known my intentions with Clara. It explains why he tried to deter me from them because he wants her for himself. I have no idea where that leaves Nina. I hope this doesn't make Nina hate Clara more because Mason wanted Clara all along. I can't believe he is the spy, yet somehow it makes sense. There were many times where if felt like the villains had intel on us because of places they would attack or they would somehow know to show up at times they shouldn't have even been up to pop up. It explains how they were able to avoid us on many occasions. These are things only League members would know. It's also impossible to hack our system, so there is no chance of anything being planted that we wouldn't know about.

Fuck, Cyanide was clever planting Mason. He went to great lengths to ensure Mason would be a spy we would never see coming. He also went to decent lengths to suppress Clara's superpower, but how did he even know what they were? As far as I know, there is no way to know a Bio Meta's superpower until it fully emerges. There might be hints to it, but that's more for physical superpowers and Clara's superpowers are not physical. Fuck, how did Cyanide get such an advantage over us?

# HEROES & VILLAINS

For years the League thought we had the upper hand, but Cyanide has been five steps ahead a long time. I'm not sure he ever lost the upper hand. He is the ultimate villain. I don't even want to imagine what he will do if he gets his hands on Clara. I'm glad she wants to help our side because I'm not sure we can win without her. Clara is vital to us winning the war. Maybe Cyanide knows that. It's possible he feels threatened by Clara which might explain his need to control her. One thing is for certain Cyanide or Mason won't get Clara. They will have to go through me, and I will die protecting her. Clara belongs to me. I won't suppress or control her, I will let her evolve into her full potential and let her be everything she can because that's what she deserves.

# CHAPTER 19

## Collin

The next morning I wake to Clara half draped on me. I chuckle at her. She certainly made herself comfortable. She looks peaceful when she is sleeping, but I know her mind is far from peaceful. I can't say my mind is in a better state. I have to tell my dad today about Mason. As much as I want to put it off, I know I can't.

I gently shake Clara awake, so we can get to training. We need to stick to our schedule. Mason will be back at headquarters soon. We need to give the illusion that everything is normal. I don't want him to be suspicious on any level. I need him to think that Clara is still afraid to tell me the truth and that I know nothing.

Clara and I both freshen up by taking quick showers to make sure we don't smell like sex. I don't care if Mason smells sex on us, but I don't think my parents or anyone else needs to know. We head to the kitchen-dining hall floor and grab a quick breakfast before heading to train.

As we are on the way to the training room, we encounter Mason heading to the dining hall. Mason stops when he gets to us. I knew he wouldn't just move on. "Anything good in there?" He questions, keeping things casual.

"The oat pancakes aren't half bad with some fresh fruit. How was fighting crime last night?"

"Eh, could of been worse. How come you weren't out there last night?"

"I spent the night with Clara. I need some relief if you get my drift." I nudge him. I hate to be derogatory in front of Clara, but it's Mason's language and now that I know he's actually a villain it makes sense.

"We all need a good fuck once in a while. I get it. Can't fight crime if you're pent up. Right?" He asks looking between us like he isn't being a total ass.

"Collin, we should get to training." Clara's voice is quiet. I'm not sure if she is truly intimidated by Mason or putting on an act. Either way, it's working because Mason quickly smirks before rearranging his face to a more neutral appearance.

"We should. I have a tight schedule today and I need father dearest lecturing me about how I need to manage my time better." I add because I need to get away from Mason before I punch him in the face. I need to act normal not start a fight.

Mason sucks air in through his teeth. "Yeah, you don't want that. The almighty Thomas is uptight." Mason comments. "See you guys later." He says with a wave moving past us.

Once we are on the elevator, I pull Clara into my arms. "Are you okay, Little Villain?"

"Yeah, but I definitely need to punch something."

I chuckle. "I can get behind that. It took everything in me not to rip him to shreds. I'll make sure he pays for what he did to you."

"Now who's the anti-hero." She questions raising an eyebrow at me.

"I never said justice couldn't also align with a little revenge if the person deserves it. Mason deserves it for what he wrongfully did to you." I defend.

"It's all a morally grey area give or take. I hope you make him suffer. Maybe let me get a hit in or two." Clara adds.

"I should be able to arrange that." I reply as the elevator doors open.

We head to training like normal. However, during this training session, I notice a new spark in Clara. She's more determined and not holding back. I'm fairly certain she is taping into her anger and I can work with that. She has a right to be angry, and I'm angry for her. I show her some particular moves that she can use against Mason if he ever tries to make her do anything she doesn't want. She has to get him to let his guard down, he has to think he's winning and that might mean temporarily putting herself in a compromising situation. Ultimately, she could get away. By the time Mason would recover from the initial shock and pain of the attack Clara should be far enough away before he could use his super speed. That's the theory though. Clara has to be fast with getting away and to safety.

After training, I send Clara to try some mediation. It's a new method I'm trying to get her to focus on strengthening her visions. We still don't much about how her superpowers work and it would appear her visions are completely random. She can't control whether she sees minor or major events or how far into the future.

Other than her vision of Yuri trying to start a war, she hasn't had any major visions. I've only seen her have one vision when she was awake and it was the weirdest thing. Out of nowhere, her eyes turned completely white and she was stuck in a trance. Definitely not ideal if she is fighting. Clara's superpowers are unique and require a bit more study. There's also the fact that her super superpowers were suppressed for years. I initially didn't think it mattered and her superpowers seemed to have emerged fairly quickly once she stopped the pills, yet there's a possibility of a delayed effect. It's hard to say.

I head to meet with Dad. We usually have at least one meeting a day to touch base, go over reports, business stuff, and so on. This time it's not going to be fun because I have to tell him about Mason. I have no idea how he will react.

Entering my dad's office I find my mom is there with him. That's not actually a bad thing in this case. I might need her help if my dad decides to question Clara, which he probably will. "Right on time." My dad comments.

"Yeah, but when I tell you what I found out last night, you might wish I was late." I counter before I fill my parents in on everything.

"Are you sure Clara isn't lying?" My dad questions.

"I'm positive. I know you don't trust her, but I do. The more I think about it, it makes sense that he is the spy. I'm not any more happy about it than you are, but Cyanide has out done himself with this, even you have to admit that." I'm not surprised he is having a hard time accepting this. My dad does not like being outdone by Cyanide and this time Cyanide got the League good.

"Well, I guess there's one way to find out. Clara said Mason confronted her in her room?" My dad questions.

"Yes. She told me he used his super speed to get into her room." Clara explained more of how he confronted her this morning when we were showering as I was curious where he confronted her. It didn't surprise me that he made sure to confront her in a private setting. Easier for him to take advantage of her and fewer people to overhear his confession.

"Well, I put a bug in her room to record anything suspicious she might do behind closed doors." Dad informs us.

"Are you fucking kidding?" I rage.

"Thomas, that is a complete violation of privacy!" My mom scolds.

"It's just audio. You two might trust Clara's intentions, but I do not. I wanted to ensure she was truly on our side. Now, should we find out if she's telling the truth?" My father defends as he challenges us while he pulls files up on his computer. Unbelievable. I can't believe he would do that, yet I'm not surprised.

He pulls up the file for around the time Clara told me Mason confronted her. Sure enough, after sifting through the file, we hear the entire conversation. My dad cuts it off when it's clear that Mason is forcing Clara to give him a blowjob. You could hear her choking and gagging. It was clear he was forcing her. It made my blood boil, but right now I can't do anything about making him pay for it.

"Satisfied?" I ask my father while making sure to give him an I told you so look.

"Yes. We need to figure out what to do about Mason. He doesn't know we know yet. We might be able to use that to our advantage but I don't know how. It's best he doesn't figure out that we know as to prevent him from doing anything rash." My dad muses like he totally wasn't just in the wrong. I knew he would pull some aggressive move against Clara. I should have known it would be a move no one would know about. My dad has a habit of keeping major plans and ideas to himself. It's a problem that my mom and I don't know how to solve.

"The Home Day celebration is around the corner. If he's going to go back to the Villains it might be around then when there's a big enough distraction for him to slither off like the snake he is." My mom suggests.

"That's highly possible. He did tell Clara soon, and that would be soon. The question is do we bother capturing him or just let him go back to the villains? He won't give us information about Cyanide or whatever plans of war that are in the works. Even if we tortured him he won't give in. He's clearly too loyal to Cyanide and would rather die than betray him. The problem is if he goes back to the villains we don't know what he could give them information wise." I contemplate out loud.

"You are right about capturing him. He won't tell us a damn thing. I don't think there is much more he could give the villains. I'm sure they have more than we care for as it is. He's been feeding them information for years. We know Mason can't access certain important information and even if he found a way, I'm sure he's already handed the information over. The best is to kill him before he can leave, but we can't do that without jump starting the war. We need to put the war off for as long as possible to be better prepared, especially now. I hate to say it but the best option might be to let him go when the time comes. One thing is for certain he can absolutely not take Clara with him." My father adds.

"She won't go willingly with him, but that doesn't mean he won't try to take her. We need to figure out ways to keep her safe without him being able to take her or becoming suspicious." Clara has to be kept safe.

"I can help with that by making her busy with helping me set up for the Home Day celebration the League always throws. All the ladies of the League are helping me in various ways, so I will include Clara as well. I didn't initially include her because I didn't want to overwhelm her with too much at once since she is not used to this life just yet. However, now it will serve as a purpose to keep her around trustworthy League members." My mom suggests.

"I'll make sure I'll spend my nights with her when I'm here and when I'm not then we will have to find a way to make sure Mason doesn't go near her. He already attacked her in her room. He knows that's a place she is usually by herself." I add.

For the next hour, the three of us strategize on different things involving Mason. This certainly is a mess. Cyanide achieved something I never would have even thought of. Who thinks of planting a spy as a baby and slowly brainwashing them to be a spy from a distance so they grow up doing your dirty work. It's fucked up, but Cyanide isn't sane. Look at what he did to Clara, even Janna. His family values are skewed that's for sure.

The important thing is to keep Clara safe. At least, my dad now believes her loyalty. I'm not thrilled he bugged her room, but he has his own type of paranoia. I know my mom threatened him if he didn't remove the bug. I'm sure she will lecture him enough for both of us. Now, we just have to figure out Clara's superpowers, what the hell is going on with Altron, if and when Cyanide is going to appear again, and how to win a damn war against a psychopath who seems to be five steps ahead of us. Fuck me. Whoever said being a superhero was glamorous had no idea what they were talking about. Yet, I wouldn't trade it for another occupation because I do like helping people and protecting our city. I have to trust that somehow everything won't go to total hell and that we can stop whatever horror Cyanide plans on unleashing.

# BIRDY RIVERS

# CHAPTER 20

## Clara

A couple of weeks have passed since I told Collin about Mason. True to his word Collin has done everything he can to make sure I'm safe. We are maintaining that everything is normal and Mason doesn't seem to be the wiser. Although, the asshole enjoys giving me dirty looks, and when no one is looking, he's looking at me like I'm his personal plaything.

I've been roped into helping plan the League's Home Day celebration. Home Day is basically where Bio Metas celebrate being part alien. Home Day is celebrated on the anniversary of the day the aliens came to Earth. Don't ask me why it's called Home Day. Oswald and Crona created the day.

Huge parties are thrown. Yuri's always held his at an abandoned warehouse or at his home. He'd have a dance floor, strobe lights, a DJ, most people would wear an alien mask, and of course lots of drugs and alcohol. The

League's Home Day celebration is a little more sophisticated and less like a rave.

Although, right now I'm not sure how I feel about Home Day. It was fine when I didn't fully remember what happened. Now that I remember that night, it keeps playing over like a bad movie in my mind. I also keep seeing the video he showed me, so I have two horrible ways to remember it. However, Collin is slowly but surely making me only remember his touch, the way he feels, and giving me good memories.

Every night that Collin isn't out fighting crime, he's with me. I spend most nights in his room, but sometimes we change it up and stay in my room. When Collin is out fighting crime, Veronica keeps a close eye on me. She's been motherly to me since I arrived, and at first, I wasn't sure how I felt about it. I've decided I like it. I'm starting to feel safe here. I'll feel much safer when Mason is gone, but I don't know when that will be. I hope it's soon.

One good thing about helping with the Home Day celebration is that it's allowing me time to bond with the other girls. Well, not Nina. She's still living up to her name of Ice Queen. I get it, she controls and manipulates ice, but her superpowers extend to her personality as well. Nina is also the Queen Bee in the sense that she has dozens of followers on her social media accounts. She has her own fashion line. I think she even models. She has endorsements and all kinds of things that make her one very popular superhero. I'd like to say she's shit at fighting, but I've unfortunately had to square off against her in training. I hate to say it, she kicked my ass. More like froze my ass like a damn popsicle.

Collin has me training with different League members now to have some new opponents to try out my skills on. I've trained with Veronica and Thomas both of which were even more challenging than Nina. Claire and Nora were a little nicer and didn't kick my ass. I haven't trained with Oliver or Mason yet. Mason is for obvious reasons. Oliver does a lot of patrol, so he's harder to pin down than the others. Training with them and fighting them proves I have a lot of work still to do, but I also realize that I haven't been training for as long as everyone else in the League making the progress I have made impressive.

Claire and Nora are warming up to me. Since I've been helping with the planning, it's been easier to talk with them and get to know them. I know I can't isolate forever and it's better that I don't. I don't want to end up isolated and alone like my mom did. So, I'm making an effort with Claire and Nora. I would with Nina, but she's not my biggest fan.

I don't see Oliver enough to really bond with him. He seems to be very dedicated to League business. When he's not on patrol, he's out at night fighting crime. I'm not sure he sleeps. I don't think he eats much because I don't see him often in the dining area that also has a full fledge kitchen where we can make whatever we want. There's also a chef that makes us food on demand. The chef is good friends with Veronica. Her superpower is related to cooking, or so I've been told.

I'm starting to get frustrated that I'm not learning more about my superpowers. It seems like everything Collin has me trying to do to further develop my superpowers doesn't work. I still get absolute truths and I can predict silly things like what someone will say before they say it or something someone will do. Sometimes it happens when I'm training. I'll get a vision of what my opponents move will be so I can counter it, but it's not consistent. Part of me is wondering if I'm having some sort of mental block. I am processing a lot at once, and I just unlocked some traumatic repressed memories. I'm definitely in my head, and I hate it.

Collin is confident I'll be able to get my superpowers to fully emerge. He has a lot of faith in me. He certainly has more faith in me than I do myself. It's nice to have someone believe in me. I've never had anyone have my back before. I'm lucky to have him as my destined mate. I'm not so sure he's lucky to have me, but I'm thankful he's giving me a shot. I'm relieved he didn't judge me and he believed me without question.

Somehow, Collin has even gotten Thomas to come around. He finally believes I'm on their side. Collin didn't give exact details of how exactly Thomas came around. Honestly, I don't care how Thomas came around, I'm just relieved that he did. Now, just to get the other League members on my side.

I'm in my room getting ready for bed. My days used to be so dull and uneventful. Now my days are filled with a schedule and are never boring. I'm always doing something whether it's training, planning something with Veronica, working on my superpowers, or spending time with Collin. At first, I didn't think I'd like being so busy, but I actually don't mind it. My days are filled with meaning and that gives me hope for the future.

My phone dings and I pick it up giddy knowing it's most likely a text from Collin. He said he would try to come to say goodnight before heading out to patrol the city for a few hours. When he comes back he will get into bed with me. Unfortunately, this text isn't from Collin. It's from Mason. A pit forms in my stomach as I open the text. He's never texted me before and the fact that he is doing it now sends a wave of dread over me.

You can avoid me all you want, Clara, but soon it will be time to leave. Don't think that Collin will save you. He will break your heart and then you'll see you belong to me. When I say it's time to go, it's time to go. Don't fight me, you won't win, and Collin won't be able to protect you because I'll make sure he doesn't want to. Ready or not your chains are coming, Clara.

I reread the text several times. Shit. I screenshot the text and send it to Collin. At least, he didn't attack me to tell me this. A shiver runs down my spine at the thought of him touching me. I don't want to think what he would do to me if he did manage to get those chains on me. I have a feeling my life would be me endlessly saying no and him doing it anyway. Not to mention my father would be there to back Mason up if I got out of line. I don't even let my mind wander to the horrors of whatever punishment they would have in store for me.

I'm not going with Mason. I will fight him or die trying. I think I'd rather die than end up in his hands. My life would be a living hell. Collin and the League won't let Mason take me with him. They know me getting in the enemy's hands is a bad thing. I wouldn't help my father willingly, but I fear he would have a way of making me. I won't let my father control me, he's controlled my life for too long. Even from afar, he was controlling my life through Yuri and Mason. Siding with the League means a better life, one where I'm free.

I can't believe Mason's twisted lies. He will make empty promises. I know he will abuse me. He won't love me or appreciate me. I will be his slave, his property. He will do awful things to control me. I don't deserve him. I might not deserve Collin, but I certainly do not deserve Mason. I deserve better than a controlling psycho. I won't be like my mom. I won't settle for the villain and I won't be controlled. I have to stand my ground against Mason and eventually my father when the time comes. Time to be a tough bitch and prove to myself I'm worthy because I won't let the devil win when I know I have the superpower to stop him.

# CHAPTER 21

## Clara

It's the day of the Home Day celebration. The street that Oswald Tower is on is closed down and heavily patrolled. There are a lot of Bio Metas and humans out to celebrate today. I have to say Veronica knows how to throw an event. There are local vendors selling goods, food trucks, crafts for kids, entertainment with music, and a parade. It's family oriented which I find nice. It's totally different from Yuri's rave party where everyone is wasted and bad things happen. Oh, not to mention Veronica is using her weather superpowers so we have gorgeous weather for the day.

Collin and I are walking the street holding hands. It's honestly nice being open about our relationship. Of course, people are snapping pictures of us. It's probably the one downside to being out in public. At least, this time it's positive. Before I'd go out in public and it was a nightmare. People would bully me, trash talk me, and refuse me services. Now that I'm officially associated with the League it's different. It shouldn't be that way, but it is because of that lovely morally grey area that many pretend doesn't exist.

Normally, I'd hate having pictures taken, but I look good today. I haven't been one for fashion and I'm still not. However, Veronica has helped me find some style. Right now, I'm dressed in a sleeveless light grey dress that has a handkerchief skirt with a black vine-like pattern paired with black flats that have a connecting strap around the ankle. My makeup is light and I'm sporting a sexy black cat eye and my hair is in light beach waves. I feel good about myself and I like that Collin is showing me off on his arm as we walk around the festivities. He's proving he's not ashamed to be with me.

Harold is here with Nina today. They are with Mason. As far as I know, Nina has no clue about Mason being a spy. Collin and Thomas made sure they only told who needed to know and given how close Nina is to Mason, I'm not sure they would have clued her in. Although, she isn't straight so maybe this won't hit her as hard as if she was truly in love with him. According to Mason, their relationship is a sham. At first, I thought Mason was lying about that, but after observing Nina and

Mason together it's clear they are only putting on a show. It's a good show, I'll give them that.

After strolling the streets we head up to a private area that's set up on the steps of Oswald Tower. It's reserved for the League and their guests. The parade should be starting soon. I've never actually seen a parade, so I'm a little excited. The parade is mixed with Bio Metas and humans, but mostly Bio Metas showing off their skills.

We join Thomas, Veronica, Harold, Nina, and Mason in the VIP area while we wait for everyone to gather for the parade. I'm not thrilled Mason is so close to me, but I'm with Collin and plenty of others who will protect me. Still, Mason is too close for comfort. I don't know how long we have to pretend that he isn't the spy. Mason said it was time to leave soon. I hope he does leave soon because I think I might relax easier when he's not around to threaten me.

"It's a lovely day." Harold comments.

"I made sure it was." Veronica replies with a smile. Controlling the weather must come in handy when you are in charge of planning big events like today.

"I think it's cute we include humans in a celebration that is just for Bio Metas." Mason randomly states.

"Mason!" Nina swats his arm appalled.

"Care to elaborate?" Thomas prompts.

"Humans aren't as evolved as Bio Metas. Most of them are only good to help create Bio Metas, but eventually one day we won't need them at all." Mason replies.

"That sounds a lot like something Cyanide would say." Oliver points out as he, Claire, and Nora join us.

"Cyanide was on to something." Mason casually replies as if he didn't just insult the entire League and what they stand for.

"You can't possibly mean that, Bullet?' Nora questions, appalled. Why do I have a feeling Mason is about to self-sabotage his way out of the League, and he's going to try and take me with him?

"Oh, like the League's little pet didn't narc on me?" Mason turns his attention to me. "Or did you finally realize where your loyalty truly lies."

"I'll never go with you, Mason." I declare, stepping closer to Collin who wraps his arm firmly around my waist. Harold, Veronica, Collin, and Oliver don't look surprised at what's about to happen, but everyone has clear confusion written on their faces. That's okay they will catch up soon enough.

"You're really going to pick the hero? You know your place is with me. I'm the one your father wants you with. I'm the one that will accept you. Do you really think they will accept you? They won't. I've spent my entire life around them and they will always hate you for the villain we all know you are. Now, come on, Clara, make the right choice." Mason offers me his hand.

"I pick Collin. I will always pick Collin and the League. I'd rather stay here and risk being unaccepted than go with you and be chained like an animal. I don't care if my father promised me to you, I'm not yours and I never will be."

"Clara is mine, Mason. She clearly knows where her true place is. Now, run along before I kill you for your transgressions against the League and for what you did to Clara." Collin threatens.

"Let's so who's faster." Mason challenges.

I know he's going to use his super speed to grab me and escape. I don't know if Collin or anyone could stop him from doing it. Collin instinctively puts me behind him while the others form a barrier around me. Mason chuckles like he's already won. Mason begins speeding around while Veronica shoots lightning bolts at him and Nina blasts ice at him while Claire attempts to use the nature around us to our advantage, but Bullet dodges it all while laughing as he speeds around us. It will take him one calculated move to break the circle and grab me. I'm not going with him. Something in me shifts as something deep within me activates out of desperation. I put my hands out slightly from my body with my palms forward. With a deep breath, I realize an invisible vibration leaves my body. Everywhere it touches time slows down. Even Mason now appears to be running like a regular man. Breaking the circle between Collin and Veronica, I step outside of my protective barrier careful to avoid Mason in the process.

Time might be slowed for everyone else, but for me, it's not. I position myself directly in Mason's path. When the time is just right I kick Mason right between his lungs and stomach, which sends his ass flying down several steps. I smirk as I relax my body allowing time to restore to a normal flow. Mason is attempting to catch his breath after I knocked the wind out of him.

"You might be fast, Bullet, but you can't control time like I do." I confidently state approaching Mason. "Now, run along and give my father a message for me. Tell him he will never control and chain me down again." I feel the heat of Collin behind me behind me.

"You heard her, Mason. Run along to your master." Collin firmly adds as his hands come to my hips in a protective manner. I lean into him letting the feel of him embrace me in safety. Defeated, Mason speeds away without me. "I'm proud of you my Little Villain." Collin whispers in my ear.

"I discovered a new part of my superpowers." I state, turning to face him.

"I see that. You slowed down time."

"I did. I think I can speed it up a bit and maybe even pause it. It was strange. Something woke up inside of me and I suddenly could feel time all around me like my senses were in tune with it. I could bend it to my will. It took a lot out of me though. It's something that requires a bit of stamina, which I lack right now. I'll have to explore this new superpower later." I observe.

"We will do a bit more testing later. I have some ideas now."

The rest of the day goes according to plan. Veronica refused to cancel the parade or the rest of the event. Mason is gone and the threat of him doing something stupid is over. I'm not sure how I pictured he would leave. I guess I thought he would do it secretly in the middle of the night or just never come back from patrolling the city. I didn't think he would suddenly drop the facade that he's put on for his entire life. Mason self-sabotaged hard.

Thomas disappears for a bit to do some damage control. Nina is in shock and decides to come out to her father. All to find out she's been secretly with Claire this entire time and she was trying to find a way to tell Mason she didn't want to fake date anymore. I have to be honest,

I didn't see that one coming. I don't know why Nina was so afraid to come out, Harold didn't seem to care. I guess even the almighty Ice Queen has insecurities.

I'm glad when it's time to head back inside. I'm tired. Using my superpowers today took a lot out of me. I wasn't expecting my superpowers to randomly emerge like they did. It makes sense why they did because I was truly being threatened. Whatever potential mental block there was went away the second my life was in danger. While I have no doubt that the League would have protected me, I wanted to stand my ground. I wanted to stand up to the man who took advantage of me. It felt way too good to kick his ass.

We end up in Collin's room. The minute the door is closed, Collin pulls me into his arms. My arms snake around his neck. "I'm truly proud of you for standing your ground, Little Villain. Don't believe Mason. You will be accepted. After today, I'd say it's hard to deny that you are truly on our side. You proved yourself. Most importantly I will always accept and love you for who you are. I'm glad you stayed with me."

"Did you ever doubt that I would leave with Mason?" I question.

"No, but I thought you might get inside your head and convince yourself you didn't deserve to be with me or something along those lines." Collin truthfully answers.

"I had thought about something like that, but I decided I'd fight my own demons and stay with you." I confess.

"Always stay with me even when you doubt yourself or us. I promise it will be worth it."

I nod my head before I kiss Collin firmly on the lips. Enough talking. I want to be with him and I know he wants the same thing. Collin lifts me by my ass and carries me over to his bed before he lowers me onto the bed with him on top of me. We both make quick work of taking our clothes off until we are skin to skin.

Collin flips me so I'm on my stomach. "Grab the headboard." He commands and moves off me to allow me to do as he commands.

I quickly do what I'm told as anticipation builds in my core. Collin comes behind me as he adjusts me into the position he wants. Soon I feel his head at my entrance. He teases my clit with the head of hard cock. I resist wiggly my ass to get him to come on because I know he's teasing me on purpose. I also know that if I tease him back by wiggling my ass, he will make me wait longer. I'm also not in the mode to be punished as I want this way too badly right now.

Collin places his hands on my hips before he finally sinks into me after making me very wet with his teasing. I feel so full from this angle and I love it. I want nothing more than to be completely filled by this man. Collin beings to fuck me on a primal level. He's marking his territory, and I'm here for it. I want nothing more than to be his. I never want to forget who I belong to or that I'm worthy of this man. I didn't just prove myself to the League today, I also proved my worth to myself. I have a newfound confidence that I don't plan on letting go.

With each rough thrust from Collin, I grip the headboard tighter as his cock rubs my clit the right way. Fuck, this angle is amazing. Between his teasing and the way his pleasuring me with his cock right now, I'm close to the edge of orgasm. My orgasm builds deep within me threatening to send me to a place I don't want to come back from. Collin knows how to send me into pure pleasurable bliss.

My walls clench around Collin as he grunts his release. The two of us collapse onto the bed out of breath. I snuggle up with Collin under the covers. My back is against his chest as his arm drapes over me. Now, I'm extra spent. I close my eyes knowing I'm safe. Mason didn't take me. I know he is still a threat, along with my father and his other followers. Thankfully, I don't have to face the threat alone because I finally belong somewhere.

# BIRDY RIVERS

# CHAPTER 22

## Clara

During sleep, I find my dreams are not really dreams as the grainy film of my vision starts to play. I'm in a dimly lit room with pool tables, couches, TVs hung up on the walls, a bar, and surrounded by my father's followers. They surround me in a circle. Then to my great dismay, the circle breaks and my father enters followed by Mason. I don't see Yuri anywhere, but that's fine because I don't need a third enemy to fight off.

My father looks like he's barely aged other than some wrinkles and a few strands of grey hair in his dark blonde hair. I haven't seen him since my mom died. "I see you came when I summoned you, Clara. I guess I still have some control over you after all." My father states with a smirk.

"Did hero boy finally break your heart? I knew you would come crawling back to me." Mason adds his own snide comment.

"I only came so you didn't follow through on your threat to hurt innocent people. What do you want from me?" I reply as if I'm bored even if I'm a little scared being surrounded by my enemies. The villains used to be my people. They were never my allies, but they were the people that surrounded me in my life. Now, they are my enemies and those that were once my enemies are slowly becoming my family.

"You are my daughter. You belong with me." My father firmly states as if his world is final.

"The daughter you abandoned. Yeah, I'm good. You left when I needed you the most. You could have taken me with you to Altron, but instead, you abandoned me." I accuse.

"I couldn't take you there. They would have taken you from me. I have support from many Altronians, but there are those on the council of elders who have sided with the League and want peace. They have forgotten what Altron's goal was. Invade planets, kill the useless people, and enslave the rest. Earth was next. Do you really believe Wolfgang accidentally found a way to contact aliens? No, they found him and saw him as the perfect way to invade. Except some members of the original mission got distracted and Bio Metas were born. We proved useful and worth exploring. The entire goal got skewed. However, my father, Cras, made sure to never forget the original plan. I'll make sure that when I take Earth that Altron remembers the planet conquering people they are and forget their pursuit of peace." My father informs me.

Cras is one of the original five aliens that came to Earth. He fathered Benji with a human egg donor. Well, turns out my father is brainwashed too. Great. Brainwashing seems to be a theme in my family, and I'm not thrilled about it. Of course, my family would be the insane ones of the bunch.

"That's lovely," I reply sarcastically. "Except that doesn't explain why you could take me with you." I point out.

"You see there is a prophecy on Altron about the Oracle and her son. The prophecy says that a female will be born from the blood of Altronian and another race. No one ever believed Altronians could reproduce with another race. It was thought of as impossible. Then Crona gets pregnant by a human and everything changes. Everything became about the Oracle. Crona whispered all the ideas about the Bio Meta Program into Wolfgang's head. Then the prophecy was suddenly added to that the Oracle would come from the bloodline of one of the five that originally went to Earth. It took time, but I knew it the moment you were born that I had fathered the prophesied child. I suppressed your superpower for many reasons. One was to protect you because your life was threatened on more than one occasion because you were my child. I knew if anyone found out about your superpowers you would be hunted by the League or captured by the Council of Elders on Altron. Two, I needed to control you so I lied and told you that you were defective. I broke you down in order to gain control." My father informs me like he has all the answers. In some scenarios, my dad has the answers I seek, but in most cases, the man is clearly talking his own insane nonsense.

"Yeah, and how did that work out for you?" I interrupt.

My father smirks like he's proud of my outburst. Almost as if he wants me to act like this. Oh, Shit. Don't tell me he somewhat brainwashed me. "You have your mother's fiery spirit. Too bad she didn't use it to fight me like you did. I told her I would be her downfall, yet she followed me into the darkness like a blind puppy. Your mother was devoted to me. Too bad you didn't get that side of her." My father continues like I didn't just sass him.

"You still keep dodging why you couldn't take me with you. What the almighty Cyanide was afraid the council of Elders would take me from you?" I taunt. I'm not a fan of how he was talking about my mom, but that's not a battle

I'm going to fight today with him. Although, I'm really beginning to question my mom's sanity.

"They would have hunted you. I couldn't risk it. It was safer for you to be defenseless and oblivious on earth than with me where the threat was too close for comfort." My father answers. I'm not buying his answers. He's lying or bluffing. I can't shake the feeling that he's lying.

"Sounds like a lame-ass excuse to me. So, why did you really want me here? You know I'm not going to join you. So why have a family reunion?" I prompt, wanting this meeting to be over with.

"I thought it was obvious you needed to get your priorities straight. The Oracle has great superpowers that can be used to bring balance and harmony or war and destruction. You will help me take Earth, and when the time comes you will give me your son to turn into the ultimate weapon. With the two of you, we can rule all the planets. You were supposed to have your son with Mason, but I see you couldn't help by spreading your legs for the Oswald boy."

I panic deep within. How does he know I'm pregnant. I haven't told a damn soul. "That's okay, Clara. It's a shame Hero Boy impregnated you first, but you'll give me multiple kids. I'll make sure I breed the fuck out of you for this." Mason threatens. I wait for my father to be disgusted with what he just said, but my father acts neutral. My dad is never going to be on my side that much is painfully clear.

"You can do whatever you want to her once she has the baby. After that, she's yours to do with as you please." I almost vomit at my father's response. Yeah, he is definitely not on my side.

"You will never get your hands on my son, Cyanide!" I yell at my father. Saying his villain name is code for Collin who is listening in with his super hearing that it's time for him and the League to attack. The League is nearby, they were never letting me into a potential trap without backup.

Fuck me, my family is twisted. I know I'm damaged and slightly twisted myself, but not this bad. Mason and my father are fucking delusional and insane. It's terrifying. The next thing I see is a total bloodbath between the League and my father's followers. The worst part is I wake up before I know if my father successfully captures me.

I rapidly sit up from my sleep to find Collin already sitting up next to me. Fuck. My father is coming back. I was right, he won't be happy with my choices. There's also the baby and prophecy factor. I know I need to tell Collin, but I quickly decide I won't tell him the baby part. I need him focused on my father coming back and the prophecy. I can tell him about the baby part of this vision later. Plus, I don't even know if I'm pregnant yet. Although, that vision wasn't too far into the future, so I might already be pregnant. It's not like we have used protection. I shake the baby thoughts from my mind. I can focus on that later.

"You started shaking in your sleep. I take it that means you had a vision."

"Yeah, and not a great one. My father's coming back, and he is not going to be happy I've sided with the League." I reply.

I proceed to fill Collin in on my vision. I include everything about the Oracle prophecy, my dad coming home, about Altron being torn between wanting peace with humans or my father's plan, the brainwashing, and the blood bath at the end. I left everything out pertaining to the baby. At first, I didn't know how my father even knew I was pregnant when I didn't tell anyone yet. I realize my father didn't actually know if I was pregnant. He and Mason were bluffing to gauge my reaction. I fell for their stupid trick and gave myself away. My father's plan is much more twisted than I initially thought and I'm more a part of his plan than I would care for. What's worse is he doesn't just have plans for me, he has plans for my son too. War is certainly coming, and I'm going to have a child during it.

# HEROES & VILLAINS

## CHAPTER 23

### Collin

I'm not surprised Cyanide is coming back from Altron. It was only a matter of time with war on the horizon. The dark leader had to emerge from the shadows at some point. I never believed he was dead and neither did my father. The way his followers carried on his plans made it clear he was still alive and simply in hiding. Now, he's coming back and all hell is about to break loose.

Clara's vision also gave some insight into what is happening with Altron. We haven't heard anything from them because they are having their own civil war. They are divided between peace and carrying out old traditions. I wonder if the Council will join forces with the League. Maybe we can help each other and with Clara being on our side that's a huge bonus.

I'm a little shocked to find out about the prophecy about her. I didn't even know prophecies were real. It's safe to assume that things are different on Altron than they are on Earth. The Oracle is super powerful and we need to make sure that if we work with the Council of Elders that Clara is kept safe. She can't be turned into a weapon on any side. She needs to bring balance and harmony, and I know that's what she wants to do. Clara is not a villain despite what many initially thought about her. As much as Clara fears she will become a villain, I know she won't because her heart and intentions are good. She might have her own agenda with things, which is fine because in the end, she does the right thing. That is all that matters to me.

I'm sensing there is something else about the vision Clara isn't telling me. I wonder if it's personal. The vision was of a meeting with her dad, it's possible part of their interaction opened some old wounds. I'm sure whatever it is Clara will tell me in her own time. I should be upset that she is hiding something from me, but I know she's not doing it on purpose. Knowing Clara she needs to process whatever it is first. Then when she is ready, she will tell me. I trust her.

After Clara fills me in about her vision, I roll out of bed to search for my cell phone. I need to fill my dad in on Clara's vision. Just as I pick up my phone it pings with a text. My dad has called an emergency League meeting.

That's not surprising and spares me from having to fill him in right now.

I turn to face Clara who is out of bed and holding her cell. "I got invited to the League meeting." She says out loud as she looks at her phone. Complete disbelief is written all over her face.

I grin forms on my face. "See, I told you that you would be accepted. My dad inviting you to the League meeting means you are officially on the inside." I reply, pulling her into my arms. Finally, my dad believes Clara is on our side. I think everyone else finally does as well.

"Don't you ever get tired of being right?" She questions with a playful scoff.

"What can I say? It comes naturally." I joke.

"Everything comes naturally for you." Clara replies as she slips out of my arms and heads to the bathroom. I follow her. Something in her tone is off.

"Everything okay, Little Villain?" I question as I follow her.

I'm fine with her taking her time to tell me things as she processes whatever it is that is bothering her. However, I don't like when I can sense her self-doubt. Clara has a tendency to compare herself to me and the other League members. I don't believe she does it on purpose, but more because she has been judged so hard for all her life she can't help it.

"I don't want my dad coming back to drive a wedge between us. He will try because he doesn't want me with you. He is determined I end up with Mason." Clara confesses. Okay, not the direction I thought this was going in. It's not self-doubt about her superpowers or abilities. It's her fear of losing me that has her upset.

"I won't let that happen, Little Villain. I will never believe any of Cyanide or Bullet's lies. I will only ever believe you." I say coming up behind her and rubbing my hands up and down her arms before planting a kiss on her right shoulder.

"Good. Now, let's shower and get ready for this meeting." She deflects. I let her go, knowing she is clearly trying to process her overwhelming emotions. That's how Clara works. She likes to process on her own and then when she is ready she shares with me. Tonight, I'm sure she will be a snuggle bug.

I understand her need for space to process things. Normal life can be overwhelming as it is. Then you add in superpowers, being in the public eye, protecting the city, and everything else that comes with being associated with the League of Metas. It can be a lot. I get it. I need time to decompress myself, which is usually something physical like training, running, or even flying.

Clara knows I'm here for her when she is ready. It's best not to push Clara and let her let down her walls. I'm sure she is probably anxious for her first League meeting too. She doesn't want to mess anything up. The only way she could do that is if she went back with her father and Mason. Since she clearly has no intentions of doing that, she has nothing to worry about. However, I know her, and she's already played the worst scenarios in her head. She might be edgy for a few days, but it's nothing I can't handle. The important part is that she is safe, so as long as she doesn't do anything reckless, things should be okay on that front. Everything else is another matter that we will deal with soon enough.

# BIRDY RIVERS

# CHAPTER 24

## Clara

As Collin and I get ready for the meeting, my mind races in dozens of directions. My vision was a lot. It seems I'm no longer struggling with my superpowers. Whatever mental block I had broke when I fought Mason yesterday. I guess I've had a mental block stopping me from fully using my superpowers. I didn't want to hear it when Collin suggested, but of course, the mighty hero was right. I should know by now Collin is right more often than not. The truth is, I just didn't want to hear the truth because the truth is often hard to handle.

One truth I have to face is having a baby. I did not see that one coming. I guess I should have because we haven't been using protection. Not that we even talked about using protection, we were both so caught up in the ecstasy of the sex we were having, we didn't think. I hope Collin wants kids. We never even talked about it. Then again, we haven't been together long. I can't focus on that right now.

Right now, I need to focus on this meeting. Collin wants me to tell everyone about my vision, which means I have to speak. I'm not good at public speaking. I had a hard time telling Collin about the vision. Now, I have to tell the League while making sure I don't slip up about the baby. A baby I don't even know if I'm pregnant with or not. I'll have to take a pregnancy test at some point, but I can't bring myself to do that. I also need to sneak a test somehow. I don't want anyone to know I'm taking a pregnancy test. That will be rumors and drama I don't need.

As Collin and I head to the meeting I push thoughts about being pregnant to my first official League meeting. I want to come off as confident and competent. I might have earned a spot at this meeting and the League's respect. I don't want to follow up my badass moment with an embarrassing one.

I've never been to the conference room where the League meets. There were clearly things left out of my original tour, which doesn't bother me. I wasn't expecting to be handed the golden keys to Oswald Tower, and to be honest, I don't want them. Collin holds the golden key to the Oswald legacy, and I know that it's a heavy-duty to carry. I don't envy Collin or Thomas. At least, I don't have the have burden of carrying on my father's legacy. That's certainly not a deranged legacy I want to be involved in.

We enter the conference room. It's a rather simple large oval room with an oval shape table surrounded by nice black leather office chairs. The walls are a sleek grey. There is a coffee bar table with a single serve coffee maker surrounded by all the things one would need. In the center of the table is a black square device. I know it's a type of projection unit. I've seen similar devices throughout the tower. I thought there would be more to it than this, but then again I'm not sure what I expected in the first place. Some members are already here while the rest file in with us. As we take our seats I take a deep breath. I can do this.

"Well, we clearly have some orders of business to take care of." Thomas starts. "I'm sure none of us are happy about Mason's betrayal. We might have lost a member of the League of Metas. However, we gain a new one in Mason's place. I think Clara has more than proved her loyalty to the League. That is why as of today she is an official member of the League and will go by the Oracle." Thomas announces. Everyone claps as my mind reels with the news. I didn't think he'd actually make me a member, but I'm glad he did. I can't help the proud smirk that crosses my face. I'm finally accepted. I'm also not sure how he came up with my name. Did Collin tell him about the prophecy or was it destiny that he would pick the very name that I'm given in the prophecy? "With our first order of business out of the way, time to move on to the next order which is what our next moves should be."

"I might be able to help with that. I had a vision last night." I proceed to tell the League everything including the prophecy and how the meeting ended in a blood bath. While I tell them about the Oracle prophecy I look for hints that Thomas might have known or anything to indicate why he gave me the superhero name Oracle without him knowing about the prophecy. Thomas didn't give me a didn't hint. He has mastered a damn good poker face. At the end of the day, it doesn't matter how he came up with my superhero name. I'm just happy to finally have one. I'm also destined to be the Oracle, so it makes sense it's my superhero name. I guess sometimes we can't escape our destiny.

While I fill the League in, I make sure I leave out the baby part. I'm careful to make sure I don't even hint that there is more to the vision. I'm not ready for that can of worms to be opened yet. Plus, I don't want Collin to find out in front of everyone. That is a private thing between us. Collin does need to know about the baby at some point, and the rest of the League will follow then. For now, the focus is on my father coming back to Oswald City and what our next moves should be. We also have to consider reaching out to Altron to see if they are with us or my father. They might even be neutral and not want to be involved at all. It's hard to say because we haven't had contact with them in at least a decade, from what I understand.

"Do you have a time frame of when he might arrive?" Thomas inquires, pulling me back to the meeting.

"No, not a day, but within the month. I'm sure he will make it known when he arrives." I answer.

"Do we know what Cyanide might do to start a war?" Veronica questions.

"That I don't know, but knowing him it will be a show of sorts. Like all villains, my father likes to make a spectacle out of himself." I reply. Thomas nods his head in agreement.

The rest of the meeting is strategizing and making dozens of different plans that I struggle to remember. I should have brought a damn notepad. Then again, this is my first meeting, and I'm still processing being made an official member, which I'm sure will go over so well with my father. I'm pretty sure me joining the League is certainly not in his plans for me. I don't care about his plans because I'm the one in control of my destiny.

After the meeting, Collin informs me he will be busy for the day. Normally, I would be a bit annoyed and feel like I'm being blown off. However, we had all day yesterday together, and I need a moment to myself to get composed, process the last twenty-four hours, and mentally prepare to take a pregnancy test. It's a lot to take in at once. My life has drastically changed in the last several months.

I'm glad so much in my life has changed for the positive, but there are more changes coming. Changes I'm not entirely sure I'm ready for. I don't even know where to begin to process the fact that there is a prophecy about me. For so long, I thought I was insignificant and defective. Turns out I'm more significant than I ever imagined, and I'm certainly not defective. My father wanted to break me down so I would be easier to control. His plan temporarily worked, but now I'm in control. I won't let anyone control me again. I'm going to master my superpowers and use them to stop my father. There is one thing I realize. Part of the reason my father suppressed my superpower is that I wouldn't use it against him. I have the ability to help stop him and put his ass in a grave. He knows this and he did everything in his ability to make sure he had control over me before I figured it out. Fortunately for me, I figured it out sooner rather than later. I will stop at nothing to end my father's reign of terror.

# CHAPTER 25

## Clara

It's been a little over a week since the Home Day celebration and my vision. It's been crazy. Nina came out to the public. She and Claire have announced the relationship publicly as well. She gave a huge speech about her motives for hiding her sexuality and her relationship. Some think it's a cover up to not face the embarrassment of Mason being a traitor, which the public also now knows. Maybe it is a cover up, but there is honesty in it as well. I don't envy the position Nina has put herself in, but I also know she will recover from it because she is a little too good at giving a flawless appearance to the world.

Everyone also knows I'm an official member of the League and that I essentially replaced Mason. Man, I would have loved to have seen the stupid look on Mason's face when he found out I replaced him in the League. I'm sure he's not happy, and my father won't be either. I don't really care what they think because I'm all about what I want. I want to be with my destined mate and be a part of the League.

I haven't gone out and fought any crime yet. I'm still getting in tune with my superpowers. Controlling time isn't easy. I can temporarily pause it, speed it up, or slow it down. It takes a lot of energy to do and my stamina for holding it isn't great. So, Collin has me working on my stamina and helped me arrange my diet to be filled with more energy foods that should also help.

I'm surprisingly having fun exploring my superpowers. I was so hesitant at first because I was afraid. I spent most of my life content to believe I didn't have superpowers because my life was easier that way. I also feared what would be done to me if I did have superpowers. I feared the League would hunt me and my father's followers would force me to lead them in a war I didn't believe in.

Fear is a super powerful motivator. It has the ability to completely cripple us. I let it cripple me for far too long. Now, I'm embracing the fear of the unknown. It also helps that I can see into the future. I do have visions when I'm awake or asleep. I haven't figured out if I can control my visions or not. Collin also wonders if I can have visions of the past, but so far I haven't had any yet. We have learned a lot about my superpowers, yet I think there are a couple more things left for me to master.

There is also the whole baby thing. It's been a week and I still haven't found a way to tell Collin about it. He's busy with Thomas working on things for the impending war. He spends time with me mostly for training and to sleep. I've moved everything into his room. There's no point in us being separate anymore. We haven't told anyone we are destined mates. It's not that we are hiding it, it's just we don't know how to explain it because Bio Metas aren't known to have destined mates. Plus, it seems so minor compared to all the things going on.

I just finished up some training with Collin before he heads to a meeting with his dad. I need to find a way to get my hands on a pregnancy test. I know deep down I'm already pregnant. One of those annoying absolute truths I simply know. However, this time I want to see the physical pregnancy test with the two fucking pink lines that say I'm pregnant. I know I'm not going to be able to sneak one on my own. I can't leave Oswald Tower without anyone with me. Not because I'm not allowed to leave on my own but because it's not safe. I'm clearly wanted by the enemy and I know the villains will stop at nothing to get me. So, I'm going to recruit Veronica because she is honestly the only other person I trust with this besides Collin.

Normally, I would tell Collin and do the test with him. However, he's crazy as it is, and I don't want to tell him until I've confirmed it myself. It's not that I don't believe my absolute truth because I do, but there is something about the physical proof of a test that gives a true confirmation. Once I have the positive test, I'll tell Collin. I'm not trying to hide our baby from him. It's the other stuff that comes with it. My father wants our son to turn him into an ultimate weapon. Whatever superpowers my son might have, my dad wants them. I don't know if there is something written in the prophecy about what his superpowers are or not. Either way, what should be a happy occasion is shadowed by my father's evil plan.

I find Veronica on the media floor, a floor I try very hard to avoid. She and Nina do all the media stuff for the League. Nina is also with her, and I'm about to chicken out when Veronica sees me and flags me over. I walk over to them where they are standing near some cameras going over a script. I'm sure it has something to do with all the damage control from Mason's betrayal. That's going to take the League a while to recover from.

"What brings you by?" Veronica questions as I get close, curiosity brimming in her features. I don't come to this floor often so I'm sure she is surprised to see me here.

“I was wondering if we could do lunch. I have something I need to talk to you about.” I answer causally.

“What I don’t get an invite?” Nina teases, but I can't tell if she is trying to be funny or is actually offended I didn’t invite her.

“I would invite you, but I really need to talk to Veronica on my own. Please don’t take offense.” I reply, biting my lower lip. I don’t want to upset anyone. I’m not even planning on going to lunch. I just want to get my hands on a damn pregnancy test.

“It takes a lot more than that to offend me. I’ll leave you two be, I have lunch plans with Claire anyway.” Nina states before she walks away, swaying her hips. Seriously, does she ever turn off her supermodel, ice queen personality?

“Where would you like to go for lunch?” Veronica asks as she hands the papers in her hands off to someone.

“It doesn't matter, but first we need something else,” Veronica looks at me curiously. “A specific test for women that we take when we miss a certain something." I hint trying to not be too obvious with my request because I have no idea who could be listening in.

It’s a little different for Bio Metas because our periods aren’t like human ones and neither is our pregnancy length. Bio Metas give birth at seven months. Altronians give birth at five, so Bio Metas are in the middle. Our periods are more similar to humans but we have longer cycles. Instead of getting a cycle every month, we get them more like every month and a half to two months.

"Ah, I can help with that." Veronica replies with a smile as she leads me off the media floor and into the elevator.

The next thing I know I'm in a private bathroom peeing on a stick. It doesn't take long for the damn two pink lines to show up. My hand shakes as I hold the test. I already knew I was pregnant, but holding the positive pregnancy test in my hands makes it all too real. I step out of the bathroom and show the test to Veronica who beams a smile. She's about to become a grandma.

"I need to tell Collin." I state, staring back at the test.

"He will be thrilled. He's always wanted to be a father. I also know you two are destined mates." Veronica informs me.

"I assumed he would tell you and Thomas at some point. You don't seem to have family secrets." I note.

"We are open with one another because we trust one another. You have no idea how much my son loves you. I think he's loved you for a long time from afar, unsure of what to do with his feelings. Ever since you two had the encounter at the fair, he's secretly been smitten with you. Yes, I know about that. I'm a mom. I know these things. You'll soon find out what I'm talking about. You're about the same age your mom was when she got pregnant with you."

"I know. She used to say twenty-three was better than eighteen." I have no idea why my mom said that.

"Eighteen was when Janna was first pregnant. She miscarried shortly after finding out. She convinced herself that she was too young at eighteen anyway to have a baby. I think it was her way of hiding her grief. She was so thrilled when she had you." Veronica gently informs me.

"I didn't know she was pregnant before me," I say quietly. My mom was full of secrets just like my dad.

"She was. I'm not even sure Cyanide knew about the first baby. When I got pregnant with Collin at twenty-one, I feared Janna would hate me. She did say she was happy for me even if she hid her sadness. Then she got pregnant two years later with you and Lois was pregnant a year later with Nina. We all had our kids close in age like we wanted. Except nothing else that we dreamed when we were younger came true. Out of the three amigos, I'm the only one left." A sad smile crosses her face at the memories.

"My mom was full of secrets, and I don't think any of us could have saved her from herself. My dad didn't kill my mom. He only said that because in his own twisted way, he thought he was protecting her reputation. My mom committed suicide. In her note, she said she couldn't handle the loss, the isolation, or Lois's betrayal anymore. She had demons of her own that no one knew about. Demons my father used to control her. Before you ask me about Lois's betrayal, I don't know anything about it. I do know it has to do with why Cyanide killed her, but that's all I know." I inform Veronica.

"I don't think Janna ever wanted to be saved. I think in her own way she thought your father would save her or maybe she went with him because she knew he never would and that is what she wanted. I'm glad you are with my son, a part of our family, and a part of the League. You are forging your own path and destiny, Clara, and that is a super powerful thing you should be proud of." Veronica beams a warm smile at me as she puts her hand on my shoulder in a comforting manner.

Veronica and I do end up getting lunch. We chat and bond. I'm enjoying having a strong female figure in my life to look up to. It's not that I never admired my mom because I did, but she died when I was still fairly young. My memories of her a faded and warped now. I also question if she knew what my father was doing to me. She clearly had her own secrets and demons that she wrestled with.

After lunch, I head back to the room and take a hot bath to relax. Telling Collin I'm pregnant is the easy part. Telling him that my father wants our son for his evil plan to make him a weapon, not so easy. Oh, and I need to toss in there that our son is part of the oracle prophecy. It's a lot to unload on someone. While I have no doubt that Collin can handle it, I hope that I can. Being a mom isn't something I ever thought about, but I know it's something I want. I rub my belly and promise myself I will do better than my parents. I have to do better than them because I want my child to have a good life and never question their worth.

# BIRDY RIVERS

# CHAPTER 26

**Collin**

The last week has been insane. I'm used to being busy and on my toes, but with war on the horizon, it's been more than I'm used to. My father has been an uncontrollable fire with Cyanide coming back. He's determined to kill Cyanide this time. He's also determined to keep Clara safe, which is something I can get behind. He fears what would happen if Cyanide got his hands on her. I can't deny that I have my own concerns about him getting his hands on her. I know Clara won't go willingly with her father or help him willingly. The only way I see Clara willingly help her father is if he threatened someone she cared about, like me. That's why it's best to keep Clara safe and out of her father's psychopathic hands.

Clara has been acting a little off lately. I suspect there was more to her vision she had last week. I keep expecting her to tell me, but then again I haven't been around much. When we are together we are training. She is so focused on her training I don't want to distract her. Clara is finally accepting and willingly working on her superpowers. I've never seen her so focused and determined before. I don't want to interrupt her progress. In the evenings we aren't always together for one reason or another. The nights we are together we are tired and end up passing out early.

Then there's processing Mason's betrayal. While he was here I was so focused on not letting him get away and take Clara that I didn't process the emotional part. We were best friends for years. If we were even friends to begin with as I'm sure he befriended me on purpose. Still, it felt genuine. However, it does explain some things like why Mason never wanted Oliver to hang out with us. He wanted to make sure no one else took his best friend status.

Of course, I never ignored Oliver like Mason wanted me to. Oliver and I are friends, but not as close as we could be. I regret not fighting harder for Oliver to join us. Mason was difficult though and when we did hang out with Oliver he was a bit of an ass. At the time, I didn't understand why Mason was so against Oliver. Oliver is a good guy. A little military minded, but he's actually a fun guy to hang around once you get to know him.

Now, I see Mason was keeping Oliver away because he was threatened by him. Mason knew he needed to keep me close in order to have the best information to feed the enemy. I hate that he used me, used us all. In some ways, it's not his fault that he was brainwashed. Cyanide and Yuri got their claws into him early. Mason didn't stand a chance at not doing Cyanide's evil bidding like his father. Mason fails to see Cyanide is using him like a pawn. Cyanide likes using people as pawns, but he won't be doing it forever.

I just finished training with Clara and now I'm headed to another meeting with my father to talk the man down off a ledge from doing something crazy. I'm concerned about my father because I've never seen him so frayed on the edges before. I know Cyanide is never a fun topic to talk to him about, but with Cyanide returning my father is losing his cool. Luckily, no one is seeing him lose his cool other than me and my mom.

As I'm headed to my dad's office I run into Oliver. "Hey, Collin." He greets.

"Hey, Oliver. You headed to the meeting too?" I question.

"Yeah, your dad told me to come," Oliver pauses. "So, how are you doing from Mason's betrayal? You two were thick as thieves."

"It stings like a bitch and I blame myself for not seeing the signs earlier." I honestly confess.

"Don't blame yourself like that. He had us all fooled. None of us saw his red flags, and when we did we chalked it up to Mason being Mason." Oliver replies as we continue down the hallway.

"I know. It's also embarrassing for the League, though. We had a spy in our ranks for years and the only reason we figured it out is because of Clara. Granted, my dad and I had our suspicions about a spy, but never did I imagine it would be someone so close to us. Someone who I regarded as a friend." I add.

"I get it. We look like fools because of it. It sucks because now people will question us, but what they fail to realize is we are half human. We make mistakes too. I'm sure even a pure blooded Altronian makes mistakes. We trust people, fall in love, make friends, have families, and do all the things that humans do. Sometimes, we unfortunately trust the wrong people."

"Has anyone ever told you that you are wise?"

"On occasion." Oliver replies and we both chuckle.

We enter my dad's office. At least my father looks more put together today. The man has been holed up in his office overthinking and over strategizing. Even my mom is struggling to get through to him. He's on a slow descent into madness that we can't seem to pull him out of. I know my father won't do anything extreme, but I worry that the stress is getting to him. I know he's certainly feeling some type of way about Mason's betrayal and how Cyanide too cleverly got the upper hand on us in a way we never saw coming. That's eating at my father on levels I can't imagine.

The meeting is basically my father asking Oliver to be my second in command when the time comes for me to take over. I had no idea my father was even thinking about me taking over anytime soon. Maybe he's not, and he's just preparing for the future. It's hard to tell. Either way, I'm okay with it. Oliver just proved through our conversation he is someone I can talk to about things, even the hard stuff because let's face it. Mason is a hard topic for many of us right now.

I'm glad Oliver accepted to be my second in command. He's got the right mindset to be a leader. I actually always preferred him over Mason to be my second in command because I know Oliver is cut out for the position. Oliver and I are going to start working together more often and hanging out more to build our friendship so that we can be leaders who understand one another. We can't lead anyone if we don't even know the person we are supposed to be leading with.

By the time my day is over, I'm ready to head to my room and curl up with Clara. However, as I'm heading to my room I get a text from Clara telling me to come to the roof. Curious, I head to the roof to find Clara wearing a cute black skater dress and black combat boots. There's a table set up with two chairs. On the table, there are two covered plates.

"What's all this?" I question, walking over to her.

"We haven't had a second date. Although, I think we are way past the second date at this point. Mainly, I wanted some time with you because we need to talk, Mighty Hero. Both of our lives are about to change. I figured it would be nice to talk over dinner." Clara pauses. "Okay, the talk over dinner was your mom's idea, but I liked it."

"I'm not even sure how to respond." I honestly admit as my curiosity brims. I guess this is the part where Clara tells me what the hell has been going on with her since her vision last week. I knew she would come around on her own.

"Well, I doubt you will know how to respond at all when I tell you what I need to tell you. You might actually want to be sitting for this." Clara gestures to the table and chairs.

We take our seats at the table, but not before I help Clara with hers. I was raised to be a gentleman, after all. Clara is silent as she takes the lid off her plate to reveal chicken fried steak, mashed potatoes, and roasted broccoli. She picks at her food as I uncover my plate. I'm not going to push her to talk. I know it's hard enough for her to open up as it is, so we eat in silence for about half the meal before Clara drops her fork on her plate, and folds her hands on the table to stop herself from fidgeting while looking up at me.

"I've tried to come up with some creative, fun way to tell you without just blurting the news, but I coming up blank. Blunt and direct is how I do things, so here it is. I'm pregnant." Clara informs me.

My lower jaw drops slightly in shock. That is not even close to what I had in mind. "That's not exactly bad news, Little Villain. Are you worried I'd be mad?"

"I was, but your mom talked me down off the ledge. She told me you always wanted kids and to not worry about you not wanting the baby," Clara pauses taking a deep breath. "Honestly, telling you about the baby is the easy part. This next part is harder. In my vision last week, I left some things out.  In the vision, my dad explained that the prophecy of the Oracle wasn't just about me, but my son as well who will have a great superpower like his mother. My father wanted my child to be with Mason, so he could have easy access to my child to brainwash it into being his perfect weapon. I don't know what our son's superpower will be, Collin, but he's going to be super powerful. We can't let my father get his hands on our baby. I won't let him turn our son into his personal weapon. Look at what he did to me, to Mason even. Now imagine what he would do to our son." Clara emplores.

I get up from my seat and kneel next to her as Clara scoots her chair out a bit so she can pivot to face me. I take her hands in mine. "I won't let Cyanide or anyone take or hurt our son. Over my fucking dead body. I'll protect you and our son. We also have the League to back us up too. It will be okay." I reassure her as my fingers gently stroke her hands as I hold them.

A half smile forms on her face. "I know you will protect us, Mighty Hero. We also have to worry about making sure our son doesn't have a dark side. It tends to be a thing with my family. A trend I'd rather not continue, but if he does we have to make sure we help guide him with it so he stays a hero, even an anti-hero, and never the villain." Clara's voice quivers a bit. She is emotional, and I understand her fears.

"You will be better at guiding him with that than you think. We will do it all together, Little Villain. I truly am happy we are going to start a family together even if we are facing challenging times." I declare before kissing Clara.

We finish our dinner and then spend some time talking on the rooftop. Then we head to bed because we both need rest with war on the horizon. I let Clara know I'll make an appointment for her on the medical floor. I want her to have the best medical care she can have. I'll make sure everyone knows to keep the pregnancy to themselves. Clara is already enough of a target for the enemy. I don't need to widen that target on her back. Clara needed to be protected before, but now she must absolutely be kept safe because it's not just her we are keeping safe anymore. Cyanide will have to go through me and the entire fucking League before he will get his hands on them. We will all feel better when Cyanide is dead.

# CHAPTER 27

## Clara

In the span of a week Collin has had me examined, changed my diet, changed my training routine, and made sure I have my own personal security detail, which is basically various League members following me around. The man is taking protecting me and our baby to a whole new level. It's sweet that he cares, but it's also annoying as fuck because all I want is oranges and chocolate ice cream. Thankfully, Veronica is on my side and sneaking me what I want, which is oranges and chocolate ice cream.

While Collin is only slightly driving me insane with his over protectiveness, I do appreciate it. I've never had someone care or look out for me the way he does. I already know he's going to be an amazing dad. I'm a little worried about being a mom. It's not like I have the best of influences. My mom's sanity was questionable, and she died when I was young. My dad is a fucking psychopathic villain. I'm not really working with the best set of cards for parenthood.

I've been anxiously awaiting my father's arrival. Thomas has a satellite that is supposed to tell us if something enters our atmosphere. It's only a matter of time before he returns. I don't know what he's going to do when he realizes I've joined the League. I wonder if he will send Mason to come fetch me. After all, Mason is his bitch boy. Not that I really want to face either of them.

I'm more worried about facing off with my father. Mason is a little shithead. I kicked his ass once before, I know I can do it again. However, my father is an entirely different evil to deal with. Mason and my dad teamed up is a dangerous cocktail that might render me mentally unstable. In my vision, they fed off each other, almost like a creepy father-son vibe and I was their target. My father wants to control and use me while Mason wants to fuck me and break me to be his own personal whore. Two men with two very different twisted things they want to do to me. The thought alone sends violent shivers through my body.

"How are you feeling this morning?" Veronica asks as we walk into the elevator. She is my assigned guard for the day.

"Eh, the morning sickness comes and goes. Collin keeps trying to make me drink these nasty drinks that are supposed to help, but it makes it worse." My face twists in disgust at the thought of the nasty tan drink Collin insists will help with my morning sickness.

Veronica giggles. "Oswald men are fiercely overprotective. When I was pregnant with Collin, Thomas was like a guard dog following me around. Cyanide was still a part of the League at that time, and it had Thomas on edge. Those two never saw eye to eye. Even when we were kids they couldn't agree on anything."

"Well, Collin is worse because he has a medically smart brain. He is designing my diet based on his intelligence. The problem is he doesn't know how to make shit taste good. He clearly doesn't know how to cook. As for my father, well, I don't think he gets along with anyone unless he brainwashes them like Mason." I reply.

"Oh, neither Thomas nor Collin can cook. I'll see if I can help him enhance the flavor of his drink and meal ideas." Veronica responds with a look that suggests the problem is already handled.

"Thank you, I'd appreciate it. I swear the taste makes me want to barf more than my morning sickness. I love that Collin cares enough about my health during pregnancy to invent special drinks for me, but they taste like shit." I gripe. I instantly feel shitty about griping, decreasing my mood even more.

"I bet they do. I'll help him. That way you can drink it and you both can be satisfied." Veronica says with a warm smile as we make it to the training floor.

I trust Veronica. She has such a motherly vibe about her. It's strange to me that I'm starting to see her as my role model. I thought after my mom died that was the end of female role models in my life. I never dared to dream I would get another female role model in my life. I was surrounded by Yuri and his sons for a good decade or so before Veronica came into my life. I'm thrilled that she did. It's nice to have other females around.

Veronica and I do some training. I'm slowly getting a better hang of my superpowers. Controlling time is still a challenge when it comes to holding it and not draining my stamina in the process. I'm also trying to get the hang of controlling time while fighting. I still don't know what triggers my visions. I'm starting to think I don't have much control over them at all. I certainly don't control when they come. I never know if I'll be awake or asleep when I receive my vision. I also don't seem to control what I see. It's almost as if I see what I'm meant to see. It's a spiritual connection I can't fully place.

After training, Veronica and I are head to see Thomas, Collin, and Oliver who have asked us to come see them. It sounds like they have news. The pit in my stomach tells me that I'm not going to like whatever they have to tell us. It either involves something to do with my father, Mason, or one of his other henchmen. Either way, I doubt I will like it.

Oliver has officially become Collin's future second in command. I know Collin was shocked his father started making such plans, but with war around the corner, I believe Thomas is preparing for all outcomes. I don't blame him because who knows what we are going to face and who we might lose along the way. I hope we lose no one, but I've learned the hard way that things often do not go the way we plan. Sometimes things turn out better and other times not so much.

We enter Thomas's office. Thomas, Collin, and Oliver are around Thomas's desk. The moment we enter Collin is at my side. He is definitely overprotective, but since I've never had someone protect me like this before I actually like it. Plus, my Mighty Hero is a little possessive of what is his, and to the dismay of some I am his. To my happy heart, I am his and he is mine. I love that Collin was never ashamed to claim me as his, his destined mate.

"So what's going on?" I ask Collin as we and Veronica walk over to Thomas and Oliver.

"A ship has entered the Earth's atmosphere." Thomas informs me and the crazed look in his eye makes me question if Thomas is alright. My father is his mortal enemy and he got a serious one up on him with the whole Mason thing, which I'm sure has been eating at Thomas.

"My father." I state. There's no doubt who it could be. My vision showed him coming soon.

"I assume so. Any ideas what he might do first?" Thomas questions.

"If you are asking if I had any visions recently, the answer is no. From what I remember of my father's habits, he will go to his lair and assess the situation. I'm sure he will not be thrilled about what he learns. Then he will most likely try to reach out to me. He won't take me by force, not at first. He will want me to come of my own free will to him. It will be a trap of sorts, I'm sure. In my vision, when I met up with him and it didn't go his way, he turned it into a bloodbath." I answer.

"We know you can't have that meeting with him. Not in your condition." Thomas states.

"I agree, but my father will make threats that we all know he will make good on. One thing my father doesn't do is bluff." I add.

"That is true. Cyanide is not a bluffer. Never has been. We need to avoid him killing in masses. That tends to be his go to move. At least it was in the past. When his demands weren't met, he would go to a populated public area and kill as many as he could with his poisonous gas. When you refuse to meet with him, he will do something drastic to gain attention, especially now that he is back. He has been gone for years, he will want to make a spectacle. Cyanide was always one for showmanship in all the wrong ways." Thomas contributes.

"How long do you think it will take for Cyanide to reach out to you?" Oliver questions.

"Not long. It won't take long for him to realize I'm not with the villains. He will ask where I'm at, and I'm sure Mason will happily toss my ass under the bus. I'm a valuable asset to my father and so is our son." My hand goes to my stomach, caressing it knowing the life I carry is more precious than I anyone can imagine.

"We won't let him get our son." Collin reassures me as he rubs my shoulders.

"No, we won't. I think Cyanide will find he has to go through the entire League of Metas and then some to get to you and your son." Thomas declares with a fierce determination in his eyes that makes me glad he finally changed his mind about me.

We spend the next couple of hours strategizing, and it feels like we have gotten nowhere. There's no good way to stop my father from throwing a tantrum when he doesn't get his way. It's not like we can wrap each citizen of the city in their own protective bubble so his poisonous gas doesn't affect them. We also can't risk meeting with him. It's a no win situation right now that is giving me a pounding headache trying to figure it out. This is one of those moments I wish I would get a vision that would tell me what to do. I think everyone in the room is thinking the same thing, but no one is saying it out loud. Sometimes I get the vibe they think I have all the answers.

As I'm getting ready to leave Thomas's office with Collin, my phone in my pocket dings. I casually take it out thinking it's one of the other League ladies texting me. Claire and Nora have become very friendly toward me. They were always more on the warm and friendly side, but now they are even more so. Nina is still a cold hearted bitch, but that seems to be her personality.

Looking at my phone I realize I have text from an unknown number. My stomach drops and a pit forms. This time it's not the morning sickness making me nauseous. I stop dead in my tracks as I open the video message. It's my father. He hasn't changed one bit since I've seen him last. His dark blonde hair is cut short, his blue eyes sparkle with vengeance, he looks like he just shaved, and I can tell he's in his lair given the background. He must have gotten my number from Mason. Even if he didn't, I know he has tech people on his side just like we do. He could have easily had one of them hack my phone to send me this video message. Collin stops next to me as he realizes what's on my phone. I take a deep breath before I hit play.

"Clara, my dear. I'm very disappointed in you. I thought I raised you better than to trust the heroes. Thomas and his pathetic league will only use you against me. Then they will turn on you because they will never truly accept you. Thomas will never be able to look past the fat that you are my daughter. You are my daughter, Clara. The darkness runs in you like it does me. You can pretend to be a good girl, but I know you have the heart of a villain in you. How could you side with the people that drove your mother to suicide? Come home to me, my darling girl. I will be the king of the planet soon enough and you can be my princess of chaos. Come home where you belong, Clara, because if you don't I will kill people until you do. You have forty eight hours to get your ass home before I go on a killing spree." The message ends and I struggle to hold back my vomit.

Collin puts his arm around me. "Well, that escalated quickly." Oliver sarcastically states.

"I told you he would be violent." I retort, trying to hide my frustration, disgust, and fear.

"We need to bring Skinwalker into play. I know none of us want to. I know we have all been avoiding suggesting him, but we don't have a choice." Collin fiercely states, and everyone in the room grows silent.

"Who is Skinwalker?" I ask because clearly I'm the only one who doesn't know what the hell Collin is trying to suggest.

"A secret member of the League, but he is a little deranged. Sam Drake has the ability to shape shift into anyone he sees. He has to see the person in order to copy them, but he can not replicate a Bio Metas superpowers. He can only replicate appearances. It's a handy ability, but the shifting between different people screws with his mind. He starts to believe he is the person he is impersonating. He has a special padded room in the basement where he stays to attempt to regain his sanity." Collin informs me.

"Bringing Skinwalker into play means we need to have a vote. We never bring him into action unless we have a vote because it's always a risk bringing Sam out of his cell." Oliver adds.

"Wait, you guys have a secret member of the League that you keep locked up?" I ask astounded.

"It's not like that. When Sam was completely sane before the negative side effect of his superpowers took over, Sam locked himself in the padded room. He asked us to keep his identity hidden and to put precautions in place. There's even a video recording of Sam requesting all of this in case someone every questioned the League's intentions with Skinwalker." Thomas informs me. "I'll call in emergency meeting first thing tomorrow morning. We vote on whether or not to bring Skinwalker in to impersonate Clara to hold off Cyanide from killing people. I assume that's where you are going with bringing Sam in." Thomas looks at Collin who nods his head in agreement.

I can't seem to wrap my head around this damn day. Ever since Yuri set up my abduction and had my ass beat within an inch of my life before dropping me on Collin's doorstep everything has been changing at a rapid rate I can't keep up with it. It's one revelation after another and I don't know how to keep up. Learning to master my superpowers, preparing for war with my father, and getting ready for the arrival of our son. It's a lot to handle all at once, but at least I'm not alone. I have my destined mate and our family of metas behind me. I'm ready to face what is to come.

# BIRDY RIVERS

# CHAPTER 28

## Collin

The next morning the League is in the conference room having one of our meetings. I think these meetings are the least glamorous part of being a superhero, but they are required.

I knew that when I brought Sam up it was the suggestion none of us wanted to make. It's why we spent so much time trying to think of something else, but when Cyanide sent Clara that video message I knew I had to suggest the one thing none of us wanted because Sam is the one thing that can keep Clara and the city safe. I hate to use him like a sacrificial lamb, but I don't see another way. I have to protect Clara and our son along with the people of this city. I would love to think that Cyanide is bluffing, but I know he isn't.

Sam is a sensitive subject for all of us because he is the one person we can't seem to help. Sam like Oliver, Claire, Nora, and Mason came from the Bio Meta Program that my grandfather started with the Altronians to help expand the Bio Meta race. It's how most Bio Meta came to be. The ones like me and Nina are lucky because we have parents. Most of the Bio Metas in the program don't have parents. There is an option for the donors to know and even raise their children, but many prefer to be donors. So my grandfather built a home for them where they can thrive, grow, and eventually train their abilities. A select few get recruited to the League.

The side effects of Sam's superpowers were not evident at first. He went years shapeshifting from person to person without consequence. Most of us don't seem to have any negative side effects to our superpowers. In fact, we didn't even know it could be a thing until Sam. Sam was sixteen when his multiple personalities started showing. He started acting differently and taking on the whole personalities of those he had shapeshifted as. We did everything we could for him. We tried medications, therapy, and even had the best medical professionals we could find to try to help Sam. It went on for a couple of years. The endless amounts of tests, meds, doctors, and none of it was able to truly help Sam.

In one of his lucid states, Sam expressed his concern that he would become a villain afraid that one of the personalities of someone evil would completely turn him. Sam didn't want to be an asset to the enemy, so he chose to lock himself away and only come out to help when we absolutely needed him. We were hesitant to let Sam lock himself away, but who were we to deny his wishes. Sam started to feel uncontrollable and locking himself away was the only way he felt he could regain some type of control over his frayed mind.

Over the years, we haven't used him unless absolutely necessary, hoping that we would find a cure for him so he could be a fully restored member of the League and help us fight crime like he used to. We have been working for a cure. I've tried to create several medications to help him, but I've failed. I will keep trying and never stop trying to save my friend's mind. I hate what I'm about to ask Sam to do knowing he might get killed in the process. No one ever said being a hero was easy or that there isn't a massive morally grey area that we often find ourselves in. Deciding what is best for the greater good isn't always easy.

My dad starts off the meeting by explaining the situation to the rest of the League then presents the idea of using Sam to copy Clara and send him to Cyanide instead. I know it's a risky ask. I know it's not something anyone wants to do. I'm not even sure I want Sam to end up in Cyanide's hands if he realizes that Sam isn't Clara. Still, I'd rather him have Sam instead of Clara and our son, which I feel like shit for thinking. However, I know Sam, and I know he would understand. The vote has started and so far everyone is on board even if some are reluctant. I understand their reluctance.

"Uh, what the hell is wrong with Clara?" Nina questions, pointing to Clara who is sitting next to me. Her eyes are completely white and she appears to be in some sort of trance. I wave my hand in front of her face, but she doesn't flinch.

"I think she might be having a vision." I answer.

"I thought she only had them when she was sleeping?" My father questions.

"We thought so too until recently she discovered she could. It's only happened a couple of times." I inform them. Things have been crazy and I haven't had a moment to even discuss Clara's training or development with my dad.

Several moments pass as we continue to vote about Sam. Everyone agrees to send Sam. It's the only way to keep the majority of people safe. I wonder if we can get Sam to fake visions. That part would be easy, but there is no way for him to fake controlling time. Thankfully, we don't have to worry about faking the pregnancy. Cyanide only found out in the vision because Clara gave herself away that she was. Clara is still silently beating herself up over that. Her father easily gets under her skin. The other problem is I don't know how to get Sam out once we send him into the lion's den. Finally, Clara snaps out of her trance. She blinks her eyes several times as she slightly shakes her head before looking at us.

"We have to go to Altron and talk to Crona." She states. Well, that's not what I thought she would say. I was certain her vision would have to do with Cyanide.

"Crona is still alive?" My dad asks in disbelief. I know that has to shock his system as Crona is his mother who we all thought died when Wolfgang did. Although we never found her body, we simply assumed that one of the other Altronians took her body back to Altron before they left.

"She is and she is on Altron. We need to go as soon as possible. They don't support my father's plan. They can help us." Clara answers.

"We will address that in a moment. It's all agreed we will send Sam as Clara to Cyanide. It's highly possible Sam will end up dead or Cyanide might convince him to join his side as we all know Sam is not always mentally stable enough to make good choices. It's a risk we have to take because it's better than risking Clara and the baby in Cyanide's hands." My dad concludes.

"Sam won't join my father. He would rather die than become a villain. I can tell you that much." Clara adds. Her absolute truths come in handy. Clara grabs my hand. "You will cure him. The answer is on Altron. We have to go there for more than one reason. Altron is the key to winning this war, curing Sam, and me finally mastering my superpowers."

"Well, to Altron we go. I've been wanting to use that damn spaceship we've been holding on to. Collin, Clara, and I will go. Veronica will be in charge with Oliver as her second in command. In the meantime. Nina, Claire, and Nora will be a badass trio protecting our city. I will prepare the spaceship to go to Altron. Clara and Collin will go prepare Sam for his assignment. Hopefully, he is lucid today because we need to send him to Cyanide before Cyanide gets impatient." My dad instructs, ending the meeting.

With our assignments, we each go our separate ways. Clara and I head to the basement where Sam's room is. On the way there I distract myself with thoughts of leaving Earth. I can't believe we are going to Altron. I've always wanted to go. I used to dream about what the home planet was like. As a kid, I imagined going there. Now, I finally get to go there, and I get to do it with my destined mate. Maybe while we are there we can understand destined mates more along with many other things. It will be nice to hopefully get some answers.

As we approach Sam's room we run into his doctor. Dr. Wells has been treating Sam for years. Well, more like helping Sam manage his psychosis. Dr. Wells smiles as he sees us approach. "Mr. Oswald." Dr. Wells greets. He's always formal, even though I've insisted he call me Collin.

"Good morning, Dr. Wells. How's Sam today?" I greet back.

"Lucid. It's a good day to visit. I know he will enjoy seeing you." Dr. Wells replies before looking down at the chart in his hands. It's most likely Sam's chart, but Dr. Wells does assist with other Bio Meta health concerns.

"Good. I do have a mission for him." I inform Dr. Wells whose smiling face morphs into concern. "We need him or else you know I wouldn't even ask."

"I know. He should be up for it. I just worry it might set him back. He's been making great progress with his therapy. You should go see him while he's still in a good frame of mind." Dr. Wells suggests.

I nod my head and lead Clara down the white lit hallway. "Okay, I thought the basement is where you guys kept your prisoners." Clara comments.

"We do. That's on the other side. The basement of Oswald Tower is vast. We offered to have Sam's room built on the medical wing, but he didn’t want that. I still don’t understand why he wanted his padded room down here, but we couldn't convince him otherwise. So, we simply honored his wishes.” I inform her.

Clara nods her head as we stop at a thick door with a small narrow horizontal window. I punch in the code on the padlock of the door. The door beeps before opening to reveal Sam’s padded room. The walls of the room are padded with light grey pads. There is a simple twin bed with no frame, just the mattress on the floor. There is a grey bean bag chair in the corner where Sam sits reading a book. He lowers the book to reveal his oval shaped face with sharp blue eyes, sandy shaggy blonde hair, and his black framed squared glasses. Sam is dressed in all white scrubs with white socks.

“Collin.” Sam gives a small smile.

“Sam.” I greet back.

“To what do I owe the visit, and who is your friend?” Sam inquires nodding his head toward Clara.

“I have a mission for you, and this is Clara Cole.”

“Ah, the Oracle. I heard the daughter of the villainous Cyanide joined the League.” Sam comments. We do keep Sam informed of what goes on with the League when he is in a lucid state of mind. Dr. Wells is in charge of relaying the information to Sam when he feels Sam can handle it.

"We need your help, Sam. Cyanide wants Clara back and is threatening to hurt a lot of people if we don't return her. We can't let Cyanide have Clara because she is valuable to his evil plan. Not to mention she is pregnant with my son who Cyanide also wants for evil purposes." I inform him.

"So, the great Cyanide returns." Sam states in a bored tone. "Congratulations on your son. I know how badly you want to be a father. I take it you want me to shapeshift as Clara and go in her place to Cyanide?" Sam is smart as a whip when he's lucid. He has a scientific mind like me. Unfortunately, he doesn't get to use his brain like he should be able to. One day I'll get him a cure so he can reclaim his life.

"Yes. It's risky, I know, but it's needed." I firmly state.

A clever grin crosses Sam's face as he sets his book down before he stands. In a blink of an eye, he is Clara. "Okay, no offense that's just creepy." Clara comments.

Sam chuckles in Clara's voice only adding to the creepy factor of his superpower. "You wouldn't be the first person to say that. So, what do I need to know?"

"My father wants me for my abilities. You can fake visions, but you won't be able to fake my ability to control time. However, as far as my dad or Mason is concerned I've only ever controlled time once. You can say you haven't done it since then. My visions are unpredictable so use that to your advantage. My father doesn't know I'm pregnant. The only reason he figured it out in my vision is because he used his stupid tactic on me that I fell for. When you go to him he will try to figure out if you're pregnant by simply stating that you are and wait for your reaction. I stupidly gave myself away in the vision because of my reaction. Lucky for you, you aren't pregnant so he will buy it when you say you aren't. The problem then will be he will want you to become pregnant, which is where I assume he will have Mason attempt to make you so. My father promised me to Mason as some twisted reward for being a spy." Clara informs Sam.

"Mason that prick. I'll enjoy making it hard for him to do anything." Sam never liked Mason and rightfully so. I wish I had seen what Sam did in Mason so that I didn't waste years of friendship on someone who didn't deserve it.

Clara goes on to give Sam as much information as she can to help him impersonate her better. He might look like her, but he also needs to act as Clara would to not make anyone suspicious. Clara also had good ideas for how Sam can fake her superpowers. I guess I underestimated Clara's ability to strategize, but then again, she knows her father and how to deceive him. I'm also sure Clara has spent years thinking of ways to make her father's life difficult if he ever returned. The man is the key to a lot of trauma and I'm sure she wants a little revenge for what he did to her.

After our visit with Sam, we head to pack for our trip to Altron. I'm not sure what to bring or how to pack for going to a foreign planet we don't know much about. When the Altronians were here they didn't give much detail about their home planet. I assume that was on purpose. Wolfgang never questioned it too much as he was simply fascinated that aliens existed. My grandfather might have been brilliant yet he was also a simple man. Wolfgang was more concerned with working with the Altronians to see how they could help advance things on Earth than he was with their motives.

Then there is the matter that my grandmother, Crona, is alive. I know that has to be messing with my dad. I wonder if he feels abandoned the way Clara does with Cyanide. Clara might hate her father, but all she ever wanted was for him to be in her life. She wanted to be worthy enough to be at his side. I know she doesn't have the heart of a villain and wouldn't have become evil like her father even if he did raise her. Still, there is a part of her that wants her father in her life even if he is toxic. She lost her mom at a young age, and she needed her father at an extremely difficult time in her life. Cyanide wasn't there for her. He might have suppressed her superpowers and been cruel to her, but she can't help but want that father-daughter bond.

Going to Altron is going to be interesting. Clara said I would find the answer to cure Sam. I hope she is right because I would love for him to be able to live a normal life. He deserves it. I don't know what fully awaits us on Altron, but I do know we have to go. I can't deny I'm excited and nervous to go to Altron. I think we all are feeling the same way. However, I trust Clara and her visions. If she says we must go there then that's what we must do. I'm not a fan of her traveling in space while pregnant, but it's necessary. We must go where our destiny calls us, so to Altron we go.

# BIRDY RIVERS

# CHAPTER 29

**Clara**

The next morning we send Sam to my father. I'm officially creeped out by his abilities. He looks exactly like me, and with him now wearing my clothes, well it's creepy as hell. It's like having a doppelganger, and I'm not a fan. He's managed to copy my mannerisms, and he only met me once. While I'm completely creeped out by Sam's abilities, I'm also grateful he is risking his life to cover for me with my dad while we go to Altron.

I hope Mason doesn't blow Sam's cover. Mason knows about Sam, but he also knows the League hardly ever brings him into play. According to Collin, Mason never paid much attention to Sam because, according to Mason, Sam was crazy and locked up in a padded room. I also think Mason will be so busy trying to get into my pants, he won't even notice it's not me. I shiver at the thought of him touching me. He's already gotten enough from me as it is. I hope Sam gets a little revenge on Mason while he's impersonating me. I have a feeling Sam will make Mason pay for his crimes in a physiological way.

Once Sam is sent off to my father, Thomas, Collin, and I head out of the city to the private air hanger at Oswald Manor. I didn't even know there was a fucking private air hanger here. Granted when I was here last, I was a prisoner and recovering from having my ass beat within an inch of my life. Apparently, this is where Thomas keeps his personal spaceship. Of course, the Oswalds have their own damn spaceship in a private hangar. Their money knows no bounds and with the Oswald empire bringing them in money on a daily basis they can afford just about anything. They do own the entire fucking city.

We enter the private hangar after driving from the city. Collin would have flown us here, but we are trying to stay under the radar. The spaceship is sleek and made from shiny metal. I have no idea what it's made of, I just know it's shiny. We enter the ship, which is also shiny inside. It's simple with six sleek black chairs that have harnesses over them. The six black chairs sit behind a larger chair with a console in front of it that is toward the front of the ship. Thomas sits in the chair behind the console while Collin tosses our bags in some storage area. It's a simple ship, but I don't even want to know how much it costs to have it. Collin and I take our seats as Thomas fires up the ship. None of us have traveled to space before, so I hope Thomas knows what the fuck he is doing.

The hanger ceiling opens as the engines of the ship fire up getting ready for our trip into space. I don't know what to expect as my stomach does flips. I grab Collin's hand as we start to take off. I close my eyes and take a deep breath. I'm just going to pretend I'm on a fucking ride at an amusement park because I don't know what else to do. The only time I've ever flown is with Collin. I've never even been on a damn plane yet here I am in a fucking spaceship.

As we travel to Altron I completely zone out trying not to get in my head about our trip. I know we need to go to Altron, but I'm not exactly sure what to expect. They have a prophecy about me and that is a little overwhelming to think about. I haven't processed the prophecy about me and my son. I know we are super powerful. Plus, I have the ability to bring peace or destruction, which is a lot to put on a person. I want to believe I'll do the right thing, but I'm the daughter of a villain so I have bad blood coursing through my veins. I don't know why I fear I'll turn evil like my father or even turn my back against the heroes like my mom did. Fear is sometimes irrational and I know I'm worrying about my son too. Thankfully, he's half Oswald so that should hopefully counter the bad blood he'll get from me.

The next thing I know, Collin is telling me we have landed on Altron. We exit the ship and are met with a gorgeous warm orange sky that has three full moons hanging in the sky. Against the warm orange sky is a backdrop of a chrome city with intricate and elegant buildings stretching to the sky. Altron is absolutely, breathtakingly beautiful. Even Thomas and Collin are standing in awe of the beautiful planet we have landed on.

It doesn't take long for the Altronians to realize we have landed on their planet. A group of them approach us, but there is one we all recognize. Crona. She is dressed in a light purple Greek inspired gown, or perhaps the Greeks got their inspiration from the Altronians. It's uncertain of the amount of time they visited Earth. Crona's long white hair is in a fancy braided updo allowing her pointy ears to show. Her tail with its pointed end swishes behind her as her warm light golden almond shaped eyes meet mine.

"Welcome to Altron, Oracle, Son, and Grandson." Crona greets. "We have been waiting for your arrival." Her tone is warm and soft. Well, at least we are welcome here.

"Mom." Thomas states under his breath with a hint of disbelief.

"Come, we have much to discuss." Crona waves her hand for us to follow her.

We follow Crona through the city. Altronians look at us as we pass through, but we look at them as well. They all have pointed ears, almond shaped eyes in varied colors, and white hair in a variety of different fancy styles. All of them are dressed in Greek and Roman inspired attire. The city is impressive as we make our way to wherever Crona is leading us. We eventually end up in front of a large building in the center of the city. We take the stairs and enter the building. We enter into a massive great hall where six seats sit in a throne like manner. The seats are all filled except for one, which Crona walks up to take.

"The council of Elders welcomes you to Altron. I am Salter as you may know. You already know Crona and Trest. Allow me to introduce the rest of the elders. Ressan, Jull, and Lantran." Salter has his hair cut short on one side with the other side long. His dark red eyes should be scary but they aren't. They are actually soft and welcoming.

"Where are Tressa and Cras?" Thomas questions.

"Deceased. They, like Benji, or Cyanide as you call him, believed in our old ways of conquering planets, killing, and enslaving. The council has been convinced that peace is better. We have been wanting to have open communication with Earth for some time now, but we have been trying to get things in order on Altron so that when we have communication, there is peace. There were several Altronians who wanted what Cras, Tressa, and Benji wanted. Benji was our prisoner for years until he escaped back to Earth to carry out his plan. Over the years, the Elders have worked hard to get Altronians to eradicate our old ways and embrace new ways. We will help you defeat Cyanide." Salter answers. I guess my father was bluffing in my vision when he said he had support from some Altronians. He was a prisoner, that's what took him so long to come back. It's also why he didn't bring me with him. He feared they would take me in and teach me the exact opposite of his views and plans.

"Peace is important to us and now that the Oracle has her superpowers peace can be preserved." Jul says as her dark orange eyes land on me. Well, no pressure.

"I need help with my superpowers." I confess.

"I can help you with that." Crona responds with a friendly smile.

"I need help with curing one of the League members." Collin adds. I know he is desperate to help Sam.

I understand why the League keeps Sam as a secret member. His condition is hard to manage and it was Sam who requested he be kept a secret. From what Collin has told me, Sam was training with him and the others that joined the League to fight crime. He was, for a time, fighting crime on the streets with the League until the side effects of his power became too much. I know Collin will figure out a cure for Sam, I just hope Sam lives long enough to take it.

"I can help you with that as Sam is my son. I was the egg donor for him. I know how to cure him." Jul answers. I guess the Alrtonians have been keeping tabs on us. It's not necessarily a bad thing that they have. The Altronians have some advantages over us with technology and even medicine. As long as they use the advantages to help us we won't have a problem.

"We will help you with whatever you need while you are here. You only need to ask. We will have a feast in your honor, Oracle, and to celebrate the life growing inside of you." Crona declares.

"You know I'm pregnant?" I question.

"Yes, Altronians can sense these things. It is a great honor to have you in Altron. We will find you accommodations so you may rest from your journey and prepare for the feast." Crona informs us.

So far our arrival to Altron has been smooth and positive. I knew we needed to come here, and I didn't doubt that we would be welcome. Still, I didn't know what to expect. Even now I'm not sure entirely what to expect.

Crona leads us through the building until we reach two doors across from one another. Thomas is shown into one while Collin and I are shown into the other. I guess even on Altron they know we are a couple.

The room's walls are chrome, like the building itself. There is a huge dark metal bed on the right side. It's bigger than a king-sized bed on Earth. Walking over to the bed the bedding appears to be metallic silver but when I touch it it's the softest thing I've ever felt. Plush white pillows grace the bed as well. There is a huge, plush, light grey, oval shaped couch in the center of the room with white throw pillows. Off to the left, there is another door leading to an open concept bathroom with a giant soaking tub built into the floor. There appears to be a type of toilet and sink to the one side while the other side has a vanity with a mirror covering most of the wall over it.

Crona tells us she will have clothes delivered for us to dress in for the feast. Our clothes from Earth stick out sorely among the Altronian's elegant attire. Collin and I settle into our room completely ignoring the fact that we have bags of our stuff on the ship. I don't think we were expecting the Altronians to provide anything for us. However, they seem to be willing to provide everything we need and more.

Collin and I don't say much as we simply take in the beauty of Altron as we step out onto the balcony off our room. The temperature is perfect here. It's not too hot nor too cold. Time seems slower here or maybe we are simply used to the hustle and bustle of Earth's cities. I'm not sure there is a day and night here as the sky doesn't seem to change at all. There's not a cloud in the warm orange sky. Just the three moons that hang over the city. I lean on the railing while Collin wraps his arms around my waist.

"I wondered for so long what Altron was like. I never imagined this." Collin breaks the silence.

"It's uniquely beautiful." I add, turning in his arms to face him.

"Not as beautiful as you."

"Oh, that's cheesy, Mighty Hero." I jest as I playfully shove him. Collin chuckles at my pathetic attempt to move him.

"Maybe, but it's true. We should find out more about destined mates while we are here." Collin suggests as I turn back around to see the city.

"I agree. I'll ask Crona. I have a feeling she will be spending a good amount of time together while we are here." I reply, finding it hard to take my eyes off the city before me.

Collin and I chat some more before the clothes are delivered to our room. We are told when the feast will start and when to arrive. I'm given a light grey Roman style one shoulder dress with strappy silver matte sandals that wrap around my ankles and up to my mid-calf. Collin is given a dark blue Greek inspired toga with golden details.

We get ready as I ponder the prophecy that surrounds me on the planet and the fact that this whole feast is to honor me. I'm not used to getting attention or being in the spotlight. Even during my time with the League, I've managed to stay out of the spotlight as much as possible. I'm more or less the mysterious Oracle that people know is a part of the League and dating Collin Oswald. Once I joined the League people seemed to forget I was the daughter of a villain and became more obsessed with me dating Collin because he's a well known member of the League.

On Altron, I'm somehow more popular than Collin, which is not something I'm used to. Collin doesn't mind it. In fact, I think he's enjoying the break from the spotlight because as much as he seems to thrive in the spotlight he secretly hates it. Collin loves being a superhero, but he hates being a celebrity and in Oswald City, the two are mutually exclusive.

Once we are ready, we join Thomas and head to the feast in my honor. The feast is lively and there tons of Altronians here all wanting to meet me. Some of them almost seem to worship me, which is certainly not something I'm used to. They are interested in Collin and Thomas as well since Bio Metas are almost legends around here given our unique nature. You would think that compared to aliens we aren't that cool. I understand why humans are completely fascinated with us, but the Altronians being so intrigued with us is not something I expected. Bio Metas certainly take after our human ancestors in the looks department as we have no physical traces of being part alien. The only thing that gives us away to being a Bio Meta, and part alien, is our superpowers.

The feast is lively and I am enjoying myself. Even Thomas and Collin are enjoying themselves. The food seems similar to ours on Earth. Although, they do call things by different names here. Crona kindly translates to something we can relate to and understand. I originally questioned how we could understand the Altronians in the first place, but part of their race's ability is to understand and speak any language they encounter. It's a handy ability to have. I wish as Bio Metas we inherited that ability, but it doesn't seem we have.

After the feast, Collin and I retire to our room. I'm exhausted. The feast went on for hours. Well, what we would call hours. The Altronians tell time differently, and I'm trying to understand their culture, as are Thomas and Collin. Their culture is interesting, and we are enjoying our time here. Tomorrow we will start to get some answers to our questions. I curl up with Collin in the massive bed and let sleep overtake my body.

# BIRDY RIVERS

# CHAPTER 30

**Clara**

The next morning there is food delivered to our room, and we eat even though I'm still stuffed from the feast. We dress in the clothes we were given for the feast. It allows us to blend in better and not stick out like sore thumbs. We already stick out due to our physical appearance being human. Yet the Altronians don't seem to care. They are very welcoming to us. I guess they are used to seeing different races as they have conquered many planets in their existence, whereas humans are still wrapping their heads around the fact that aliens and Bio Metas exist.

Collin goes off with Jul to help find a cure for Sam while Thomas goes with Salter and Ressan to develop strategies to fight my father. I'm glad that they have changed their ways and don't want to conquer Earth any longer. I wasn't sure how we would fight my father along with an entire race of aliens invading our planet. My father is good at bluffing and he was certainly bluffing in my vision when he said he had Altronians on his side. It seems those who followed the old way have either been banished or executed. I'm not sure why they didn't execute my father. His superpowers do make it hard to kill him because he can normally kill his enemies before they can kill him. I wonder how they held him captive for so long and how he escaped. I'm sure these are all questions that Thomas will be asking Salter and Ressan.

I meet up with Crona who takes me outside the city to a temple like building made from what appears to be cream marble. Inside the building is a giant room with a sweet, relaxing fragrance like roses and lavender, but I know that's not quite it because those plants don't exist here. The room is open with pillars lining the sides. It has a Roman feel to it and I'm truly starting to believe the Greeks and Romans took a lot of their culture from the Altronians.

"This is where we come to meditate, think, and pray to the goddess of Destiny. The goddess is the one who gave you your superpowers. She is the one who told us about the Oracle. What do you know about the prophecy?" Crona prompts as we walk around.

"Only what my father told me in my vision. He told me I have a great superpower, the ability to bring peace and harmony or destruction and war. He said that my son would be super powerful as well. He told me that for a long time, Altronians didn't believe the Oracle was real because she would come from Altronian blood mixed with another race, but that changed when you had Thomas." I give her a quick summary.

"That is all true. You are the reason me and the other Altronians who wanted peace and to change our old ways were able to convince the Elders to change. I wasn't always on the council. Neither was Salter or Trest. We became Elders after our time on Earth." Crona informs me.

"Why change your ways when you could easily use me for war and destruction like my father desires. Altron could conquer the universe with the Oracle?"

"War takes its toll on the soul. Conquering planets became exhausting. Humans have shown us so much. Wolfgang showed us that we didn't have to conquer planets to learn from them. We could work together and that was further proven when Bio Metas were created. We could work together to bring forth a new and thriving race that would be the best of both worlds. A race the Oracle would be born from." Crona answers. "You have to understand that we never believed the prophecy of the Oracle would come true. We never thought we could mix our biology with another race. The council of Elders always promised that if by some chance the Oracle could come into existence they would choose peace and harmony and would give up war and conquering."

"You said my superpowers come from the goddess of Destiny. Is that why I only see what I'm meant to see? I've tried controlling what I see, but I can't." I'm slowly trying to piece together my true abilities.

"That is correct. You will only ever see what you are meant to see. There are some things you will see to prevent from happening and other things you will see to prepare for the aftermath of what happens. You will know which is which when you have your visions. You can control time. You can pause it, slow it down, and speed it up, all temporarily of course. You will have absolute truths that you simply know because the goddess allows it so. The only true thing you will be able to control is time. However, you will never be able to control your visions or absolute truths. They will come to you when you need them. You will see what the goddess deems you need to see. I know you have seen into the future, but have seen you seen into the past yet?"

"No, I haven't. I didn't know that was even possible to see into the past." I answer honestly wondering what answers the past might hold.

"I'm sure you will when you are meant to. As far as your son, my great-grandson. Well, we don't know much about what his superpowers will be, but he will be super powerful. He will be a great asset or weapon. I'm sure we will have a new prophecy strictly surrounding him soon enough, and when we do one of us will inform you." Crona informs me. Well, I was hoping for some more answers for my son, but I'm getting other answers about my superpowers, which has been helpful and enlightening. I'm curious how they get prophecies from the goddess, but I have other questions that are more pertinent at the moment.

"I have some questions about destined mates. I know from my absolute truths that Collin and I are destined mates, but we wouldn't have known if I didn't have my vision."

"Destined mates are gifts from the goddess of Destiny. Altronians know exactly who are destined mate is from the moment we meet them. It's as if there is an invisible teether tying us to our destined mate that snaps into place once we meet them. For Bio Metas it's a bit harder because of your human DNA. You will feel an extreme attraction to one another that's unexplainable. That's the best way for me to describe it." Crona explains.

"I felt that way with Collin. After our interaction as teenagers, I was extremely attracted to him. I didn't know why and it only grew when we finally reconnected as adults. I felt this strong connection to him. I was drawn to him on every level. Was Wolfgang your destined mate?" I inquire. I've always been curious about Crona and Wolfgang's supposed love story. Even before I joined the League and lived among villains it was something I was curious about.

"No, Cras was my destined mate. Altronians can't have humans as their destined mates, but Bio Metas can because they are half human. Cras and I were two very different people with different views. We clashed in many ways making it hard to fall in love. When I met Wolfgang, I was attracted to him because of his kind heart and his brilliant brain. He was unlike any other male I had ever met. I never expected to fall madly and deeply in love with him. When we had intercourse for the first time, I wasn't even sure it would work, but our reproductive biology was incredibly similar allowing us the ability to have intercourse. I was blown away when I realized I was pregnant. At first, Cras was furious I was pregnant by another male, but when he realized what it meant, he changed his tune. Cras went on to father Benji with a human egg donor. Then Tressa, Salter, and Trest had children of their own with donors creating the original five Bio Metas. Wolfgang and I went on to create the Bio Meta program getting donors from both Altronians and humans and using surrogates.

The expansion of the Bio Meta race became important for the sake of the Oracle and because Bio Metas served as a bridge between our two very different worlds." Crona informs me.

"Did you and Cras ever have children of your own?"

"No, we never even had intercourse. As I said we were two very different people. We weren't even really attracted to one another. Keep in mind this is all rare. Destined mates are supposed to fall in love. Cras and I were an odd exception. I used to be so frustrated that my destined mate wasn't the love of my life until I met Wolfgang. Then when I got pregnant I realized that the goddess of Destiny had other plans for me. I was meant to discover the race that would create the Oracle and that was an honor. It was worth the sacrifice of true love because here you are in the flesh, breathing, alive, and already thriving, even if you don't see it."

I can't help the small smile that forms on my face. Months ago, I would have never seen myself as worthy for someone to sacrifice something over me for. Now, I see myself in a different light. It's not just because of Collin. Yes, he is a big reason why I do see myself differently, but it's more than him. It's the entire League coming around and accepting me. It's the people of Oswald City no longer shunning me but embracing me. It's standing up against my father. Claiming what I want for myself. Once I wanted to run away from everyone and everything, now I run to my destined mate and the League, knowing it's where I belong.

"Crona, why did you leave Earth? We all thought you had died."

"It was not my first choice to leave. I love Earth and its people. I can't wait to get back to embrace your world more. Well, I hope to go back one day at least. I left because of Cras and Tressa. We were summoned by the council of Elders to give our reports from Earth, especially the Bio Metas. The Oracle had been born, and Wolfgang had passed away. It was hard to go back in my grief. There was also the fact that civil war was being threatened on Altron. Cras, Tressa, and their followers were not going to go away peacefully. There was too much going on here for me to return. I hated leaving Thomas and the other Bio Metas on their own." Crona answers. I realize the hardship, tough choices, and sacrifices Crona has made. I respect her, and in many ways, I admire her strength to persevere through hard times.

"Final question. Why did you not kill my father when you had him captured?" I have to know. I know Thomas will find out as well, but I want to find out for myself.

"Benji was a topic of disagreement among the council. Some thought we should kill him, while others thought we should let the League handle him. In the end, the goddess spoke to us and said it was Benji's fate to perish at the hands of the League. The council of Elders receives messages in our mind from the goddess telepathically. It's how we get prophecies, which there aren't many, and how we get answers for things like what to do with Benji. So we kept Benji prisoner waiting for the time to hand him over to the League, but with so many changes happening here it was easy to forget Benji was even here. Then he escaped back to Earth and we all knew in time he would be eradicated from existence." Crona explains. Yeah, this goddess, visions, and telepathic communications from said goddess make my brain hurt. It's a lot to wrap one's mind around.

For the next several hours Crona and I talk. She shows me around the temple and explains more to me about the goddess of Destiny. If I thought I had pressure on me before, well I definitely do now. I'm the only Bio Meta with superpowers from a freaking goddess. I'm meant for greater things than I ever planned for. It's overwhelming yet strangely it's overwhelming, in a good way. I'm feeling more confident in my superpowers and in myself. Crona even gives me some pointers on how to better control my time since it's the only aspect of my superpowers I actually have control over. I feel better having a better understanding and grasp of my superpowers. It was the confidence booster I needed to kick my ass into gear.

After my time with Crona, I head back to my room. Collin is still with Jul, so I decide to take Crona's suggestion and take a bath. The water on Altron is loaded with minerals to help relax, energize, and has anti-aging properties, which explains why the Altronians have flawless skin. I head to the bathroom and turn on the water allowing the tub to fill with warm water. I slip out of my clothes and sink into the tub, allowing the warm water to soothe my soul. The water here has a slightly minty smell to it, which I like, adding to my relaxation.

Altron is a different world from Earth. It's a beautiful planet. Earth certainly has its own beauty. It will be nice to see Earth and Altron at peace, working together for a brighter future. First, we have to take care of my father and his followers. I know Thomas is working on that. I know we will take him down, but the question is what we will sacrifice in the process.

"There you are, Little Villain." Collin's voice breaks my train of thought as I smile at him as he enters the bathroom.

"Here I am, Mighty Hero. Care to join me?" I gesture to the tub.

A seductive grin graces his handsome face as he starts to strip. "How was your meeting with Crona?"

"Successful. I learned a lot about my superpowers and about destined mates. I'll fill you in later. How about you? Did you find a cure for Sam?" I inquire as Collin steps into the giant square tub.

"I did. A plant called Nightthorne is the key. I had been treating his human side, but not his Altronian side. I simply didn't have what I needed on Earth to help him." Collin answers as he pulls me onto his lap so I'm straddling him. He's already semi-hard.

"After we take care of my father we can have an open line of communication with Altron. Things will be different and better."

"Is that a vision you had or one of those absolute truths you know?" Collin questions as his hands land firmly on my hips.

"Absolute truth." I answer.

Collin studies me for a minute. "What's wrong? You seem upset."

"I'm feeling shaken finding out that my superpowers come from the goddess of Destiny. That I have the ability to be good or evil and with my family history, evil seems to win. I've always struggled to accept myself, to love myself. I feel unworthy of my superpowers yet somehow I'm the chosen one." I confess feeling a weight lift off my shoulders. I might be feeling more confident but that doesn't mean my self-doubt is totally gone.

"Oh, Little Villain, you won't turn evil. If you wanted to, you would have already. You have more than enough chances to follow in your father's footsteps and to join him." Collin says as his hand strokes my cheek.

"What if the only reason I haven't is purely because I want to defy him? I'm not a hero like you. I only agreed to help the League knowing it would piss my father off. I didn't help because it was the right thing to do. I did it because I gained something in the process."

"No one said you had to be a hero like me. I don't expect that of you, no one does. There's nothing wrong with you being an anti-hero who has their own motives. As long as those motives don't help the enemy and help the League, then who cares why you do what you do." Collin reasons.

"Will you love me until I learn to love myself?" I plead softly.

"I will love every version of you, Little Villain because you are mine." Collin declares before his lips land on mine.

I thread my hands through his thick hair as his hands guide my hips up and onto his now raging hard cock. Collin guides me slowly up and down his cock, so I can feel how his cock fills me as his tongue invades my mouth, finding my tongue before they swirl together in their own dance of passion. Collin slowly increases my speed, guiding me as he shows me exactly who's in control. I've never been in control when it comes to Collin, and he is the one man I will always hand the reins over to willingly. No one makes me feel safe and loved like he does, which is probably why he is able to bring me to my knees like he does. Collin might be in control, but he never controls me.

Collin fills me to the brim with his large cock as he increases our paces. Eventually, his hand let go of my hips and find their way to my breasts. He palms a breast in each of his hands before letting my nipples slip through his fingers so he can play with them. The position we are in is hitting my clit in the right places and all the pleasure is building in my core from the multiple sensations. Everything is extra sensitive because I'm pregnant and fuck me does it add to my pleasure. Moans escape my mouth, but Collin's mouth catches them causing them to be muffled as we continue our love making. Sometimes Collin fucks me senseless and other times he makes love to me. Right now, he is making love knowing it's what I need because he always knows what I need. I will always need him.

We both find our release as we break our kiss. I lean my forehead against Collin's. "I love you, Mighty Hero." I confess.

"I love you too, Little Villain." Collin replies without hesitation.

We finish our bath. Collin helps me out of the tub and dries me off before drying himself off. Then he carries me to bed where we cuddle, enjoying the feel of one another. I might have new confidence with my superpowers, but I'm still struggling to accept that I'm worthy of them. I used to dread having superpowers, and now that they are no longer suppressed I find myself embracing them. I have to believe I'm worthy of them. The goddess of Destiny didn't make a mistake when she chose me to be the Oracle. I simply have to believe in myself, and that is easier to do when I have someone who believes in me like Collin does. Crona said our destined mates are gifts from the goddess of Destiny. Well, she sure as hell gave me one hell of a gift with Collin. I will do anything to prove I'm worthy of him and my superpowers. I will not let my past define me, and I won't let the unknown control me. I accept the calling of my destiny. I am the Oracle.

# CHAPTER 31

## Collin

Now that we have answers, it's time to return to Earth. I'm not sure any of us are ready to leave Altron, but we have to. With peace established, I'm sure there will be plenty of chances to come back. Right now, we need to get back to Earth and put a full plan in motion to stop Cyanide before he destroys Earth because that is his goal. Cyanide might not have the allies he claims he does on Altron, but that won't stop him from attempting to prove he is right.

I'm also eager to get back to Earth to help develop this cure for Sam so that when he is done with his mission, he can finally have the life he deserves. No more being locked in a padded room. He can finally be a proper member of the League and fight crime with us. He can have his life back.

Sam, Oliver, Mason, and I were close as kids, but as the side effects of Sam's superpowers became evident he distanced himself. Then Mason did his best to make sure we spent less time with Oliver so he could have me to himself. I used to think it was because Mason was a dick, I mean he is, but his motives were much darker than I imagined. I still plan on making him pay for his betrayal.

That's the thing that Clara fails to realize. She thinks I'm this pure hearted hero with good intentions all the time. Perhaps that is the image I have portrayed to the world, but I have my own underlying dark side. I have my own need for revenge on Mason. He broke my trust, which is not something I give freely. He betrayed me and the League. He also sexually assaulted Clara on more than one occasion, and while she got her revenge for that, as her destined mate, I want my own turn.

Heroes and Villains are more alike than we would ever care to admit. It's not all black and white. The morally grey area is where we all dwell. The difference is that Heroes aim for good. However, that doesn't mean our intentions don't have underlying reasons. Heroes walk on a razor's edge of doing what's right while not being consumed by our own revenge. Villains give into their darkness and never look back. Anti-heroes, like Clara, walk the finest line of us all because they have a higher potential to turn into the thing they swear they will never turn into, a villain.

The truth is, heroes do kill. They kill for the greater good. That's exactly what will happen when we fight Cyanide. Cyanide won't make it out of this war alive. One of us will kill him for the greater good. Sometimes mercy is granted. Other times mercy is not the answer and death is. With Cyanide and his many followers, including Mason, death is the safer option for the greater good. For most villains and criminals we show mercy. We allow them to serve sentences for their crimes. The League has a special island for the worst of the worst. Our own personal Alcatraz. The basement of Oswald Tower is only a temporary holding cell before they are transferred to Nullum Island.

While our trip to Altron has been short, it has been informative. My father has several new strategies to help fight Cyanide and his followers. I finally have a cure for Sam, and Clara seems to have a better understanding of her superpowers. It's almost as if Clara is at peace with her superpowers even if she isn't sure she is worthy of them. Her self-doubt has always been an issue, even in her training it's caused some problems. However, her self-doubt and lack of worth isn't her fault. It stems from years of emotional, mental, and even physical abuse. She is working on finding her worth and confidence, and I will do everything I can to help her.

The council of Elders and several Altronians see us off, and before we know it we are landing back on Earth at Oswald Manor. Space travel is interesting and there is absolutely nothing more breathtaking than being surrounded by millions of stars against the darkest canvas of space. I can officially say I've checked something off of my bucket list. Kid me is doing flips right now because I have always wanted to go to space and to Altron.

"I should get back to the city. I'm sure your mother is more than ready to hand leadership back over." My dad states as we exit the spaceship.

"I want to stay here. It's safer if I'm out of the city as to not blow Sam's cover." Clara adds.

"That's a good idea. To be honest, I would have left you on Altron if I didn't think we needed you here." My father comments as we walk out of the hangar.

"I agree. I will go back and forth as needed to the city. I think Mom should come to the manor. We do have a baby to prepare for, and she is the best person I know for that." I add.

"I agree, but be careful not to draw too much attention, though. Cyanide is no doubt watching the League's every move. I don't even like the thought that he knows we went to Altron." My father cautions.

"I can be discreet. Mom knows how to hide her purchases. As for me going back and forth, I can even play it off that I'm heartbroken Clara joined the villains to help Sam's cover, and that I need space. Is there any way we can find out how he is doing without risking his cover?" I question. I would be lying if I said I wasn't concerned about him. I know he is great at what he does and I'm sure by now he has fully embodied Clara's personality and is selling our scheme to Cyanide. Still, he's in the vipers' nest and I don't like it.

"I don't know. I don't want to risk blowing his cover. I will see what I can manage." My father replies heading to the garage.

Clara stops dead in her tracks. Her eyes turn white and glaze over. She's in a trance. She's having a vision. Several moments later she snaps out of it. "Okay, that is going to take time to get used to." She comments as she shakes her head attempting to snap back to reality. "Sam is fine. He's playing his part a little too well." She comments. Sam's superpowers creep her out. To be honest, it creeps us all out. It's bad enough he looks just like the person he is shapeshifted as, but his ability to copy a person's mannerisms and even personality is what ups the creepy factor.

"I will never grow tired of your superpowers, Clara." My father comments. "Collin, settle Clara here and make Harold aware that the manor will be in use for a bit. I'll head back to the city. I will inform your mother she is needed here. I'll also have her inform you of everything we missed while on our trip." My father directs before he enters the garage to select one of our cars to head back to the city.

I take Clara and our things into the manor. Harold greets us at the door. "Master Collin, Miss Cole." Harold greets.

"Oh, we aren't starting that. It's Clara. Please, I don't need any more reminders of who my father is by being called Miss Cole." Clara immediately interjects.

"As you wish, Miss Clara." Harold responds in a friendlier tone than normal.

Clara goes to open her mouth, but I interrupt her. "Don't even bother trying to get him to drop the Miss part. I've been trying my whole life to get him to drop the Master part before my name, and he won't do it unless his not happy with me."

"That is correct. Are you two staying?" Harold questions as he takes the bags from my hands.

"Yes, it's safest for Clara to be here in her condition and to not compromise Sam's mission. My mom will be joining us, and I will be going back and forth as needed." I inform Harold.

"I will make the appropriate arrangements. Will I be taking all the bags to your room, Master Collin?"

"Yes, please," I turn to Clara. "I think it's time I gave you a proper tour of Oswald Manor." I say offering my hand to Clara.

"I've been dying to see the place in its full glory. I know Oswald Tower is impressive, but the rumors say nothing compares to Oswald Manor." Clara replies by taking my hand.

I chuckle. "I guess you will have to let me know better. I'm sure the fans would love to know your opinion."

"Don't even go there. I'm not doing anything social media related ever. It was weird enough being practically worshiped on Altron. I don't know how Nina thrives in the spotlight." Clara comments.

"I wouldn't tell her about that part, she might get jealous. Now, come on let's give you a proper tour."

I give Clara a tour of the manor and then we head to my room, which I guess is now our room. I don't mind sharing anything with Clara. I love that she is a part of my life and that we are starting a family together. I'm still wrapping my head around the fact that she is pregnant, and I know she is too. We both have concerns because we know our son will be super powerful and we don't want Cyanide to get his evil hands on him. Still, I'm going to enjoy this as much as possible. It's why I wanted my mom to come here. My mom is nothing short of amazing, and I know she will do everything to help us prepare in every way possible.

Clara rests while I go about taking care of formulating this cure for Sam with the Nightthorne. I have my one little lab in one of the extra buildings built on our property. My dad has his own tech lab on the property as well that used to be my grandfather's before he passed. We have certainly made use of the vast land we own. There is still much of it undeveloped.

In my lab, I get to work creating the cure for Sam. It's not a one and done cure as Sam will need to take this for the rest of his life. I'm going to try to develop it in pill form so it's easier for him to take. It will be like any other antipsychotic drug except this one will be formulated with Nightthorne to help his Altronian side and human antipsychotic meds to help his human side. It might take a few tries to figure out the right combination and dosage according to Sam's DNA, but this is the closest I've ever been to helping my friend and fellow League member. I'm determined to help save him from himself.

# CHAPTER 32

## Clara

It's hard to believe that I'm three months pregnant already and starting to show. It's a good thing I'm hiding out at Oswald Manor. Sam is still impersonating me, and according to my visions and absolute truths Sam is killing his mission. It doesn't seem my father or Mason are any the wiser. I don't know how the hell Sam is convincing them of my superpowers or stalling Mason's advances, but he is. I'm not questioning it too hard. While Sam is pretending to be me, Collin is working hard to develop the right dose for Sam's medication so that when he comes home he can be cured.

Veronica has been helping me prepare a nursery for our son. I'm glad she's here it's been nice having a mother figure during this time. Part of me wishes my mom was here to bond with me over this life event, but I'm not sure she would be with me if she was alive. My mom was loyal to my father. She chose him over the League. My father even said she was loyal like a dog to him no matter how he may have isolated her from everyone and everything causing her to be depressed. Even from the stories from Veronica, it sounds like my mom was loyal to my dad, so even if she was alive I'm not sure she would be enjoying this life event with me.

Crona said I could see into the past, but so far I haven't. While part of me wants to see in the past in hopes of seeing my mom again. However, I'm afraid of what the visions might reveal. I still wonder if she knew that my dad was suppressing my superpowers. If she did know, I don't know how I'd feel about it. My father suppressed my superpowers to control me, or at least attempt to control me. He knew about my superpowers because of the prophecy, and he used that to his advantage to attempt to control me.

While I worry about my son's superpowers and how super powerful he will be, I will never control him. I will help him understand his superpowers and embrace them in a positive way. I won't let my father control him and turn him into his personal weapon. I won't suppress his superpowers and lie that he is defective like my father did to me. At first, I thought my father did me a favor, but I quickly realized he did more damage than good. I won't repeat my parents' mistakes.

Collin is back and forth between the city and the manor, but he mostly stays at the manor. Veronica and him are here to protect me and our baby. Not that I can't protect myself. I've been spending my time here training and perfecting my skills. I've gotten good at controlling time. It does require an enormous amount of strength and stamina, which I have worked tirelessly on as well. I've gotten better at my hand on hand combat too. I can't go too intense with training because I'm pregnant, but I'm pushing myself to improve, and I have. Once I have the baby, I'll be doing more intense training.

I'm still not sure when we will have our last showdown with my dad. It's coming, that much I know. Thomas is eager to take my father out, we all are, but my father is being tactical and not rushing this war. Sure, the villains and my father's followers have upped their game, and the crime spike in Oswald City is no joke. I wish I could help, but I have to protect my son. I'd also blow Sam's cover, which would make things worse for everyone. I don't want to imagine my father's wrath if he ever figures out we tricked him.

In fairness, my dad pulled a huge one over on the League for years with Mason. It's only fair we get him back in return. Except my father would go ballistic and hurt innocent people in his anger. I know that even when we kill my father the crime won't permanently go away. I'm sure his followers will lurk in the shadows for years to come like they did after he disappeared to Altron. However, things will be better, and I know it will be much safer for me and my son.

I also feel better knowing Mason is locked up on Nullum Island or dead. I can work with either option. I know Collin is itching to get his hands on Mason and make him pay for his betrayal along with what he did to me. Mason didn't just piss Collin and me off, though. He pissed off the whole League. Oliver and Nina are also itching to get their own punches in. Especially, Nina because for years he deceived her. She thought he was her friend and she trusted him. Nora and Claire aren't happy with Mason but they are more like Veronica and about peace than revenge. I guess if you piss some heroes off enough they want revenge and I don't blame them because I'm itching to get some more punches on Mason. I'm also wanting to take out my years of suppression on my father, but I don't think I have it in me to kill him. Thomas, however, will have zero problems putting my father in his grave.

One thing I'm learning while being at Oswald Manor this time is that I finally have a home and a family that accepts me. Veronica and Thomas have made me feel welcome and like a part of the Oswald family. The rest of the League members have all accepted me into the League. Claire and Nora have become very friendly with me and text me often to see how I'm doing. Nina is still a bit icey toward me, but I'm learning that's more or less her personality. She is, however, more accepting of me being a part of the League than she ever has. The only two people who seem to melt Nina's icy heart are Claire and her father. Speaking of Harold even the grumpy butler has come around as well, but I sense his reservations because of Lois.

Everyone is realizing I'm not my parents. I'm not a villain. I'm my own person who wants to do good. I might have my own motives for why I do good, but ultimately I'm not a bad person. I'm learning to embrace myself and love who I am as well. It's a process and I'm working through years of mental and emotional abuse from my father and Yuri. Not to mention years of being neglected, rejected, and bullied for simply being Cyanide's daughter. Then you add in the sexual assault from Mason and I'm working with a cocktail of damage.

However, I've been doing talk therapy with Dr. Wells. He's helping me process my trauma in a healthy way and helping me accept my past while embracing my future. Ironic that the Oracle who can see the future and the past with the ability to control time and know absolute truths needs help coping with her past. I'm still wrapping my head around what I learned on Altron. Being given such a gift from a goddess is intense. At first, I didn't think I was worthy of her gift or of Collin, but I'm learning that I'm more than worthy and that I deserve it.

they had the chance. His superpowers were dampened; they could have executed him easily. They executed Cras and Tressa. Crona explained that Cras and Tressa were Altronians and they had the right to execute them. However, Cyanide is a Bio Meta. They felt it was more appropriate for the League to handle him. She also mentioned something about the goddess of Destiny, but I had stopped listening at that point. Why the Altronians didn't just hand his ass over with a pretty bow is beyond me. It seems the Altronians have spent the last several years getting their shit together, and are still finding their footing with their new ways.

The Altronians couldn't figure out a way to neutralize Cyanide's superpowers, but they were close. Now, it doesn't matter because Cyanide is too much of a threat, he must be killed. Even then his followers are many and they will carry out his plans in his name, so we have to neutralize their threat as well. Although, many of them can be imprisoned and with the new superpower dampening tech we have from the Altronians capturing and imprisoning bad Bio Metas is easier than ever. We will need it in the coming war against Cyanide and his devoted followers.

I've been going back and forth between the city and the manor. It's exhausting. I try to do my best to stay at the manor for Clara's sake. She gets anxious when I'm gone. I know she feels safest when I'm with her. I'm glad she is finally feeling safe. I'm also proud of how far she has come in her training. She has a wonderful handle on the parts of her superpowers she can control. We can't do too much physical training because of her current condition. Still, her progress is impressive. To think when she started this journey she wanted nothing to do with her superpowers and now she is embracing them.

Clara has also made progress with healing from her past. Dr. Wells has been helping with talk therapy. Clara is healing and learning to embrace her future. I'm thrilled that she and my mom have bonded so well. My mom has taken Clara under her wing much like she did with Nina, Nora, and Claire. Nora never knew her mom. Clara and Nina both knew their moms, but they are gone now. Janna killed herself, which was news to the League as we thought she was killed by Cyanide, which was a cover up designed by him to preserve Janna's reputation. We still don't know why Lois was killed, but we do have an idea it has something to do with a betrayal involving Janna. We have been able to fill in many gaps with Clara between what she knows and her visions.

Clara doesn't know what Lois's betrayal was. Harold and Nina believe Clara is hiding it. They want to know because they want answers about her death. Harold has warmed up to Clara, even if Lois's death is still a sore subject. I know Clara is telling the truth. The only reason they don't want to believe that she isn't telling the truth is because I believe there is a part of them that doesn't want to believe Lois could betray Janna. There is also the possibility that they feel Janna betrayed the League first so she deserved whatever Lois did. Lois's death has always been a touchy subject for them and one we try to avoid bringing up around them.

Nina, Claire, and my dad are coming for dinner today. Nina is close to Harold. They have a special father-daughter bond especially because Lois is gone. Nina is very serious with Claire, and I think she wants her dad to get to know Claire better. I will say she brings Claire around her father more than she ever did with Mason. I always thought those two were so in love, but they were simply good at faking their relationship. I would have never thought Mason's end goal was to have Clara as his and for Nina to hide her true relationship with Claire out of fear. I didn't even think Nina could be fearful with the icy exterior she wears like armor. I guess underneath all the ice is a girl with her own insecurities.

I find Clara in the nursery as she is trying to prepare for our son's arrival. I wrap my arms around her waist and let my hands rest on her belly. “You have been in here for hours, Little Villain.”

“I know, apparently it’s called nesting. I only have three months left before our son arrives. I want to be prepared.”

“The nursery looks great. We have to get ready for dinner. Nina, Claire, and my dad are coming.” I remind her.

“I’m aware. Harold wouldn’t stop talking about it during breakfast. He is excited for Nina to visit.” She replies.

“Why do I sense you are not as excited?”

“Nina and I have our differences, that's not a secret, but every time I see her I see the accusation in her icy blue eyes. She wants answers that I don’t have. Harold is a little easier to deal with when it comes to Lois’s death. Plus, Nina thinks because I have a prophecy surrounding me that I somehow think I’m better than her. She accused me of being a know it all bitch the last time I saw her. Ever since I got my superpowers and became the Oracle, everyone expects that I have answers. The problem is I don’t always have the answers, and when I do, they don’t always like my answers.” Clara confesses.

“You carry a weight that I don’t envy with the prophecy. I’m always here for you, Little Villain.”

"I know, Mighty Hero. I wouldn't be able to do any of this without you," Clara pauses and then sighs. "Come on, let's go get ready for dinner so we aren't late. We don't want to upset Mamma Storm Witch or we might find our asses electrocuted with lightning." Clara jokes as we head toward the door.

I chuckle. "No, we do not."

We head to our room. I should have known my room would be our room the first night I brought Clara here to tend to her wounds. Clara has made her way into my heart. She did it when she was a wounded teen in the parking lot of a fair, I just didn't know it then. She's my destined mate, and I wouldn't have it any other way.

We get ready for dinner and then head down to the main dining hall where my mom has everything set up in. Nina, Claire, and my dad have already arrived. We take our seats, and Harold and my mom bring the food to the table. Harold has prepared a feast of roasted chicken, mashed potatoes, roasted brussel sprouts, and freshly baked bread. Harold is a great cook and having him around has always been amazing. The Gavin family has served the Oswald family for a few generations now. My dad and Harold grew up together, and they are still good friends. Lois met Harold through my dad.

Dinner is smooth and lively. Nina is a bit icy, but that's just her. I know that Clara takes Nina's attitude personally, and I can't blame her. I grew up with Nina so perhaps I'm just used to the way she acts. It also doesn't help that Nina has never been Clara's biggest fan because Cyanide killed her mom. What Nina fails to realize is that Cyanide hurt Clara too. Just because she is his daughter doesn't mean he treats her with love. Clara doesn't have a parent she is even close to. At least Nina has her dad. Nina could bond with Clara over losing a mother at a young age instead she chooses to hold something against her that she didn't even do.

I hate that Clara's image is so tainted by her parent's reputation and choices. If people aren't assuming she is a villain like her father, they assume she isn't trustworthy because her mom left the League to be with Cyanide. I know it will take time for people to look past the negative of what Clara's parents have done and finally see her as her own person. The main thing is that most of the League is very accepting of her now. Nina is really the only one left with her skepticism and that's tied to Lois's death.

After dinner, we retire to the sitting room for dessert. My mom made a seven layer chocolate cake with raspberry drizzle and vanilla ice cream. My mom is quite the baker. It's her hobby that she has greatly perfected over the years. The conversation is light as we all make ourselves comfortable while Mom serves dessert. Clara and I sit on the light grey loveseat while Claire, Nina, and Harold sit on the matching couch. My dad is sitting in the plush light chair, Mom will take the matching chair next to him when she is finished serving dessert. While we are having a conversation Clara's eyes go white and she enters a trance state. She's having a vision. I secretly always hold my breath when Clara is having a vision or tells me she's had one because I don't know what she will see. I always hope it's something helpful or good.

The rest of the dinner party realizes Clara is having a vision and the room grows quiet as we all hold our breath. You could cut the tension with a knife. My dad clenches his jaw so tightly I swear I see it tic. My mom has completely stopped serving dessert. Several moments later, Clara returns from her trance state as she slightly shakes her body like she is shaking off invisible water. Clara looks around the room, all of us stare at her waiting for her to tell us what she saw.

"Fuck, I really hate having visions while awake. I suppose you all want to know what I saw?" We all nod our heads. None of us are capable of using words because we are on edge. Clara sighs. "I saw the past. It was weird because this time it was a montage like vision. It started off at my old house. Lois came to visit. I was a little over one. My dad wasn't home. My mom was shocked to see Lois, but let her in. My mom went into the kitchen to make some tea, leaving me in the living room with Lois. Lois claimed she was there for peace, to see her friend that she missed. Her intentions were much more sinister. Lois tried to smother me with a pillow. My mom came out of the kitchen and caught Lois. She almost killed her, but Lois was pregnant so she stopped herself. She told Lois to get out before she changed her mind. My mom didn't tell my dad until many years later. That's when he went after Lois and killed her, afraid she would try to kill me again. My mom gave him the idea to suppress my superpowers. She was doing it to try and keep me safe, afraid that people would fear me if they knew I was the Oracle. My dad took her idea and used it against me to control me." Clara reveals.

"Lois wouldn't try to kill a child. She would never do something so horrible." Harold defends.

"Actually, she would." My mom states quietly. "I never thought in a million years she would do it. I thought she was just venting her frustration, and maybe a little hormonal. We were setting up for Collin's birthday and Lois was halfway through her pregnancy. We were talking about how we wished Janna was with us while setting up.

We talked about how we wished our kids could all grow up together. It was a bittersweet conversation until it turned dark. Lois started rambling about how she couldn't believe Janna had Cyanide's daughter. She talked as if Clara was going to be evil too and how all Janna did was carry on Cyanide's villainous lineage. She said someone should rid the world of the next supervillain. I told her that was an awful thing to say about an innocent child. We had no idea how you would turn out, Clara. I had to believe there was good in you like I believed there was still good left in Janna. Lois wasn't so easily convinced. I never thought she would ever try to kill you. If I did, I would have stopped her." My mom reveals as she lets go of a secret she has been holding on to for far too long.

"Well, that's another piece of the puzzle that Cyanide has created. We almost have a complete picture now." My father comments.

"Lois couldn't have such horrible desires." Harold is in pure denial.

"Harold, it's true what she attempted to do. Whether she would have actually gone through with it if Janna hadn't stopped her is something we will never know. I don't even think Clara could give us the answer to that. Let's just think of the good in Lois, and that she would have stopped herself if Janna didn't walk in to stop her. However, in the end, Lois did get herself killed. I don't know why Janna waited so long to tell Cyanide, but let's be glad she did because Nina wouldn't be here." My mom reasons.

"I need some air." Clara says as she stands before she heads out of the room. I follow her. I know all of this must be taking a toll on her. I find her in our room, sitting on the bed. I go over to her, and get into the bed with her before pulling her close to me.

"Are you okay, Little Villain?"

"I don't know. I wondered if my mom knew what my dad was doing to me, I never thought she would be the one to give him the damn idea. However, her intentions were out of her fear for my safety. Her intentions may have been misguided, but ultimately they came from a good place. My dad on the other hand took her misguided intention and used it to his benefit. He was always manipulating and controlling my mom. I can't decide if them being destined mates is a good thing or a bad thing. If they were even destined mates." Clara confesses.

"That one I can't answer. Your dad is a manipulative narcissist who unfortunately had his claws in your mom. Whether they were destined mates doesn't matter because Janna was going to follow Cyanide no matter what. She loved him and love can make people do foolish things.

How about a nice relaxing bath and I will bring you chocolate cake in bed." I suggest.

"That would be nice. Thank you. I'm really happy you are my destined mate. I could be stuck with Mason." Clara comments as she leans her head on my shoulder.

"You will never be his. You are only mine, Little Villain. The goddess of Destiny deems it so." I kiss her on the head.

I help Clara get her bath ready and once she's settled I head back downstairs. By the time I get back to the sitting room only my parents are left eating dessert in silence. My mom asks how Clara is and I tell her she will be okay. It's true she will be okay. I know she carries a heavy burden as the Oracle. I grab the cake and bring it back to Clara for when she is done with her bath. I lay out clothes for her before I head to see how everyone else is doing. It's becoming more and more clear that Cyanide is an evil villain who needs to be stopped. He has caused so much pain to so many, even those he loves. The sooner he is dead, the sooner Clara and our son are safe.

# CHAPTER 34

## Clara

Sometimes I love going to sleep, and other times not so much. I much rather get my visions in my dreams because it gives me time to process what I've seen before I have to tell anyone. Most of the time when I have vision while I'm awake I'm with people, and they immediately want to know what I saw. Just like what happened a couple of months ago at dinner. I would have liked a bit of time to process what I had seen before I dropped that particular bomb. Instead, I ended up ruining the evening, even if it was unintentional. It was also the first time I saw into the past.

Last night's vision wasn't any better. I'm about three to four weeks out from giving birth. I'm so close, and I have so much anxiety about my father coming after our son. Then last night, I had a vision confirming my worst fears. My father will come for our son. He's going to figure out that Sam isn't me in a matter of days and when he does he's going to torture Sam. Sam will end up telling my dad I'm pregnant just to escape the torture. My dad will kill Sam and come for our son. So, now we have to save Sam and I need to go to Altron to give birth. It's not a bomb I want to drop on anyone, but here I am about to drop the bomb at breakfast to Collin and Veronica.

We are eating in the kitchen in the breakfast nook. Harold is busy serving us waffles, eggs, and sausage while also making sure our coffee is full. I take a sip of the decaf coffee that Harold makes for me every morning. I like lots of cream and a smidge of sugar in my coffee. I take in the simple pleasure of having coffee in the morning before I set my cup down and take a deep breath gaining Collin and Veronica's attention.

"Oh, no. I know that look. You had a vision in your dreams last night, didn't you?" Collin points his fork at me in a slightly accusing manner.

"Yeah, and it's not great either. Sam's cover is about to be blown. My dad is going to torture him and in the process Sam will tell him I'm pregnant. He's going to kill Sam and come for our son. We need to get Sam out now. We have three days to get him out. Meanwhile, I need to go to Altron for safety in case we can't save Sam. My dad can not get our son." I inform them.

"Well, fuck that's a shit storm." Collin comments, dropping his fork before pulling out his phone to call his dad.

"I'm going to Altron with you, Clara. You are not giving birth alone." Veronica encouragingly smiles at me.

"I'm going too. I'm not going to miss the birth of my son. Dad and Oliver can help Sam. I need all the details you can give me Clara so they know how best to pull him out." Collin directs. I nod my head and give him every single detail I can remember. Collin then informs Thomas of everything. They set their plans in motion.

Within a few hours, there's a fully laid out plan. Collin, Veronica, and I are getting ready to head to Altron. Luckily, Thomas taught Veronica how to fly the spaceship. So, she will be flying us to Altron. In the meantime, Thomas and the rest of the League have a plan to get Sam out. I hope they can save Sam. The part of my vision that I didn't tell Collin, is that I know the League won't save Sam in time before he tells my dad about me being pregnant. The League will be able to prevent Sam's death, but they won't be able to prevent his torture. That's why I have to go to Altron. I have to get my son as far away from my father as I can.

As much as I'm dreading the final battle that's going to come soon, I also want the threat of my father gone. My son and I will only be safe when he is dead. My father's tyranny is coming to an end, whether he likes it or not. The League of Metas will make sure of it. I'll make sure of it. I won't let him live. I don't want to kill him, but I will if I have to. I can only hope someone else kills him because I'm afraid to kill him. Killing is what my father does, and despite the good in me, there is still a dark side that hides in the shadows, threatening to come out. If I have to kill my father, it will be for revenge, and I fear what that will do to me.

Right now, I can't focus on that. I need to focus on my son. In just under twenty-four hours, the three of us are boarding the spaceship. We don't bother bringing anything because we know they will have everything for us on Altron. I didn't think we would be going back so soon or that that's where I would give birth. I just assumed I'd give birth at Oswald Manor. We had talked about having the doctor and a midwife come to help with the delivery. I never imagined I would be doing it on another planet.

Veronica fires up the ship as we take our seats, getting strapped in. I close my eyes trying to relax. I hate to say it but I really hate flying. I don't think I'd like an airplane either. I can't believe I've been on a spaceship twice now and I have still never been on a plane. Being a Bio Meta certainly isn't boring. I find myself at the center of a lot of different situations. Joining the League has also opened up a lot of scenarios. Yet in the midst of the chaos, there are some of the most precious moments in life that nothing can replace or compare to.

I don't care where I give birth. I care that I have people around me who care about me and love me. I'm so relieved and happy that Collin came with me. Part of me thought he would choose his duty to the League, his city, and his friend. Collin instead delegated everything so he could be with me because being with me was his priority. I'm so thankful Collin is my destined mate because he's the dream guy I never even knew I needed.

I'm also glad that Veronica came with me. She's been a mother figure to me. Something I need and want in my life. I know no one can ever replace my mom. I know she loved me. She only wanted what was best for me. She did her best, and it was more than enough for me. She did her best to make up for my father's cruelty. Even if my mom wanted to go back to the League and take me with her, my father would have never allowed it. He would have killed her, and she knew it was better if she was around. Then her own mental health broke, and she simply couldn't hold on anymore. My father broke her along with so many other tragedies. My mom's life wasn't easy. I need to be stronger than her. That's why I lean on Collin to help me be strong.

We arrive at Altron, and we are welcomed with open arms once more. Veronica is blown away by the beauty of Altron. It is certainly enjoyable coming here. It's strange but I can see Altron being a home away from home. We are safe, welcomed, and embraced here. I still find it strange that I'm so admired here. The Oracle prophecy feels incredibly sure when I'm here. I'm not used to being in the spotlight, but being in the spotlight on Altron is very different than being in the spotlight on Earth.

On Earth, I feel like a performer. I have to put on the best version of myself and parade around for entertainment. The supporters who appreciate what we do and respect our privacy are appreciated by the League. However, there are those who see us more as entertainment for magazines, blogs, social media, and such. On Altron, it's the admiration and respect that is genuine on every level. We are equals, yet we are put on pedestals like legends. It's a little intoxicating, but I don't think I could live here permanently. Earth is a nice dose of reality that keeps one in check. Besides, you can have more than one home.

We get settled into our room. Crona is prepping for my birth. I'll give birth in the room I'm staying in with the best healers around me. Altronians give birth in a similar fashion as humans and Bio Metas. Between Veronica and the council of Elder's knowledge plus Collin's medical mind, I'd say I'm in good hands. I have an overwhelming amount of support that I'm grateful for. Maybe I'm blessed by the goddess of Destiny after all. I guess I just had to have a rough road to get to my reward. I would take any path through hell if it led me to my happy place. Now, I just wait for my son to make his entrance into this world.

# CHAPTER 35

## Collin

We have been on Altron for a couple of weeks waiting for Clara to give birth, and it's finally here. She went into labor early this morning. Crona and the healers are preparing our room. I'm ready to meet my son. I know there is so much serious shit going on right now with fighting Cyanide, but I'm soaking up this life changing moment. I do know that the League managed to get Sam out, but not before he was tortured. Cyanide knows we are going to have a son, which is why I'm glad we are on Altron. We will be leaving our son here when we go back to Earth for the final battle that is coming soon.

Clara is in a simple flowy light grey dress. She's walking around holding her back trying to work through contractions. She's not fully dilated yet, but she will be soon. I tried to help her walk around, but she insisted on doing it on her own. My mom is helping Crona and the healers set up. Clara is putting on a brave face, but I know she is nervous. I'm doing everything I can to support her.

I didn't like having to choose between my friend and my destined mate, but I knew Clara needed me. Sam had the rest of the League to save him. Only I could be with Clara. Besides, it's a special moment for both of us. Sam is safe and healing. When I get back, I will give him the cure I've developed for him. The truth is, I will always put Clara and our son first. They are the most important things to me. I think Sam would understand that.

Soon Clara is in full labor. She makes her way to the bed. The healers help her get into position. Clara grabs my hands as I sit on the bed next to her ready to help her in any way she needs. Clara is coached by the healers to push. I completely lose track of time as I soak in the very moment our son comes screaming into the world. The healers cut the umbilical cord and then clean him up before placing him in Clara's arms. Clara is sweaty and worn out, but the pure love on her face as she holds our son is a moment that will forever be etched into my mind.

"What should we name him, Mighty Hero?" Clara asks gently rocking our son who is wrapped in his soft blue blanket. We haven't much time to discuss names.

"I was thinking Aiden Thomas Oswald." I reply, letting my finger stroke his little cheek.

“It’s perfect.” Clara says kissing him on the forehead.

Clara and I take some time with Aiden and enjoy our little family. After some time, I take Aiden so Clara can get cleaned up and the room can be changed over. I let my mom and Crona help Clara while I watch Aiden. Once Clara is all cleaned up, Crona gives her some medicine that will help her heal up quickly. Clara gets comfortable in bed before she feeds Aiden. The two of them are both asleep by the time Aiden is done eating. I let Clara rest while I lay Aiden in his bassinet next to the bed.

All of Altron is celebrating Aiden’s birth. I don’t like that we have to leave him here, but he is safe here. We can’t risk Cyanide getting his hands on Aiden. I’m eager to get back to Earth and end this. However, there is one thing I want to do before we go back to Earth and that is to marry Clara. I want to go into this battle united in every way. I’ve been wanting to ask Clara to marry me while we were here, but she was so focused on giving birth that I figured it was better to wait. I pull the gun metal ring with a black fire opal surrounded by a halo of black diamonds. I had it custom made for her a few months back. I had to do it in secret as to not raise any attention for many reasons. Now that Aiden is born it’s time to put this ring on Clara’s finger.

It's been a few days since Aiden's birth and Clara is making a great recovery. We are going to go back to Earth in two days. Clara is sitting on the balcony of our room overlooking the beautiful chrome city. I approach her as she bounces Aiden lightly in her arms.

"I just got him asleep." She gives me a sleepy smile.

"Well, that gives me time to ask you something." I say kneeling next to her and pulling out the ring. "I want to marry you, Clara, here on Altron before we leave. I love you, and I want you to be mine in every single way. Let's fight this battle as destined mates united by marriage. Let's fight to protect our son united."

"I would love to be Clara Oswald. I want to fight united and I want the world to know I'm yours." Clara leans in and kisses me on the lips careful not to squish Aiden. I break our kiss and put the ring on her finger.

"I'll tell my mom and Crona the wedding is on. We get married tomorrow." I inform her.

"Of course, you have this all planned out. I'm glad you do because I don't think I have it in me to plan a wedding." Clara replies.

"I didn't plan it. I let my mom and Crona do their thing. I knew you would rather have the whole thing planned out for you than plan it yourself. I know you, Clara Cole, aka the Oracle."

"Correction, it's Clara Oswald, aka the Oracle, and yes you do know me, my Mighty Hero."

"You know me too, Little Villain. I'll let you rest. You have a lot of training to get to once we get back to Earth." I warn teasingly.

"I know, I'll be ready. I want Aiden home with us as soon as possible."

"Me too. He will come home, and then we will spend time bonding as a family at Oswald Manor before we go back to the chaos of the League and being heroes."

"I like the sound of that." Clara gives a genuine smile.

I kiss Clara on the lips briefly before kissing Aiden on the forehead. I let Clara have her bonding time with Aiden while I go tell my mom and Crona the good news. I wish my dad and the others could be here with us. We will have to celebrate with everyone after Cyanide is killed and it's safe for Aiden to come home. I'm sure my mom would love to plan a reception party that would somehow end up with a press around. All in good time. Tomorrow I get to marry my destined mate, and while it might not be exactly what we want, it doesn't matter because at the end of the day, Clara and I are united in every way that matters. I love her. I will never stop protecting her or Aiden. They are my world and I will do what it takes to keep them safe.

# HEROES & VILLAINS

# CHAPTER 36

**Clara**

The next day, Collin and I are in the great hall. I'm wearing a beautiful light grey dress with silver details in a Greek style. Collin is in a dark blue toga inspired outfit. Salter is marrying us. Veronica is holding Aiden. The Council of Elders is behind Salter. The hall is filled with Altronians here to witness our union. I wish more people could be here with us, but this is a surprise wedding even if I have a feeling Collin has been planning this for a bit. Although, I think his plan was to have our wedding on Earth, however, my father messed that up. I'm not thinking about him right now. Right now, I'm focused on the handsome man in front of me.

"I unite you two as one in the eyes of the goddess of Destiny. May she bless your union and your destined mateship. May she watch over you and guide you through all things," Salter pauses. "I believe on Earth you kiss your betrothed." Salter gestures for us to kiss and we do. We keep our kiss short and romantic. Everyone cheers around us.

After our union, there is a huge celebration. There is food, music, and dancing. I'll say the Altronians know how to through a celebration. The room is lively and a buzz with happiness. I know there is a dark road ahead with the coming battle, but right now I'm happy. I've found my place in the world and I won't let my father ruin it or take it from me. Tonight, I'm free and happy.

We spend time with Aiden celebrating and enjoying ourselves. I didn't expect to leave Altron a married woman, but I'm happy to be Clara Oswald. I know Collin wishes his dad and the others were here. I wish the same thing, but unfortunately, things just didn't happen that way. That's okay, I'm sure we will make up for it with a party on Earth with everyone after my father dies.

The celebration is long, and eventually, I get tired. While the Altronian medicine that Crona has been giving me has mostly healed me, I unfortunately still get tired easily. Collin, sensing I'm getting tired because he knows me, has me give Aiden to Veronica before scooping up in his arms bridal style and carrying me out of the great hall.

"I take it we are going back to our room?" I question, gently pawing at his chest because I'm eager to be with

Collin. I'm thankful for quick healing because I do want to be with Collin tonight.

"Yes, Little Villain. We only get one wedding night and I'm not wasting it."

"What about Aiden?" I question, knowing he's perfectly fine with his grandma, but I'm going to be leaving him tomorrow and that is going to be hard.

"He is fine with my mom. I know we want time with him before we go, but we also need to not lose our own special moments. We will have plenty of time with Aiden when we finally bring him home. Tonight it's just you and me, Little Villain." Collin firmly declares as he carries me through the halls to our room.

"Just you and me, Mighty Hero." I reply, leaning my head into his firm chest.

We make it to our room, and Collin doesn't even hesitate before he heads to the bed. He gently lays me down before he steps away, completely stripping himself of his clothes. I enjoy the show because Collin is a sex god on a stick that is all mine. I know he's in control because that man would never not be in control, so that's how I know this little strip tease is because he wants to not because he has to. By the time Collin is completely naked with his already raging hard cock, I'm ready to let this man do whatever he wants to me.

Collin moves to get on top of me before using his super strength to shred my dress to pieces so I'm exposed to him. I'm not wearing any panties or a bra. Fun fact the Altronians go commando all the time. They don't believe panties, bras, boxers, or anything like that is necessary. When I'm here I go commando too, and so does Collin. It certainly gives easier access to the important parts.

I can't help myself, I grab Collin's raging dick in my hands and begin to rub him. "Oh, you do like to play with fire, Little Villain."

"Only with you, Mighty Hero." I retort, bringing my lips closer to his so that our lips are just hovering over one another.

"Two can play that game, Little Villain." Collin smirks as his hand finds its way between my legs.

His fingers skillfully find my clit before he starts rubbing my clit. Collin then kisses me before he breaks our kiss, giving me another devious smirk. Collin then lowers his head to my breast as he sucks a nipple into his mouth while he keeps rubbing my clit. I attempt to keep rubbing him, but fuck he's winning with the amount of pleasure he is giving me.

"Give into my pleasure, Little Villain," Collin says after he lets go of my nipple before moving to the other one. The pleasure of his mouth on my nipples as he sucks, licks, and bites them combine with his fingers rubbing my clit in skillful circles sends me right to cloud nine. I'm losing the game I started. I let my hand drop from his dick. His chuckle vibrates around my nipple causing extra pleasure. I'm so close to going off the edge. "Be a good girl and cum for your Mighty Hero, Little Villain." Collin's words send me over the edge as my orgasm crashes around me.

Collin wastes no time plunging his hard cock inside of me. I do notice he's gentle. Collin can be rough in bed and that's when he's fucking me. Right now, is one of those gentle romantic moments where he's making love to me. I wrap my arms around his neck while also wrapping my legs around his waist to give him deeper access. Collin moves at a regular pace in and out of me, letting us take in being one. His lips fall to mine as he kisses me possessively. I'm his. I've always been his. He had my heart all those years ago in that stupid fair parking lot. We were always destined for one another, and I wouldn't have it any other way. I'd endure every kind of hell knowing it would lead me here with Collin, my destined mate and mighty hero. Collin and our son are the only things that matter.

I enjoy Collin's rhythm, I love the feeling of him filling, claiming me. We are still kissing as Collin moves his hips to grind my clit in the right places. Being with Collin will never get old. He makes me feel cherished and loved. I love being his, and I love the moments when Collin reminds me who I belong to. Collin picks up his pace, chasing his own release. I thread my fingers through his hair pulling his head closer to mine to deepen our kiss. Collin moves faster and faster until he finds his release deep within me.

We take a few moments to take in the rest of the moment before Collin rearranges us in bed so we are cuddled together and in resting positions. "I love you, Mighty Hero." I declare, snuggling closer to him.

"I love you too, Little Villain. We face the battle against your father together. We will bring our son home."

"I know we will, and thank you for not letting me do anything alone." I reply, feeling the heaviness of sleep threatening to send me into the darkness of rest.

"I promised you that I wouldn't let you do anything alone. I keep my promises, Little Villain.

"You can be a cocky bastard sometimes, but I'll always be grateful I'm yours."

"You always talk like I'm the one who saved you, but you always forget you saved me too. I know I pulled you out of a bad life and showed you a better one, but my life wasn't complete until you fully came into it. I wasn't some playboy superhero fucking around every night. Yes, I had one night stands, but they weren't all the time. The entire time I was looking for the right person, I was looking for you. I think it's safe to say that we both fell in love with one another in that fair parking lot stuffing our faces with fried goodness. It was our destined mate bond kicking in, we just didn't know what it was we were feeling." Collin concedes.

"I thought about that moment all the time when I was feeling down. It was a happy memory that I could escape to. Even then you made me happy, but I was afraid of being happy because I didn't think I deserved it. I let lies rule my life until all the lies were revealed and I couldn't pretend anymore. I trust you more than anyone on any planet." I add.

"You are where you belong, Little Villain. I will always accept you for who you are. Now, let's get some rest because we have a battle coming up." Collin says before kissing me on the head.

We cuddle closer and I let the comfort of being with Collin soothe me to much needed sleep.

# BIRDY RIVERS

## CHAPTER 37

### Collin

We have been back on Earth for about a month. Aiden is safely tucked away on Altron, out of Cyanide's reach. My father is ready for Cyanide's inevitable attack. My father acquired a weapon while we were on Altron and some tech that will help us fight Cyanide. I knew my father was holding on to something when he left Altron, I didn't know what it was until now. For whatever reason, my dad has been keeping things to himself when it comes to his ultimate plan for killing Cyanide. I've tried to not push too hard knowing he's determined, and I'm not going to change his stubborn mind.

Clara has been training incredibly hard since we got back. She is determined to be prepared for her father. I also know she wants Aiden home, as do I. Leaving him was hard. Probably the hardest thing we have ever had to do. Aiden isn't safe on Earth. Not until Cyanide is dead.

We know he is going to attack Oswald Tower soon. Sam told us of Cyanide's plan. He also informed us that Mason killed Yuri under Cyanide's orders. Mason is Cyanide's new second in command. Cyanide is convinced Aiden is at Oswald Tower. He's going to attack no matter what. He's coming, and we are ready.

Sam is healing up. He's still banged up. Cyanide nearly killed him. I'm glad the League was able to pull him out before he was killed. I know Sam feels guilty for telling Cyanide Clara was pregnant. No one blames him. I can only imagine the horrors he had to endure. I gave Sam his cure. He was thrilled and for the first time in a long time, Sam was genuinely hopeful. Sam has a shot a regular life of becoming a proper member of the League. It will be nice to have my friend back.

The entire League has been training hard anticipating Cyanide's attack. Clara hasn't had a vision of when Cyanide will exactly attack, but she knows it will be soon. Within the month was the most precise she could get. It's good enough. I know Clara is nervous for her first battle. I've fought many battles over several years. Clara has never fought one single battle, and her first battle is going to be against her father. I'm confident in Clara's abilities. She has come a long way.

Clara has started finding her flow in battle training and simulations with the rest of the League. Even Sam is starting to slowly train with us again as he heals and lets the cure take effect. We are all preparing the best we can for this battle. Everyone is on edge, and the entire tower is buzzing with anxiety with what's to come.

Somehow, I always knew the League would have to face Cyanide one last time, I didn't know how we would get there, but we would. Cyanide was always a threat lingering ever since his disappearance. Without a body, it was hard to believe he was dead. Our ultimate theory that he was hiding out on Altron was correct, although, I didn't see him becoming a prisoner of the Altronians. Cyanide is fighting for old ways. Old ways that will kill several thousands, and enslave several thousand more. Cyanide will overtake Oswald City and make it his headquarters.His ultimate plan is to take over the Earth so that he can prove to Altron that the old ways are still worth pursuing. Cyanide has been brainwashed by Cras. He will never stop until he is dead.

My dad is planning on ultimately fighting Cyanide. He has been training hard. Harder than I've ever seen him train. Even my mom has stated she has never seen my dad so focused and determined before. Whatever tech and weapon he got on Altron has my dad confident in his fight against Cyanide. I'm glad my dad is confident, I just wish he would share his plan with us, but he won't. Whatever his ultimate plan is to kill Cyanide, he doesn't want anyone to know. That means whatever he has planned is something we might try to stop him from doing. It means his plan is on the extreme side.

I'm not sure how I feel about my dad being so secretive about his plan. I certainly don't like that it's on the extreme side either. My dad is the type of hero who will sacrifice himself for the greater good. He would never sacrifice my mom, me, or anyone he cared about. He is an entirely different story, which is why my mom and I are both nervous and concerned with his big plan.

The part of the plan we do know is that we are to defend Oswald Tower when the time comes. Cyanide is for my father. We can help him get to Cyanide, but we are to not interfere with his fight with Cyanide. We are to capture as many villains as we can and kill those that get in our way. It's going to be a brutal fight. The hardest one many of us are going to face. The stakes have never been higher.

The League is about to fight the biggest threat we've ever faced. The entire city is at stake along with Aiden's safety. Not to mention Clara's safety is also at stake as her father wants her to help him with his insane quest. I always wanted a family of my own, but I never realized the danger that would surround them. Aiden is barely a couple weeks old and his life was threatened at his conception. Cyanide is a disease we must get rid of, one I know we will eliminate. I will do whatever it takes to keep Aiden and Clara safe. I would have left Clara on Altron with Aiden, but we need her in the battle to come. I will fight and protect everything that I love. Cyanide wants a fight then we will give him a war.

# CHAPTER 38

## Clara

The day has come. My dad has attacked Oswald Tower. He decided to attack at dawn in front of Oswald Tower. He's trying to make his way in. The League is outside fighting. Collin, Veronica, Oliver, and Nina are busy getting citizens to safety. Nora has a healing area set up where she can heal people. Claire and I helping where we are needed. Sam is weak, but he is helping hold the line. Thomas on the other hand is on a hunt for my father who hasn't fully revealed himself yet.

Mason is now speeding around like a bullet taunting me. However, Collin puts an end to Mason's taunting when he intervenes and starts kicking Mason's ass. I smile smugly as I help give Collin the advantage over Mason by controlling time around them. I slow things down for Mason while speeding things up for Collin. It's a nifty little trick I learned during all my training.

“You’ve developed your superpowers nicely, Oracle.” My father’s voice comes from behind me.

A shiver slides down my spine as I turn to face him. “No thanks to you, Daddy.” I retort, putting on my armor. I will stand my ground. Part of me wondered if my dad would be bold and attempt to talk to me. No doubt he still wants me on his side. He also knows if he can convince me to join him, I will help him and lead him right to Aiden.

An evil grin crosses his face making his five o’clock shadow darker. “That’s what you think, but I’ve been controlling your superpowers long before you even knew you had superpowers. Maybe I wanted the League to train you for me.” He taunts.

“It doesn’t matter because I won’t use my superpowers to help you.” I counter.

“You will do exactly as I say Clara Cole, and you’ll start by helping my second in command.” My father commands.

“One, I’m an adult and I don’t have to do a damn thing you say. Two, it’s Clara Oswald now.” I correct, showing the engagement ring on my finger that is also accompanied by a matching simple band.

“You tied yourself to an Oswald?” My father sneers. “You really are no daughter of mine.”

"Oh good, now you get it." I say with a sarcastic smile.

I can't help but look over to Collin and Mason who are locked in a deadly fight. I'm not able to help Collin because I'm distracted by

my dad. I quickly locate the rest of the League members. Nina is fighting bad guys by blasting them with cold ice shards, those fuckers hurt, I would know. Training with Nina is a bitch. Oliver is now helping Collin while Sam and Claire are helping pedestrians get to safety or to Nora who can heal them. Veronica is now with Nora defending the healing site from the bad guys that are trying to bring further damage to those injured while attempting to hurt even more people. Thomas is the one person I'm looking for because I know he has the weapon and the plan to take my father out.

"You could have been a princess of Chaos, Clara. Instead, you chose to align yourself with the enemy." My dad's words bring my attention back to him.

"I choose my destined mate and the League, get over it. You failed in raising me and in doing so you lost two weapons. Maybe in another time, I would have followed you like a loyal puppy like Mom did. Maybe in another time, you raise me to be just like you because you actually stuck around and included me in your plans.

Maybe, just maybe, in another time, I'm the villain you make me into, but none of those are the cases because you abandoned me. Don't give me your weak ass excuses of how it wasn't safe for me on Altron. You should have never gone to Altron. They did after all imprison your ass for a good while. Poor choices lead to bad results. Instead of making me a villain, you made me a hero." I taunt. I'm doing my best to distract my dad until Thomas can find us.

Collin and Oliver are still fighting Mason who seems to have his own reinforcements. Except his reinforcements are good because Collin and Oliver are taking them down, but in the process it is stalling them from their ultimate goal of capturing Mason. I know Collin wants Mason dead, but Thomas says we should teach him a lesson about betraying the League. So we all agreed to capture Mason and toss him on Nullum Island. My father is the one person we all agree dies no matter what. If Thomas fails in killing him, then the rest of us will die trying.

"That's right, Benji, you failed in your mission." Thomas adds coming up behind me. "Clara belongs to my family, not yours. Does it pain you to know your daughter rather be a part of my family than yours?"

"She might have united with your son and have your last name now, but she is a part of my bloodline, my DNA will always be a part of her." My father counters.

"I might be a part of your bloodline, but I'll never be part of your legacy." I retort as Thomas puts his hands gently on my upper arms as he comes up behind me.

"I need you to clear a fifteen-foot circular perimeter around me and your father. Get some of the other League members to help you. The quicker the better. Also, ignore what I'm about to say, I'm trying to provoke your father while stalling him. I wouldn't pick anyone else to be my son's destined mate. I'm proud of who you've become, Clara. Now, go." Thomas directs quietly in my ear.

I now know what Thomas's plan is. He's going to sacrifice himself to kill my father, and I have to let him. "See even your daughter listens to me better than she ever did you." Thomas taunts my dad as I quickly move away from him.

I flag down Sam, Nina, and Veronica. Oliver joins to help us as I tell them what Thoma's instructions are. The five of us quickly begin to clear the perimeter Thomas has asked for. Collin is finishing up kicking Mason's ass. Mason is clearly getting tired. Mason always lacked stamina. We finally clear the perimeter as Collin puts superpower dampening cuffs on Mason. The superpower dampening cuffs are Thomas's latest invention with tech and knowledge from Altron. Thomas was busy when he went to Altron and came back with more stuff than we realized.

"Enough, Thomas. Time to kill everyone here." My father threatens as emits his poison in the air in green puffs.

Thomas smirks before he hits a button on his watch that puts a force field around him and my father. It's a different forcefield from the ones the League usually uses. My father's poison can't escape the force field around them. Thomas is protecting everyone from my father by enclosing them both in a forcefield. Thomas has to be in the forcefield in order to kill my father. However, my father's poisonous gas will kill Thomas in the process.

"Time to end this, Cyanide," Thoams declares between chokes. "Could I get some assistance, Oracle?" Thomas asks as he pulls out a shiny metal stick with a red jeweled handle.

I nod my head knowing what he is asking me. Collin tries to break down the force field trying to save his dad, knowing he won't be able to. I want to go to Collin and be with him for what we are all about to witness, but I have to help Thomas. I know that Collin understands that. Thomas's shiny metal breaks down like little nanotech pieces and morphs into a dagger. I put my arms out as one hand begins to slow time down around my dad while speeding time up for Thomas so he can use the advantage to stab my father through his heart. My father grabs his chest in shock, falling to the ground with Thomas who won't let go of the dagger. Thomas is choking severely now. My father dies causing his poison gas to dissipate. Unfortunately, the damage has already been done to Thomas as he now lays limp on top of my dad, still holding the dagger.

The force field drops but no one moves. Not a soul stirs as everyone stares in complete shock at the scene before them. Shaking the shock from my system, I run over to Collin who has tears starting to sprout from his eyes. Veronica is full on sobbing with Nora holding her.

"Collin, I know you are hurting, but you need to step up and lead the League of Metas before everything turns to chaos," I say, putting my hands on either side of Collin's face to attempt to pull him from shock. "What would Thomas do in this situation?" I prompt, but Collin is still frozen. "You're father would put his grief aside and be a leader. He would be a mighty hero. So, go be my Mighty Hero, and make your dad's sacrifice count."

Collin shakes his head as he comes out of his shock. He puts his hands on mine and nods his own, knowing what he has to do. Collin lets go of my hands and I drop mine from his face and stand at his side. "Sam,

Oliver, and Nina round up as many villains as you can there's plenty of superpower dampening devices to go around. Nora and Claire help the civilians and cops." Collin directs as I go over to Veronica who Nora lets out of her arms to go do what Collin asked. Veronica collapses in my arms. I hold her, looking over at Thomas and my dad's bodies. It's over. Aiden is safe to come home. I wish Thomas got to meet him. Thomas knew what he was sacrificing the moment we left Altron the first time.

Collin goes over to his father's body and moves him off my father before taking his watch off which controls the force field. Collin also takes the dagger out of my father's chest. The dagger is dripping with blood. Collin needs to collect the items before they fall into the wrong hands.

In a matter of hours, we have well over a hundred villains ready to ship to Nullim Island including Mason. Thomas's body has been taken to Oswald Tower for a funeral and memorial service. My dad's body has been taken to the morgue to be cremated. Collin has sent a message to Altron informing them of what happened and that they can arrange for Aiden to come home.

Veronica is a mess. Collin is barely holding on. The rest of the League is also in mourning. Harold is coming to the city for as long as he is needed. He is the one helping with the funeral and memorial service. We may have won today, but our victory came at a great cost. A cost I know Thomas would pay again, knowing his loved ones are safe, knowing his beloved city is protected by his legacy that will carry on in Collin and Aiden. Thomas died a true hero and he will always be remembered.

# BIRDY RIVERS

## CHAPTER 39

### Collin

The last week has passed by in a blur since my dad died. I knew when he didn't tell us his big plan it was most likely something I wouldn't approve of. I was right. I know that sometimes being the hero means sacrificing yourself for the greater good, which is what my dad did. I can't believe my dad is gone. Now, I know why he was eager to set me up for taking over as Leader of the League, and why he made sure I had a second in command. He was preparing to not make it out alive.

Aiden is home. Crona brought him the next day to Earth. Crona has come to say goodbye to her son and honor our traditions on Earth of a funeral and burial. My dad has been buried in the Oswald family cemetery on Oswald Manor property. We had the private family event very quickly. My dad had everything set up and he sent Harold instructions knowing my mom would be too much of a mess to do anything. He also knew I would be busy dealing with League business.

Today is the memorial service for the public. We are having a ceremony outside of Oswald Tower where we will reveal a statue of my father made to honor and remember his sacrifice. Mentally I'm not ready for it, but I have to be. I can grieve in private, but in public, I need to maintain a calm and put together front.

Right now, I'm in my office. My office, damn that's strange to say. I always knew that one day my dad's office would become mine. I didn't imagine it would be so soon. I thought I had years to go before I became the leader of the League. Yet here I find myself, sitting in my dad's office chair at his desk in his office, and it's all mine now.

The door to the office opens and in walks Clara holding Aiden, my mom, Harold, Crona, and the rest of the League. I'm about to carry out my dad's last wishes. The man seriously had everything planned out. He had most of his funeral arrangements handled and sent to Harold. He primed me to take over as leader with Oliver as my second in command and Sam will be my third in command when he is ready. My dad even recorded hologram messages for us all. We each have one addressed to us and then there is one for all of us to watch together.

"Thank you for coming. Today is my father's memorial service for the public. As much as none of us want to do it, we have to because the people of this city deserve the right to pay their respects to the hero who saved them. The man who made sure it was safe for his grandson to come home. We owe my father a great debt and the best way to pay that debt is to continue fighting villains and keeping his beloved city safe. My dad was prepared for his death. He has pre-recorded a hologram message for each and every one of you. He even has one for Aiden, for when he is older." I inform them as I pass out their individual hologram messages for them to watch in private. "He has one for all of us to watch together." I say after I'm done handing out their individual messages. I put the black circular device in the middle of my desk and hit play.

Seconds later a holographic image of my dad appears. "I don't know where to begin this group message. Surprisingly, the individual ones were easier to make. Let me first start off by saying I'm proud of the League of Metas. I'm proud of each and every one of you for doing the right thing and protecting our home. I know some of you might be upset or even angry that I didn't let you in on my grand plan. I did it on purpose because I knew you would find some way to save me. I didn't want to be saved.

I knew what had to be done and I was willing to make the sacrifice needed. Cyanide is gone and I'm sure we have captured many villains who are being imprisoned on Nullum Island. That doesn't mean new threats won't arise. Cyanide was more influential than anyone imagined. Even if Cyanide isn't the inspiration behind new villains, they will still come for our city. We are opened up to universal threats as well, now that we have an open line of communication with Altron. Their enemies are our enemies and vice versa. We are allies with them, and it will remain that way. I know that you all will carry on the League's legacy and pass it to the next generation. You all are my family because the League is a family. Lean on one another, support each other, and be a refuge for one another in dark times. The League of Metas is in good hands."

The message ends. Everyone takes a few moments before they disperse. We all need a moment to ourselves to compose ourselves before the memorial service. Clara hangs behind with Aiden. "Are you okay, Mighty Hero?" She asks sitting on my lap with Aiden in her arms.

"I will be." I reply wrapping my arms around her waist, holding her close to me. "What about you? You lost your dad too."

"My dad was an evil prick who deserved what he got. Thomas didn't deserve to die too," Clara pauses. "Do you know his last words to me besides giving me an order was telling me he was proud of me and that he wouldn't have picked anyone else to be your destined mate. He made sure I knew I was accepted by him before he died. He knew I would have to do the hard thing and assist him in killing my father, knowing it would also lead to his death. He trusted me not to betray him or the League, knowing I could have easily helped my father instead. I could have helped Cyanide live, and Thomas knew that. I was the key to making his plan work. He put his faith and trust in me, and that meant the world to me. I'm more upset that Thomas is gone than my own father because at the end of the day, Cyanide was never there for me, but Thomas was." Clara confesses.

"You changed his stubborn mind along with so many others, Little Villain. You showed them that your past and bloodline don't define you. You can be your own person no matter where your origins come from. You proved not only yourself but so much more. You proved people are worth second chances and that we shouldn't judge a book by its cover. You might be my Little Villain, but to the world, you are the Oracle, a symbol of hope and peace."

"I told my father I might be a part of his bloodline, but I will never be part of his legacy. I'm a part of the League's legacy. Prophecy or not, the Oracle will always belong to her destined mate, her mighty hero." Clara turns slightly so she can kiss me briefly.

"You will always be mine, Little Villain. We will always belong to one another because we are destined mates," I pause. "My dad did leave one hologram message for both of us. Should we play it?" Clara nods her head as she takes a deep breath.

I gently lean forward opening one of the top drawers to pull out a black circular device. I place it on the desk and hit the small black button to play. Another hologram of my dad pops up before us. This time he is holding the Altronian weapon he used against Cyanide. I've been wondering about it. I even asked Crona about it, but she told me that I would find out in time. I guess she knew my dad was going to explain it.

"Collin and Clara, I may not be there to help guide you on your parenthood journey, but I know you have others around you that will help. I want you to know how much I wish I could be there to watch Aiden grow. Now, on to business. I know you have questions about the weapon I used. I obtained it on Altron from Salter as I did some other gadgets and tech that you've now seen. The weapon I used to kill Cyanide is called the Converter. It can morph into any weapon the wielder desires. I helped the Elders create it for Aiden. I had to borrow it first," my father pauses before clearing his throat. He does that when he is going to tell someone something serious. "While we were on Altron the Elders revealed to me a prophecy about Aiden. He will be called the Power Collector, the Guardian of Altron, and the Defender of Earth. He is going to be incredibly powerful and there will come a day when both Altron and Earth will need him to protect us. I didn't want to tell you two prior because I wanted you to enjoy Aiden for a bit before you had to worry about another prophecy. I have faith in you two to raise Aiden to be everything he can be and more. Make sure he watches the message I left for him when he is older. I love you three, and I know you will be a beautiful family."

My dad's hologram disappears. "Looks like we can't escape prophecies." Clara comments holding Aiden closer.

"No, but we will face it together." I reply, knowing it doesn't matter what we face because it will always be together.

Today is going to be a rough day, but I know I'll get through it because I have Clara and the League behind me. I'm ready to be a leader even if I thought I wouldn't be taking over just yet. I will continue my family legacy. It doesn't matter what the future holds because I know I don't have to face it alone. Just like Aiden won't have to face his prophecy alone. We will be there for him, guiding him and supporting him. Clara and I head down to the memorial service for my dad while I hold Aiden. Today is a day of grief, but that won't always be the case. Even in the wake of heartache, there are things to celebrate, hope to be had, and a future to embrace.

The End

Our Heroes will be back in *Destiny Awaits* with new villains to face.

# EPILOGUE

## Clara

It's hard to believe it's been twelve years. Twelve years since I found out about my superpowers being suppressed and the prophecy about me. Twelve years since Thomas died. Twelve years since I joined the League. Twelve years since I married my destined mate, and twelve years since I had our son Aiden. A lot has happened in twelve years.

About eight years after Thomas passed away, Veronica moved to Altron. She taught all the League members how to fly a spaceship. She made sure Collin, Oliver, and Sam were comfortable in their leadership positions. She made sure I was good with raising Aiden while Collin did his duty to the city. She made sure Nina was comfortable as head of PR. Nora and Claire are organizers of events, which Veronica made sure they were set up for. She organized everything so that eventually she could go to Altron. The memories of Thomas on Earth are hard for her. There's no escaping Thomas's legacy. He is everywhere from the giant memorial statue in front of Oswald Tower to the memorabilia that supporters have made to remember him. Thomas was the face of the League, the Oswald family, and the face of the city. Veronica needed to breathe again, and Altron was the way. She does visit Earth for major holidays and events.

Collin and I visit Altron as often as possible. We take Aiden there to help him further his training. Aiden is twelve and his superpowers have emerged. Aiden is called the Power Collector for a reason. He can replicate any Bio Metas superpower by simply touching the Bio Meta. He can only use one superpower at a time, but he can switch between them. Aiden collects superpowers and uses them as his own. It's impressive and makes him super powerful. I see why my father wanted to get his hands on him, thankfully Thomas made sure my father would never get to me or my son again when he killed him.

Oliver and Nora are married and have a son named Dane. They also adopted a human girl a couple of years younger than Dane. Her name is Aria. Oliver saved her and somehow she pulled at his heartstrings. Oliver took her home and she never left. Aria is a special girl, and she has completed Oliver and Nora's little family. Sam has a son with a doner named Lucas. Nina and Claire used the same donor and got pregnant at the same time. Nina's daughter is named Kayla and Claire's daughter is named Carly. Their superpowers have yet to emerge but I'm sure they will soon enough.

We've started a type of academy for Bio Metas who want to join the League as well as a human vigilant program. Humans wanted to help the League fight the bad guys. Thomas's sacrifice encouraged humans to want to fight along with us except it caused a lot of chaos. So, we came up with the vigilante program for the humans to join. They have to pass a series of tests in order to join. We still have kinks to work out with both things, but we are making progress and ensuring that Thomas's legacy lives on. That his sacrifice was not for nothing.

A lot has changed in twelve years, but so much of it has been for the better. The future brings new changes, that much I know. Things we can't fathom will come true, Aiden will fulfill his prophecy, and the way we fight villains will advance. Once destiny called me, now destiny awaits my son.

# Books by Birdy Rivers

**The Coven Series**

The Coven of the Crow and Shadows: Legacy book 1 of the coven series

The Coven of the Crow and Shadows: Ghost Opera book 2 of the coven series

The Coven of the Crow and Shadows: Mayhem and Death book 3 of the coven series

The Coven of the Crow and Shadows: New Era book 4 of the coven series

**Retellings**

The Children of the Empire: World on Fire (Snow White, Beauty and the Beast, Cinderella, Sleeping Beauty, and Rapunzel)

The Children of the Empire: Reflected Mirrors

The Voice of the Sea: A Little Mermaid Retelling

A Thousand and One Wishes: Book 1 of the Wishes Duet (Aladdin)

Hunting My Wolf (Little Red Riding Hood)

Birdy Rivers also has books on Kindle Vella and various reading apps. Follow her social media pages to find out where to locate her other books, updates, and merch.

Facebook: Page: Birdy Rivers. Readers Group: Birdys Magical World

Instagram @birdyriversauthor

Made in the USA
Columbia, SC
09 June 2025